DARK POWER
POWER
COLLECTION

Other Books by Bill Myers

Forbidden Doors
Dark Power Collection
Invisible Terror Collection
Deadly Loyalty Collection
Ancient Forces Collection

Dark Side of the Supernatural

The Elijah Project
On the Run
The Enemy Closes In
Trapped by Shadows
The Chamber of Lies

FORBIDDEN DOORS

DARK POWER COLLECTION

The Society
The Deceived
The Spell

BILL MYERS

ZONDERVAN®

ZONDERVAN.com/
AUTHORTRACKER
follow your favorite authors

We want to hear from you. Please send your comments about this book to us in care of zreview@zondervan.com. Thank you.

ZONDERVAN

Dark Power Collection
Copyright © 2008 by Bill Myers

The Society
Copyright © 1994 by Bill Myers

The Deceived
Copyright © 1994 by Bill Myers

The Spell
Copyright © 1995 by Bill Myers

This title is also available as a Zondervan ebook.
Visit www.zondervan.com/ebooks.

This title is also available in a Zondervan audio edition.
Visit www.zondervan.fm.

Requests for information should be addressed to:
Zondervan, *Grand Rapids, Michigan* 49530

ISBN 978-0-310-72903-7

Published in association with the literary agency of Alive Communications, Inc., 7680 Goddard Street, Suite 200, Colorado Springs, CO 80920, www.alivecommunications.com

Interior design: Christine Orejuela-Winkelman

Printed in the United States of America

11 12 13 14 15 16 17 18 /DCI/ 20 19 18 17 16 15 14 13 12 11 10 9 8 7 6 5 4 3 2 1

THE SOCIETY

For our struggle is not against flesh and blood, but against the rulers, against the authorities, against the powers of this dark world and against the spiritual forces of evil in the heavenly realms. Therefore put on the full armor of God, so that when the day of evil comes, you may be able to stand your ground, and after you have done everything, to stand.

EPHESIANS 6:12–13

1

Rebecca's lungs burned. They screamed for more air; they begged her to slow down. But she wouldn't. She pushed herself. She ran for all she was worth. She had to.

There was no sound. She saw a few kids standing along the track, opening their mouths and shouting encouragement. She saw them clapping their hands and cheering her on. But she couldn't hear them. All she heard was her own gasps for breath ... the faint crunch of gravel under her track shoes.

Several yards ahead ran Julie Mitchell—the team's shining hope for all-State. She had a grace and style that made Rebecca feel like, well, like a deranged platypus. Whatever that was.

But that was okay; Becka wasn't running against Julie. She was running against something else.

"It's Dad ..."

For the thousandth time, she saw her mom's red nose and puffy eyes and heard her voice echoing inside her head. "They found his plane in the jungle. He made it through the crash, but ..."

Becka bore down harder; she ran faster. Her lungs were going to explode, but she kept going.

"You've got … to accept it," her mom's voice stammered. "He's gone, sweetheart. He was either attacked by wild animals or … or …"

Becka dug her cleats in deeper. She stretched her legs out farther. She knew the "or … or …" was a tribe of South American Indians in that region. A tribe notorious for its fierceness and for its use of black magic.

The back of Becka's throat ached. Not because of the running. It was because of the tears. And the rage. Why?! Why had God let this happen? Why had God let him die? He was such a good man, trying to do such good things.

Angrily she swiped at her eyes. Her legs were turning into rubber. Losing feeling. Losing control. And still she pushed herself. She had closed the gap with Julie and was practically beside her now. The finish line waited a dozen meters ahead.

Trying out for the track team hadn't been Becka's idea. It was her mom's. "To help you fit in," she'd said.

Fit in. What a joke. Rebecca had spent most of her life living in the villages of Brazil with her mom, her little brother, and a father who flew his plane in and out of the jungle for humanitarian and mission groups. And now, suddenly, she was expected to fit in. Here? In Crescent Bay, California? Here, where everybody had perfect skin, perfect bodies, perfect teeth? And let's not forget all the latest fashions, right out of *Vogue* or *InStyle* or whatever it was they read. Fashions that made Becka feel like she bought her clothes right out of *Popular Mechanics*.

That last thought pushed her over the edge. She tried too hard, stretched too far. Her legs, which had already lost feeling, suddenly had minds of their own. The left one twisted, then gave out all together.

It was like a slow-motion movie that part of Becka watched as she pitched forward. For a second, she almost caught her balance. Almost, but not quite. She stumbled and continued falling toward the track. There was nothing she could do—only put out her hands and raise her head so the crushed red gravel would not scrape her face. Knees and elbows, yes. But not her face.

As if it really mattered.

She hit the track and skidded forward, but she didn't feel any pain. Not yet. The pain would come a second or two later. Right now, all she felt was shame. And embarrassment. Already the humiliation was sending blood racing to her cheeks and to her ears.

Yes sir, just another day in the life of Rebecca Williams, the new kid moron.

☜ ☜

As soon as Becka's little brother, Scott, walked into the bookstore, he knew something was wrong. It wasn't like he was frightened or nervous or anything. It had nothing to do with what he felt. It had everything to do with the place.

It was wrong.

But why? It certainly was cheery enough. Bright sunlight streaming through the skylights. Aqua blue carpet. Soft white shelves with rows and rows of colorful books. Then there was the background music—flutes and wind chimes.

But still...

"You coming or what?" It was Darryl. Scott had met him a couple of days ago at lunch. Darryl wasn't the tallest or best-looking kid in school—actually, he was about the shortest and nerdiest. His voice was so high you were never sure if it was him talking or someone opening a squeaky cupboard. Oh, and one other thing. Darryl sniffed. About every thirty seconds. You could set your watch by it. Something about allergies or hay fever or something.

But at least he was friendly. And as the new kid, Scott couldn't be too picky who he hung with. New kids had to take what new kids could get.

For the past day or so, Darryl had been telling Scott all about the Society—a secret group that met in the back of the Ascension Bookshop after school. Only the coolest and most popular kids could join. (Scott wasn't sure he bought this "coolest and most popular" bit, since they'd let Darryl be a member. But he didn't want to hurt the little guy's feelings, so he let it go.)

"Hey, Priscilla," Darryl called as they walked past the counter toward the back of the bookshop.

"Hey, yourself," a handsome, middle-aged woman said. She didn't bother to look from her magazine until the two boys passed. When she glanced up and saw Scott, a scowl crossed her face. She seemed to dislike him immediately. He hadn't said a thing; he hadn't done a thing. But that didn't matter. There was something about him that troubled her—a lot.

Scott was oblivious to her reaction as he followed Darryl toward the hallway at the back of the store.

So far his first week at Crescent Bay had been pretty good. No fights. No broken noses. A minimal amount of death threats. But that's the way it was with Scott. Unlike his older sister, Scott always fit in. It probably had something to do with his sense of humor. Scott was a lot like his dad in that department; he had a mischievous grin and a snappy comeback for almost any situation.

Scott was like his dad in another way too. He had a deep faith in God. The whole family did. But it wasn't some sort of rules or regulations thing. And it definitely wasn't anything weird. It was just your basic God's-the-boss-so-go-to-church-and-try-to-make-the-world-a-better-place faith.

But sometimes that faith . . . well, sometimes it allowed Scott to feel things. Deep things.

Like now.

As he and Darryl entered the hallway, Scott brushed against a large hoop decorated with what looked like eagle feathers. He ducked to the side only to run smack-dab into a set of wooden wind chimes. They clanked and clanged noisily. Lately, Scott hadn't been the most graceful of persons. It probably had something to do with growing two inches in the last three months. He was still shorter than Becka—a fact she brought up to him on a regular basis—but he was gaining on her by the week.

As they continued down the hall, Scott noticed a number of trinkets and lockets hanging on the wall. He couldn't put his finger on it, but they looked strangely familiar.

Then he noticed something else. Frowning, he glanced around. Was it his imagination, or was it getting colder? There were no windows, open or otherwise, anywhere close by.

Something inside him began to whisper, "*Stop.... Turn around.... Go back....*"

But why? Nothing was wrong. It was just a hallway. Just a bookshop.

"Here we go." Darryl gave a loud sniff as he slowed in front of the last door. He smiled, pushed up his glasses, and knocked lightly.

No answer.

"Well, it doesn't look like anybody's home," Scott said, his voice cracking in gratitude. "I guess we'd better—"

"Don't be stupid," Darryl said, reaching for the knob. "They always meet on Fridays."

Cautiously, he pushed the door open.

It was pitch-black inside. Well, except for the dozen or so candles burning around a table. And the faces illuminated by the candles. Faces Scott had seen at school. They were all staring intently at something on the table. Scott squinted in the darkness, making out some kind of board game with a bunch of letters and symbols on it. Two of the kids had their hands on a little plastic pointer that was moving back and forth across the board.

"What's that?" Scott whispered.

"What do you think it is?" Darryl whispered back. "It's a Ouija board."

"A what?"

"You use it to spell out words. You know, it tells you about the future and stuff."

Scott looked at him skeptically.

"No kidding," Darryl squeaked. Scott grimaced. Even when the guy whispered his voice sounded like a rusty hinge. Darryl continued, watching the others. "The pointer moves to those letters on the board, spelling out answers to anything you ask."

"No way," Scott scorned. As far as he could tell, the pointer moved on the board because it was pushed by the two kids whose hands were on it: a big, meaty fellow in a tank top and a chubby girl dressed all in black. "Those two, they're the ones moving it."

Darryl didn't answer. He just sniffed and stepped into the room. Scott wasn't crazy about following, but he walked in after him.

And—just like that—the plastic pointer stopped. One minute the little pointer was scooting around the board, spelling out words. The next, it came to a complete stop.

"Hey," a pretty girl complained, pushing her long red hair back. "What's wrong?"

"I don't know," the meaty guy answered. He turned to his partner, the girl in black. "Are you stopping it?"

"Not me," she said. And then, slowly turning her head toward the door, she nailed Scott with an icy look. "It's him."

Every eye in the room turned to Scott.

He raised his hand. "Hi there," he croaked, trying to smile. Nobody smiled back.

"Ask it," the redhead demanded. "Ask it if he's the reason it's not answering."

"Yeah," the meaty guy agreed.

The girl in black tilted back her head and closed her eyes. Her hair was short and jet black—an obvious dye job. "Please show us," she said more dramatically than Scott thought necessary. "Show us the reason for your silence."

Everyone turned to the plastic pointer. Waiting. Watching.

Nothing happened.

Scott tried to swallow, but at the moment, there wasn't much left in his mouth to swallow.

Suddenly the pointer started moving. Faster than before. In fact, both the girl and the meaty guy looked down in surprise as it darted from letter to letter, barely pausing at one before shooting to the next. In a matter of seconds it had spelled out:

D-E-A-T-H

Then it stopped. Abruptly.

Everyone waited in silence. Afraid to move. Afraid to break the spell.

The girl in black cleared her throat and spoke again. But this time, a little less confidently. "What do you mean? What death?"

There was no movement. No answer.

Scott shifted slightly. He felt the chill again, but this time it was more real. It had substance. Suddenly he knew that there was something there, in the room ... something cold and physical had actually brushed against him. He was sure of it.

Again the girl spoke. "What death? Is someone going to die? Whose death?"

No movement. More silence.

And then, just when Scott was about to say something really clever to break the tension and show everyone how silly this was, the plastic pointer zipped across the board and shot off the table.

"Look out!" Darryl cried.

Scott jumped aside, and the pointer hit the floor, barely missing his feet. He threw a look at the girl in black, certain she had flung it across the table at him.

But the expression on her face said she was just as surprised as him.

Or was she?

☜ ☞

"You okay?" Julie Mitchell asked as she toweled off her thick blonde hair and approached Rebecca's gym locker.

"Sure." Rebecca winced while pulling her jeans up over her skinned knees. "Nothing a brain transplant couldn't fix."

It had been nearly an hour since her little crash-and-burn routine on the track. Of course, everyone had gathered around her, making a big deal of the whole thing, and, of course, she wanted to melt into the track and disappear. But that was an hour ago. Yesterday's news. Now most of the girls had hit the showers and were heading home.

But not Julie. It was like she purposely hung back. Becka glanced at her curiously. There was something friendly about Julie, something caring. Becka had liked her immediately ... even though Julie was one of the best-looking kids in school.

"The team really needs you," Julie offered.

"As what? Their mascot?"

Julie grinned. She tossed her hair back and reached over to slip on a top-of-the-line, money's-no-object, designer T-shirt. "Seriously," she said, "I'm the only long-distance runner we've got. Royal High has three killers that bumped me out of State last year. But if you work and learn to concentrate, the two of us might give them a run for their money. You've got the endurance. And I've never seen anyone with such a great end sprint."

"Or such klutziness."

Julie shrugged. "You've got a point there," she teased.

Becka felt herself smiling back.

"Anybody can learn form and style," Julie continued. "That's what coaches are for. And if you add that to your sprint, we just might be able to knock Royal out of State." She rummaged in her gym basket, then bit her lip and frowned. "Shoot … don't tell me I've lost it."

Becka rubbed a towel through her hair, then sighed. Her hair was mousy brown and would dry three times faster than Julie's. The reason was simple: Becka's hair was three times thinner. Yes sir, just another one of life's little jokes with Becka as the punch line.

Julie's search through her basket grew more urgent.

"What are you looking for?" Becka asked.

"My pouch …" There was definite concern in her voice as she continued pawing through her clothes.

"Pouch?"

"My good luck charm."

Becka wasn't sure what Julie meant, but she gave a quick scan along the bench.

"I just hope nobody stole it," Julie said.

Becka spotted something under the bench. It was partially covered by towels. She reached for it and picked up a small leather bag with rocks or sand or something inside. A leather string was attached at the top so it could be worn as a necklace.

"Is this it?" Becka asked.

Julie relaxed. "Yeah. Great." She took it and slipped it around her neck.

Becka watched, fighting back a wave of uneasiness. She tried to sound casual as she asked, "So, what's in it?"

"I don't know." Julie shrugged. "Some turquoise, some powders, herbs—that sort of stuff. The Ascension Lady puts them together for us—you know, for good luck."

" 'Ascension Lady'?" Becka asked.

"Yeah," Julie fingered the little pouch. " 'Course I don't believe in any of that stuff. But with the district preliminaries coming up, it doesn't hurt to play the odds, right?"

Becka's mind raced. She wanted to ask lots more about the

pouch and this Ascension Lady, but Julie didn't give her the chance.

"Listen, we'll see you Monday," she said grabbing her backpack. "And don't be bummed, you did fine. Besides," she threw a mischievous grin over her shoulder, "we can always use a good mascot."

Becka forced a smile.

"See ya." Julie disappeared around the row of lockers and pushed open the big double doors. They slammed shut behind her with a loud *click, boooom.*

Becka didn't move. She sat, all alone ... just her and the dripping showers.

Her smile had already faded. Not because of the pain in her knees or even because of the memories of her fall.

It was because of the pouch. She'd seen pouches like that before. In South America. But they weren't worn by pretty, rich, athletic teenagers who wanted to go to State track championships.

They were worn by witch doctors who worshiped demons.

2

"Why do I always get the grunge work?" Rebecca complained. She grabbed a pile of old newspapers by their string and dragged them across the floor. Julie's leather pouch and the mysterious Ascension Lady were no longer on her mind. She was too busy shuddering at the cockroaches that scurried from under her papers and dashed toward darker quarters.

Her mom stared at the rows of stacked boxes behind them — boxes that still needed to be moved. She sighed in answer to Becka's complaint. "Honey, we've all got our jobs."

"Fine ... then let Scotty clean out this stupid garage, and let me hook up the TV and computer junk."

"Becka, please ..." Mom brushed aside a tendril of gray, sweaty hair. It had been six months since Becka's dad died, but it looked like Mom had aged ten years. Maybe she had. "We all have certain skills, and Scotty's—"

"I know, Scotty's the electronic whiz kid, and I'm ... the bag lady." Becka bit her lip. She hated being a whiner. She knew it had been a tough week for Mom — getting moved in, getting situated, trying to find work. In fact, it had been a tough week for all of them. They hadn't known a soul in the town except for some distant aunt whose name Becka couldn't even remember. But since this aunt was Mom's only relative, here they were, smack-dab in the middle of Weird Town, USA, cleaning a house that, at the moment, seemed to have been owned by the Addams Family.

"Do you think these people ever threw anything away?" Becka asked, trying to change the subject.

Mom fought to lift a half-rotted box. It wasn't heavy, just big. "Well, at least they were honest," she groaned. "The ad said the place was a fixer-upper, and this place is definitely a fixer —"

"Look out!" Rebecca cried.

The bottom of Mom's box gave way, and a dozen lightbulbs fell out, smashing and popping as they hit the concrete. Mom dropped the box with a loud *thump,* and a few more shattering *pops* followed.

The two stood a moment in stunned silence. Finally Rebecca stooped down for a closer look. "Lightbulbs?" she asked. She shook her head in amazement. "They saved their used lightbulbs?"

"Must be a hundred of 'em," Mom marveled as she peered into the box.

"I know they were ecology nuts, but ... what's next?"

Without a word, they both turned to the stack of fifty or so boxes thrown against the back wall of the garage. Fifty or so boxes that still needed to be cleared out.

Mom pushed her hair aside, a weak grin crossing her face. "Maybe next we'll find their secret stash of used toothbrushes."

"Mom ...," Becka groaned.

Like Scott, Mom had a sense of humor in tough times. And it didn't get any tougher than being dog-tired and having fifty more boxes to move.

"Or how 'bout used Kleenexes — you know, nice and crispy."

"Mother …" Becka was weakening.

"Maybe if we're really lucky, we'll find a giant ball of used dental floss."

That was it. They both started to giggle. Neither knew what was so funny. After all, fifty boxes were still fifty boxes. No doubt about it, it had been a long week for both of them, and it didn't seem to be getting any shorter. So of course they had to laugh. Either that or cry.

Suddenly, Becka swallowed her giggles and grew still. "Listen. What was that?"

Mom quieted down and gave a listen. "I don't hear anything."

Becka scowled slightly, looking toward the boxes at the back wall. "It's stopped now. But it sounded like …" She hesitated, thinking she heard it again. "It sounded like a faint scraping sound — didn't you hear it?"

Mom shook her head and stared toward the boxes. Both of them stood in silence, listening, waiting — but there was nothing.

"Probably just the wind," Mom finally offered as she stooped down and started picking up the shattered bulbs.

Becka nodded and crossed to the broom and dustpan. "Yeah," she said, "probably just the wind."

👁 👁

For the past couple of hours, Scott had been able to put the Bookshop incident out of his mind. And for good reason. So far he had almost blown up the TV by connecting the wrong cables to the wrong box.

Now it was a fight to the finish with the computer's wireless router. He was up in his room, going for the best two out of three falls with the contraption. Unfortunately, Cornelius wasn't helping much.

"BEAM ME UP, SCOTTY, BEAM ME UP."

"Not now, Cornelius, I'm busy."

The bright green bird hopped onto Scott's arm and worked his way up to Scott's right shoulder. "MAKE MY DAY. MAKE MY DAY."

Scott let out a heavy sigh. Teaching the family parrot cool phrases was fun back in the beginning. It was a great way to impress all of his Brazilian friends. The only problem was that people quit using those cool phrases a long time ago. A fact that totally escaped Cornelius. The bird just kept repeating the same things over and over and over ... and over some more. It made Scott crazy, especially when he was trying to concentrate.

"BEAM ME UP! *SQUAWK*. BEAM ME UP! BEAM ME UP!"

Scott tried to ignore him. He finished connecting the last cable, took a deep breath, and hit the computer's on button.

So far so good—no power surges, no nuclear meltdowns.

Scott grabbed the mouse and brought up his email home page. "Got it!"

Before Scott could log in, a flurry of green feathers leaped into his face. Cornelius had grown weary of sitting on Scott's shoulder and thought he'd fly down to the keyboard to take a little stroll. Unfortunately, he strolled across the wrong keys. Immediately the screen went blank.

"Hey!" Scott cried. But that was all he managed to get out before Cornelius reached up and began nibbling on the end of his nose.

Scott sighed. It was hard to yell when your nose was being kissed.

👁 👁

"Hi there.... Rebecca, isn't it?"

Becka froze. This was about her twentieth trip to the sidewalk with about her twentieth extra-ply, heavy-duty Glad bag filled to the brim with junk. In the beginning, when she had first stepped out of the garage and into public view, she had cared how she looked. But that was eight hours ago. Before the exhaustion. Before she became a sweaty greaseball covered in grime. Now she couldn't care less about how she looked.

Or so she thought.

She turned toward the voice and squinted into the light. The sun glared behind him so she couldn't see much — except that he was tall and had incredible shoulders.

He shifted slightly. The sun flared around his face, and now she could see his thick black hair and strong chin. She caught a glimpse of something else too. His eyes. She'd never seen anything quite so blue.

Her face flushed instantly. Of all times to be looking like pond scum. She gave one final tug on the bag, bringing it to the curb. She was careful to keep her back to him, hoping he wouldn't recognize her. But since he already knew her name, chances of that seemed kind of slim.

"Need a hand?" he asked.

"No," she answered too quickly, almost sounding angry. She tried again. "I mean, this is the last of it for the day."

"Oh." Was it her imagination, or was there a trace of disappointment in his voice? After a moment, he continued. "The people that used to live here were really weird. Did some strange stuff."

Becka's mind raced. She knew the guy was trying to make conversation, and she wanted to help out. But at the moment, all she could think about was how awful she looked. "Well ...," she faltered, "we're finding some pretty weird stuff in there, that's for sure." She reached up and discreetly tried to fluff out the stringiest part of her hair.

"If you guys ever need a hand, let me know. I just live down on the corner."

Rebecca nodded.

Another pause.

She tied another knot at the top of the bag. It didn't need

it, but she had to do something. Still careful to keep her back to him, she asked, "So, uh ... how'd you know my name?"

"I've been asking around."

"Becka?" It was Mom, calling from the garage.

"Coming," Rebecca answered. She was both mad and grateful for the excuse to get away. "Well, I've gotta go." She quickly turned and headed up the driveway. "It was nice meeting you."

"Same here—see ya."

She immediately hated herself for being such a chicken. It wasn't until she reached the garage that she realized she wasn't just a chicken. She was a brainless chicken. She hadn't even asked his name!

But he knew hers. *What'd he say? "I've been asking around"?* One eyebrow lifted, and she glanced over her shoulder in the direction he'd gone. *Hmmm ... maybe life around here won't be so terrible after all.*

3

By three o'clock the following morning, Scott had twisted his blanket and sheets into a tight little ball. He thought he'd be able to forget about the Bookshop and the Ouija board. No such luck. He just kept tossing and turning and kicking and thrashing. And the dreams just kept coming, one after another. The latest was of his dad. Or at least his dad as Scott remembered him. Before his death.

They were playing football—just the two of them. Well, just the two of them on one side. The other side had a team of giant bruisers at the line of scrimmage just waiting to turn them into football shoe goo.

Scott shuddered as he and his dad huddled up. Not because he worried about getting tromped to death. He figured that was inevitable. He shivered because of the chill. The same chill he'd felt the day before in the bookstore.

"Scotty," his dad asked with a frown, "where's your armor?"

Scott looked to him in surprise. The man was wearing a full suit of armor, like something right out of King Arthur! It was obviously another one of his dad's little jokes. "My armor?" Scott chuckled. "Well, I, uh ..."

"Can't play the game without your armor."

"Yeah, sure ... I, uh ... I guess I must have left it at the cleaners," Scott quipped, "or maybe the body shop." His dad didn't laugh. He didn't even crack a smile.

They broke from the huddle and approached the line of scrimmage. Scott glanced up at the faces of his towering opponents and gasped. There were no faces. The football helmets were there, even the face guards. But inside ... inside there were no heads, no faces. Nothing. Just dark, ominous shadows. Scott fought back a shudder.

"Don't worry," Dad whispered. "Just run the plays."

"Plays?" Scott asked. "What plays?"

"The ones we practiced."

"Where ... when ... we never practiced any plays."

"Sure we did." Dad grinned. "All the time."

Scott was clueless. But before he could argue, Dad took his position over the ball. Scott had never played football in his life, but through the process of elimination, he figured if his dad was playing center, that probably made him quarterback. What a mind.

Once again Scott looked to the faces of the opposing team. Once again he only saw menacing blackness.

He took a breath. Well, it was now or never. "Ready! Set!" he yelled. He'd gotten that much from watching TV. Now what? He wasn't sure. But when all else fails, yell.

"HIKE!"

Dad snapped the ball, but to Scott's amazement, it was no longer a football. Now he was holding a small bronze shield, like in one of those old Roman gladiator movies!

Scott stared at it, frozen in surprise—but not for long. Suddenly, the entire line of shadows charged toward him. He could hear their cleats pounding the mud; he could hear animal growls coming from their throats.

He dropped back. But they kept coming—grunting, growling, snorting like bulls. He frantically searched the field for his dad. Finally he spotted him standing on the sidelines, watching.

"What do I do?!" Scott cried. "What am I supposed to do?"

Dad cupped his hands and shouted. "Use the shield!"

"What?!"

"Just like we practiced!"

The faceless crushers kept roaring toward him, closer and closer.

"Use the shield!" Dad repeated.

"I don't know—*what shield?* What are you talking ab—"

Finally they hit him. Hard. Scott cried as they knocked the wind from him, as his head snapped back and he fell to the ground.

Suddenly he shot up in bed, wide-awake. He was breathing hard and covered in sweat. His eyes darted around the room as he fought to get his bearings.

Finally he took a deep breath and slowly let it out. As he eased back onto the pillow, he tried to relax. But he knew sleep would be a long time returning. When he closed his eyes, all he saw were the shadowy giants. When he opened them, all he thought of was the Ouija board.

The faceless crushers kept roaring toward him, closer and closer. And with them came a strange buzzing sound.

"Use the shield!" Dad repeated.

"I don't know—*what shield?* What are you talking ab—"

The buzzing repeated itself as they hit him. Hard. Scott cried out as they knocked the wind from him, as his head snapped back and he fell to the ground.

Suddenly he shot up in bed, wide-awake. He was breathing hard and covered in sweat. He fought to get his bearings ... as he heard the buzzing sound again. He looked around, perplexed until—

There. On his bedside table. His cell phone.

Even though they didn't have a lot of money, Mom insisted Scott and Rebecca each have their own cell phone—for safety.

Scott grabbed the phone and looked at the screen; he had a text message.

> Welcome to Crescent Bay.
> Z

Z? Who's Z? Scott stared at the text trying to remember who he'd given his number to. He and Becka had gone to a Christian youth thing at a nearby church when they first got here. *Maybe someone there...*

> *Thanks! Who are you?*

He hit 'send' and waited nearly a minute. When there was no answer he gave up, set down the phone, and nestled back under the covers. But he'd barely closed his eyes before the phone vibrated again.

He scooped it up and saw it was the same number. The text read:

> Isn't 3:36 a.m. a little late for a freshman to be up?

Scott frowned then texted:

> *Actually, I was asleep until you called.*

He hesitated a minute, then feeling bad, added:

> *Which was okay cause I was having a pretty weird dream.*

He hit send and started to set the phone back when it buzzed again. This time the text read:

> Does it have anything to do with your Ouija board encounter?

Scott stared at the phone in surprise. Once again he felt the familiar chill creeping across his back. Quickly he typed:

Who are you? How did you know about that?

He hit send and waited ... and waited. Then, after what seemed like hours, his phone buzzed a final time. This time there were only two words:

Be careful.

Immediately, Scott texted back. But there was no response. He tried again. Then again. No answer. Finally, he sat the phone back on the table and lay back in bed, staring up at the ceiling. Any chance of going back to sleep was long gone.

👁 👁

Down the hall, Becka was having her own trouble sleeping. Granted, part of the problem was her skinned knees. Whenever she moved or dragged the blankets across them, they let her know how much they appreciated her little performance out on the track.

But that was no big deal compared to what was going on in Becka's brain. It kept racing with thoughts of Julie, the amulet, and the Ascension Lady.

Should she warn Julie about the pouch or keep her mouth shut? After all, Becka was not like Scott. She couldn't make friends at the drop of a hat. It took time. The few friends she did make, she made for life. That's just how she was ... faithful and giving to the end. But the initial work of making friends, that was always hard for her.

And now, out of the blue, one of the most popular girls in school was reaching out to her. If Becka tried to warn Julie this early in the relationship, she might ruin it. She might sound like some sort of superstitious fanatic. But if she didn't say something, what would happen to Julie?

She shook her head impatiently. What was she worried about? Nothing would happen. It was just a stupid little necklace.

But she'd seen too many things in Brazil ... heard too many stories. Lots of the missionaries her dad had flown in and out of the jungle had tales about witch doctors and hexes and amulets and spirits ... tales that made your hair stand on end and your blood run cold. Tales that they swore were true.

So the argument rolled around and around in her head. To tell or not to tell? Finally, she'd had enough. She threw off the covers, hopped out of bed, and padded downstairs to the kitchen for some munchies. Scott could have his fingernail chewing when things got tense; she preferred junk food.

She'd just shut the door of the fridge and started to unwrap last night's chicken when she heard it.

Scrape.

She froze. It was the same sound she'd heard in the garage the day before. Only now, in the stillness of the house, it seemed louder. She looked at the kitchen door leading to the garage. The sound stopped for a moment, then started ... then stopped again.

Rebecca hesitated. A tiny knot formed in her stomach. She took a deep breath and forced it away. *Mom was right,* she thought, *it's probably just the wind.*

Or a giant rat ...

Or a wild, vicious animal ...

Or a ghastly ghoul hiding in the bizarre boxes at the back of the—

Stop it! Becka forced her mind to quit racing. Which almost worked until—

SCRAPE ... SCRAPE.

She looked back to the door. What was she going to do—just stand there like some little kid afraid of the dark?

SCRAPE.

Somebody better check it out.

SCRAPE ... SCRAPE.

And since there were no other volunteers, that somebody would have to be her. With another deep breath, Becka crossed to the door.

SCRAPE.

After a moment's hesitation and an extra breath just to be safe, she turned the knob and quickly threw open the door.

A light—a beam—streaked across the garage to the back wall of unopened boxes ...

SCRAPE.

... and was gone.

Becka gasped. She fumbled for the switch. It took forever to find it and flood the garage with the much-welcomed light.

There was no movement. No sound. Everything was deathly silent.

Becka stood in the doorway, barely moving, barely breathing. That was definitely *not* the wind. And it definitely was not an animal. It was a light. But what kind of light shoots around garages in the middle of the night making strange noises?

Becka's heart pounded. She was frightened—really frightened—and she hated it. She hated being intimidated. She'd have to do something to get to the bottom of it ... to prove it was all perfectly normal and explainable.

But not tonight. Not all alone. Not in her bare feet and sweats. Becka stepped back, snapped off the light, and closed the kitchen door.

Then, after a moment's hesitation, she reached down and locked it.

4

Monday morning.

Scott knew he was in trouble the moment he entered the school. His first clue was the way a monster-sized kid, complete with skateboard tucked under his arm, picked him up and slammed him against his locker.

His second clue was the way the guy screamed into his face, "Mind your own business!"

But what really cinched it for Scott was when he couldn't lighten the mood with a joke. Humor was his specialty. That's how he stayed on everyone's good side. But before Scott could fire off some wisecrack about treating school property with respect or about not putting too many dents in the locker with the back of his head, Skateboard Kid threw open Scott's locker, tossed him inside, and slammed the door shut.

As the ringing in his ears faded, Scott could hear everyone outside laughing. No surprise there. After all, he was the new guy. Such things were expected. But he had no idea what Skateboard Kid had meant when he'd shouted ... what was it? "Mind your own business"?

Scott tried to relax. Other than the coat hook performing a

little brain surgery in the back of his skull, things weren't too bad. Besides, if the Ouija board was right and he was going to die, it wouldn't be here. This way, he figured, he was safer inside the locker with the coat hook than outside the locker in Skateboard Kid's hands. Eventually some teacher or janitor or vice principal would come to bail him out. Until then, he'd use the situation to his advantage. His humor shone best in tight situations, and it didn't get much tighter than in a locker. He began to whistle.

"What's that?" a voice asked.

"Listen," another said.

The hallway quieted down as Scott continued to whistle. It really wasn't a tune, just something he made up as he went along. But it did the trick.

He could hear the kids snickering. Then laughing.

Suddenly there was loud banging on the locker door. "Knock it off!" Skateboard Kid's voice shouted.

"Oh, sorry," Scott called. "I thought you were gone."

After a moment he began to sing at the top of his lungs:

"Mine eyes have seen the glory of the coming of the LORD. He is trampling out the vintage where the grapes of wrath are — "

BANG! BANG! BANG! "I said knock it off!"

"But I'm bored!"

More laughter outside.

Skateboard Kid's voice dripped with sarcasm. "I'm sorry if you find this an inconvenience. Perhaps I could get you something?"

So the big guy was trying to be clever. Great. That gave Scott home-court advantage. "How 'bout a big-screen TV?" Scott quipped.

More laughter.

"Sorry, fresh out." It almost sounded like the guy was starting to have fun. He continued, "How 'bout a hot tub?"

"Nah," Scott shouted, "I left my shorts at home. But, hey, can

I borrow your board? You know, work on some moves while I'm in here?"

More laughter, until the bell finally rang. The show was over. Scott could hear kids chuckling, talking, shuffling off. Unfortunately no one felt inclined to chuckle, talk, or shuffle off in his direction.

He continued to wait, trying to stay cool and calm. Nearly a minute passed before there was a quiet knock on the locker. "Scott, you there?" The squeaky question was followed by a loud sniff.

Darryl.

Scott sighed. "No, Scott stepped out for a bite to eat—but if you come back in about—"

"Stop fooling around," Darryl interrupted. "What's your combination?"

"32 …"

Scott could hear the combination dial spinning.

"25 …"

More spinning.

"12."

Suddenly the door opened and Scott stepped out—a little stiff from his cramped quarters, but still in one piece. "Thanks," he said, rubbing the coat-hanger dent from his neck.

"Don't mention it," Darryl said as he glanced around. "Don't mention it to anyone." He quickly turned and headed up the hall.

"Hey, wait up." Scott grabbed his first-period books and started after him.

But Darryl didn't slow.

"What's the hurry?" Scott asked as he caught up.

Darryl kept his fast pace. "You don't get it, do you?"

"Get what?"

"What just happened." They rounded the corner, and Darryl quickly searched the hall.

"Sure, I get it. I'm the new kid, which means I'm a walking target for low self-esteemed bullies from dysfunctional fami—"

"Stop joking," Darryl snapped.

"Who's joking?"

"It's nothing to laugh about."

"Lighten up." Scott tried to chuckle. "I'm the one who got thrown in the locker, remember? I'm the new kid who—"

"It has nothing to do with you being the new kid."

"Then what?"

Darryl's eyes kept combing the hall. "Listen, I gotta go," he squeaked. "And don't tell anyone I helped you."

"Darryl—"

Without another word, the little guy turned and darted into a classroom. Now Scott stood in the hallway all alone. Well, not quite all alone. Try as he might, he couldn't shake the feeling that, somehow, some way, he was being watched.

And, once again, that all-too-familiar chill started to move across his shoulders.

👁 👁

Things were almost as weird for Rebecca ... but in the opposite way.

Scott was the star of the family, the life of the party. Oh sure, he was a little egotistical at times—what guy isn't?—but basically he was everyone's favorite. Becka, on the other hand, made it a point to stay in the background, generally doing her best imitation of a potted plant. She wasn't a geek or anything like that—she just tended to be quieter, more thoughtful ... more boring.

But now ...

"Hey, Krissi," Julie called across the cafeteria, "I want you to meet Becka."

Rebecca winced. Something about her name being shouted

across the cafeteria made her uncomfortable. But she wasn't surprised. Ever since second period, Julie had made it her personal mission to introduce Becka to all her coolest and best friends. And since she was considered Julie's friend, that automatically made her their friend.

Of course, Rebecca knew it wouldn't last. As soon as they got to know her, they would drop her like a hot potato. But until then, there wasn't much she could do but play along.

"She's new," Julie continued as she plopped down at Krissi's table and motioned for Becka to do the same. "She's a great long-distance runner—going to help us beat Royal High in the Prelims next week."

Krissi flashed Becka a perfect smile, which was attached to a perfect face, which was attached to perfect hair, which was attached to—well, you probably get the picture.

Rebecca returned the smile and said nothing. She figured the longer she kept her mouth shut, the longer she could keep up the front.

"You're not the one who fell on her face Friday?" Krissi asked.

Becka's smile froze. So much for keeping up a front.

Immediately Julie came to the rescue. "She tripped over those stupid potholes. I keep telling Coach Simmons to fix them, but she keeps putting it off."

Krissi nodded and went back to eating.

Becka wasn't sure if Krissi had seen through her disguise or not. But she had no time to worry about it because suddenly there was another voice.

"Mind if we join you?"

Becka glanced up. An incredible-looking guy was grinning down at Krissi. And by "incredible," we're not talking your normal, everyday incredible. We're talking major "Did my heart just stop beating?" incredible. On the scale of one to ten, this guy was somewhere in the teens. Instinctively, Becka knew he was

Krissi's boyfriend. He had to be. Who else would be dating this perfect Barbie but that perfect Ken?

"Hi, Philip," Krissi said, her face beaming as she scooted over to let the guy and his friend squeeze in.

Becka looked over to the friend and quickly sucked in her breath. It was the guy with the deep blue eyes.

"Hey, Becka." He flashed her a grin. "How you doing?"

Rebecca tried to smile. She wasn't sure if she succeeded. She wanted to answer, to say something witty, but it's hard to be witty when you can't find your voice.

"Ryan," Julie asked in surprise, "you two know each other?"

"Sure do," Ryan said as he reached for the salt. "We're old friends." He gave another smile. "Right, Becka?"

Becka smiled back. She could feel her face start to burn and her mouth go dry. She threw another look to Julie, who was fiddling with the pouch around her neck, sliding it back and forth on its leather thong.

The pouch. Becka had almost forgotten. But no matter how she tried, she couldn't entirely put it out of her mind.

She glanced back to Ryan and froze. Her eyes darted to the other kids ... first Krissi, then Philip. Suddenly she had no appetite. But it wasn't because of Ryan's flirting or Julie's friendliness. It wasn't even because she was sitting with the coolest, most popular group in the cafeteria.

Becka could no longer eat because around each of the kid's necks, she saw the same, identical leather pouch that Julie wore.

It was a California scorcher. Ninety-five point four degrees in the shade. A million point seven degrees in the sun. No wind from the ocean. No clouds in the sky. It was the type of day to skip class and hit the mall or to go to the beach. Definitely not the type of day for a P.E. class to be playing baseball outside.

Then again, P.E. was taught by Coach Dorsek, a man revered and hated by all. A man who, upon awakening that particular morning, discovered his entire front lawn had been t.p.'d. A man who knew that if he made everyone suffer in every one of his P.E. classes, chances were he'd make the "more energy than they know what to do with" punks suffer too.

The score was three to five. Scott's team trailed. So far our hero had grounded out, flown out, and struck out. The way he figured it, that was enough outs; now it was time to try for some hits. As he took the plate, a new pitcher was sent in. Maybe this was Scott's lucky break. Then again ...

The first ball sizzled but was so far inside, Scott had to jump back to avoid getting hit. Some of the fourth-period lunch crowd who were watching from the stands whooped and hollered at the pitcher. But Scott turned back to him and grinned. No hard feelings. The kid was just warming up.

The second ball came in faster and even more inside. Scott hit the deck.

More whoops and hollers.

Scott rose and brushed himself off. This time he did not smile. Instead, he took his position as far back in the batter's box as possible — just to be safe.

Pitch three smoked across the outside corner for a strike.

Pitch four was a carbon copy.

Figuring the pitcher had finally found his groove, Scott stepped closer to the plate.

He didn't remember much after that. He didn't remember taking a couple of practice swings or the ball blazing toward him. And he didn't remember being hit so hard in the head that it cracked his batting helmet.

What he did remember was Coach Dorsek kneeling in front of him, holding out his fingers and yelling, "How many do you see?! How many do you see?!" He also remembered being lifted to his feet and carried toward the nurse's office.

And he remembered one other thing. He remembered the Ouija board's threat on his life.

👁 👁

By late afternoon, the sun had turned the track into a giant grill. Heat waves rippled and shimmered from its surface. And still the girls ran. They ran sprints; they ran 800s; they ran 1600s.

Julie had given Becka tips all afternoon. "Concentrate. Find your rhythm. Stay *focused*. That's the word. Count if you have to. One, two, one, two. But whatever you do, stay focused."

Now they were in their final lap of the mile, their last lap before hitting the showers. As usual, Julie had taken an early lead. That was her style. She never had a sprint to finish with, so she always took the lead early and kept far enough ahead to hold it—even against Becka's great end sprint.

But Becka was no threat to her—once again her mind was drifting. Once again it was back on Julie's pouch. Ever since lunch she'd fought with herself about talking to Julie. She'd even practiced what to say. But no matter how she worded it, she still sounded like some superstitious freak.

For example, there was, "Excuse me, did you know that necklace of yours—the one that Ascension Lady gave you—is totally evil and straight from the devil?"

Then, of course, there was the more subtle approach. "I just love your jewelry. Oh, by the way, do you know it's used by witch doctors in demonic rituals?"

Any way she worded it, Becka would sound like a fool. What was worse, she could kiss her popularity with the in-crowd good-bye—which explained why she didn't say a word. She just kept her mouth shut. And the civil war kept raging inside her head:

Julie's your friend. She deserves to be warned.

You're absolutely right, Becka agreed with herself.

But you didn't make her wear it. Don't you deserve a little popularity?

You're absolutely right, Becka agreed again.

But what about Julie?

And so the debate continued, spinning around in her head until, to her surprise, Becka noticed she had somehow stumbled across the finish line. It wasn't a pretty sight as she tripped and practically fell, but at least she'd made it.

She came to a stop a few feet from Julie. They both leaned over trying to catch their breath. Julie spoke first. "Becka, you gotta concentrate; you gotta stay focused."

Becka nodded, unable to speak.

Julie coughed, then took another gulp of air. "You can beat Royal. We both can."

Again Becka nodded.

"Numero Uno, just you and me ... but you've gotta stay focused."

"All right," Becka finally croaked. "I hear you, I hear you."

Julie cracked a smile. "Just being a friend, girl."

Becka glanced up and tried to return the smile. But she couldn't. All she could think was, *Shouldn't I do the same? Shouldn't I be a friend?*

5

That baseball hit you too hard on the noggin."

"No, Beck, I'm serious." Scott slumped in the chair in front of his computer. His head still hurt from his little "who turned out the lights" routine in P.E. But after a trip to the nurse's office, then some X-rays over at the hospital ER, they found nothing broken. "Maybe a little scrambled," the doctor teased, "but nothing broken."

Immediately Cornelius hopped off the desk and crawled up Scott's arm, chattering, "TO INFINITY AND BEYOND, *SQUAWK!* TO INFINITY AND BEYOND!"

Scott absentmindedly handed him a section of orange. Cornelius stopped talking and gratefully devoured it. Scott looked at his sister. "I really think there's someone—or some-*thing*—out to get me."

"Puh-leeese ...," Becka said scornfully. "Why? Just 'cause once in your life you're not Mr. Popularity?"

He shook his head. "C'mon Beck, you know me better than that."

Becka sighed. She did know him better than that. In fact, she knew him better than anyone. And he knew her too. They'd never admit it, but whether they liked it or not, the two were each other's best friend. Maybe it had something to do with being the only American kids living in the Brazilian rain forest ... or having to constantly make new friends as their parents kept moving from town to town.

Or maybe it was losing Dad.

Whatever the reason, on average days they fought like cats and dogs. But whenever the chips were down, like now, they were always there for each other.

Becka leaned against Scott's dresser and gave a quick recap. "So you go into some bookstore, interrupt a bunch of kids playing some game that makes a stupid threat, and now you think something's out to get you?"

"It was more than just a bookstore," Scott insisted.

"What do you mean?"

"Do you remember Takuma, the old witch doctor? Remember how creepy we'd feel whenever we got near his place?"

"With all his charms and the demonic junk inside?"

Scott nodded. "Well, that's the kind of stuff I saw in the Bookshop, and that's exactly how I felt when I walked inside."

"Hold it; wait a minute." Rebecca felt a twinge of uneasiness. "There were, like, occult things inside there?"

Again Scott nodded. "I didn't recognize a lot of 'em, but—"

"What about charms?"

He looked at her.

"You know, leather pouches with stuff inside, like Takuma would make for the villagers."

Scott shrugged. "I suppose. That kind of stuff, yeah."

Rebecca slowly sat on his bed.

"You okay?"

"This bookstore ...," she said slowly. "What was its name?"

"Why? What's—"

"Just ..." She cut him off, then drew a slow breath. "Do you remember the name?"

"They called it the 'Ascension Bookshop,' whatever that means."

Becka knew exactly what it meant. She took a deep breath. *The Ascension Lady* ... that was what Julie called the woman who made her the pouch. But it wasn't her name; it was where she worked. The Ascension Lady—just like they'd call a woman who worked at a drugstore the drugstore lady, or a bank clerk the bank lady.

"Beck, you okay? Rebecca?"

Was it possible? Was there actually a place like Takuma's where kids were given demonic charms? A place right here in Crescent Bay where kids hung out and practiced ... practiced ...?

Suddenly Becka turned to Scott. "What about this game they were playing?"

"It was more than a game. They took it pretty serious. Darryl called it a 'Ouija board.' You ever hear of it?"

Becka hadn't, but having lived in the jungles of Brazil, there were lots of things she'd never heard of. "And you think there was something wrong about it?" she asked.

Scott nodded and pulled his cell phone out of his pocket. "Not just me." He clicked through his texts to find Z's warning.

"That's weird," he said. "I thought I saved it."

"What are you looking for?" Becka asked.

"There's this guy, Z—I was texting with him Saturday night—" He stopped when he noticed a new text message he had not read. It was from Z:

Check your email.

Weird, Scott thought. *I don't remember giving him my email.*

"Hold on," He turned to the computer and brought up his email. He opened a message titled "Ouija Boards."

Rebecca rose to her feed and looked over his shoulder. The screen read:

> After our talk I did a little research. Please read carefully.
> I will have more soon. AGE: Ouija boards have been used
> in one form or another since about 600 B.C. PURPOSE: To
> communicate with the dead.

Scott and Rebecca exchanged glances. Scott paged down to the next screen:

> TODAY'S USE: Today's version is treated as a toy and sold
> in many department stores. It is a flat, smooth board with
> letters and numbers on it. A pointer moves under the hand
> of the "players" and spells out answers to questions asked.

"That's it," Scott exclaimed. "That's exactly what they were doing."

"Shhh." Becka scowled. They read on:

> DOES IT WORK?: Many "occult experiences" can be faked
> or subconsciously controlled by the subject. The same is
> true with Ouija boards. But that is not always the case.
> Often the messages given by the board go beyond what
> the players know.

Scott hesitated, then paged down to the next screen:

> Numerous tests have been performed where the players
> have been blindfolded and the board's alphabet rearranged.
> It still worked with such speed and accuracy that the only
> answer is "supernatural intervention."

Scott leaned back in his chair and took a deep breath. "What's all that mean?"

Rebecca frowned. "If that board's really working, and the kids aren't moving it themselves ..." She paused, looking at Scott, her eyes serious. "It means we're dealing with spirits."

Scott's eyes widened. "You mean like demons?"

Rebecca bit her lip and slowly nodded. "Yes ... demons."

6

The following morning, Becka stumbled down the stairs to join her family at the breakfast table.

"Hey, Buckwheat," Scott called, between stuffing his face with spoonfuls of Kix. "What'll it be — Kix without milk or . . . no milk with Kix?"

Becka scowled at him through puffy eyes. She definitely was not a morning person. Unfortunately, Scott was. And for some reason, he seemed to think it was his personal mission to make sure everyone was as cheery as he was.

"I'm sorry," Mom said, referring to the lack of milk. "I promise as soon as things settle down and I get a job, we'll get back to normal."

"Any leads yet?" Scott asked.

"A couple," Mom said, grabbing some juice from the fridge and pouring it. "Should know in a day or so."

Once again Becka felt a sadness creep over her. Mom always worked so hard to keep everyone happy. Even when Dad had died, she'd spent more time making sure the kids were okay than she ever spent on herself. Sometimes Becka marveled at Mom's strength and ability to give. Other times it made her feel sad and even a little guilty.

"Did either of you leave that door open last night?" Mom asked, motioning toward the kitchen door leading to the garage.

Scott and Rebecca both shook their heads.

"That's funny. I came down about 1:30 last night, and it was standing wide open."

Becka's eyes shot to the door.

"And there was this strange sound," Mom said, glancing to her daughter. "Kind of like you described when we were moving the boxes."

Becka froze. She threw a look to Scott, but he was too busy eating to notice. She cleared her throat and tried her best to sound casual. "Did you see anything?"

"Well, no," Mom answered. "Not that I really tried. I just sort of shut the door, locked it, and ran for my life." She chuckled, a little embarrassed.

Scott gave a snort.

Becka said nothing. Mom had enough worries. She didn't need any more. But Becka's mind was racing again, trying to piece it all together: the amulet, the Ascension Lady, the attacks against Scott ... the demons.

And now this. A door that she definitely had locked, that was now unlocked and standing wide open.

Was there a connection between all these things? Probably not. But still ... She gave another look at the door. It was shut and securely locked. And that was good enough for now.

At least, she hoped so.

👁 👁

"Excuse me ... Sorry ... Excuse me ..." Scott continued climbing up the bleachers, stepping on more than one pair of feet.

"Hey, watch it, Hairball!" It was Skateboard Kid.

"Hey, how you doing?" Scott said, then continued on, "Excuse me .... Pardon me ... Sorry ..."

He had tried to talk to Darryl all morning, but the little guy would have nothing to do with him. Every time he saw Scott coming from one direction, he'd head the other.

Until now.

Now they were all taking their seats for some sort of assembly—an antidrugs or "crime don't pay 'cause prison's the pits" talk. Every school has them, where some guy comes in and rambles on about messing up his life because he did what he did and how you should never do it because if you do, you'll mess up your life just like he did. At any rate, everyone was gathered to listen.

After crawling over a few dozen more people and toes ...

"OUCH!"

"Sorry."

"Watch it!"

Scott finally managed to squeeze in next to Darryl.

"What are you doing here?" Darryl squeaked. His eyes darted around nervously.

"We've got to talk," Scott answered.

"Not here, not in the open."

"You've been avoiding me all day."

Before they could continue, Principal Slayter had everyone stand for the flag salute. Next he introduced their guest speaker, Assistant Police Chief somebody-or-other. He was a heavy man with a great sense of humor, but Scott and Darryl weren't laughing. The reason was simple. They weren't listening.

"All I'm saying," Scott whispered, "is if those kids aren't moving that Ouija board pointer by themselves, then something else is moving it."

"Duh." Darryl said sarcastically. "Of course something is moving it. Spirits."

Scott was stunned. "You mean you know about them?"

"Of course."

"And you—you actually fool around with them?"

"That's the whole point, brainless. We call up the spirits of the dead and ask them all sorts of—"

"The dead?" Scott interrupted so loudly that Mrs. Pederson, a teacher four rows down, turned around and scowled. Scott gave an apologetic nod, then continued more softly. "Those aren't spirits of dead people, Darryl."

"What are they then?"

"Demons."

"Demons?!" Darryl half cried, half squeaked.

Again Mrs. Pederson turned and glared.

Again the boys looked to her apologetically. This time there were also a few snickers from nearby students.

The two guys looked ahead, pretending to be interested in the assistant chief's speech—something about locking up your bicycles—but they could only fake it for a few moments.

Soon Darryl was leaning back over to Scott and whispering, "They can't be demons."

"Why not?"

"Because they say they're dead people. They give us their names."

"They're lying."

"How do you know?" Darryl asked.

"The dead can't come back and talk to us. It's impossible."

"Who says?"

"The Bible."

"THE BIBLE?!"

This time Darryl was so loud that the assistant police chief stopped and looked toward their section. "I'm sorry, was there a question?"

More kids chuckled. But not Mrs. Pederson. "No, Chief," she said, rising to her feet. "Just a couple of rather ill-mannered children. I do apologize." She turned to Scott and Darryl and motioned for them to join her.

There were plenty more snickers as Scott and Darryl got up and headed down the bleachers to join Mrs. Pederson. Without a word, she escorted them toward the door. The assistant chief resumed his speech, but of course everyone was too busy shaking their heads and chuckling to hear what he said.

☙ ☙

"What do you mean, 'evil'?" Julie grinned.

Rebecca didn't grin back.

"You're not serious are you?" Julie asked.

Becka swallowed hard and gave half a shrug. All day she'd tried to work up the courage to tell Julie about the amulet. Now, as they headed down the hall toward the locker room and practice, it seemed as good a time as any. There weren't too many people around, so if she made a fool of herself, it would at least be in private and not—

"Hey, Krissi!" Julie called across the hall. "Listen to this."

So much for privacy.

"Yeah? What's up?" Krissi asked, joining them.

"Becka here's got something to tell you."

Once again Becka took a deep breath.

The girls waited.

Finally she started, "It's just that those, uh, those charms you're wearing—"

"She's talking about our lucky pouches," Julie interrupted. "She says they're evil. Satanic."

It was Krissi's turn to grin.

Becka looked to the floor. Her face grew hot.

"I don't know about 'evil,'" Krissi said brightly, "but they're definitely satanic. Sure."

Becka snapped her head back up in surprise.

Krissi continued to smile. "Oh, don't worry, not satanic like the mean ol' devil with a pitchfork. But satanic like they're supposed to unlock the deeper forces of nature or something like that. At least, that's what Priscilla says."

"Priscilla?" Becka asked.

"Yeah," Julie answered, "the Ascension Lady who makes this stuff."

"The lady at the Bookshop?" Becka asked.

"Yeah." Krissi nodded. "She says she's a witch. But a good witch—you know, someone who uses the forces for good. Hey, I gotta go. Philip's going to surprise me with this incredible earring, with a diamond and everything."

"If it's a surprise, how do you know what it is?" Julie asked.

"I'm a professional hint dropper." Krissi laughed as she turned and headed back up the hall.

Julie shook her head in amusement until she saw the concerned look on Becka's face. "Lighten up," she said as she pushed open the locker-room door. "Krissi's an airhead, you know that. Nobody believes in witches and that junk. My pouch is just a lucky charm, like a rabbit's foot."

Becka opened her mouth but couldn't find the words.

👁 👁

Detention wasn't as bad as Scott feared. Nothing like in the movies, where the hero sits next to the all-school bully who's just waiting to turn his face into pizza topping.

Nope. Detention was just Scott and Darryl sitting in the library for one hour after school. And Mr. Lowry, the librarian, was so cool he didn't even care if they talked, as long as they kept it down.

"So what makes you an expert in all this spirit stuff?" Darryl asked, sniffing and pushing up his glasses.

"We lived down in South America," Scott bragged. Pride

wasn't a huge problem with him ... just big enough. "Yeah, we had to deal with the occult lots of times."

"Occult?"

"You know, demons, Satan — that kind of garbage."

"Did weird stuff ever happen?"

"Oh sure." Scott pretended to yawn. "We had to deal with this stuff all the time." A definite exaggeration — he'd only heard the stories from missionaries and his dad; he hadn't actually seen anything for himself. Even so, Scott's words did the trick. Darryl's eyes grew as big as saucers.

"Weren't you ever, you know ... scared?"

"Nah ..." By now Scott had crossed the line from exaggeration to lying, so he tried to pull it back a little. "Actually," he cleared his throat, "Mom and Dad, they were the ones who usually handled it when things happened." He noticed a trace of disappointment crossing Darryl's face, so he quickly threw in, "But the Bible says any Christian can beat that stuff."

"Yeah?"

Scott nodded. "Jesus gave us authority over Satan and all the demons." He was still bragging, but at least this part was the truth.

"So ...," Darryl mumbled, mostly to himself, "that's why they're doing it."

"Who's 'they'?" Scott asked. "Doing what?"

"Huh?" Darryl glanced up. He looked a little sheepish. "Nothing, I just, uh — "

"Who are you talking about?" Scott held his eyes.

"No one, I — "

"Come on, Darryl. Who's doing what? What's going on?"

Darryl faltered. Scott pressed in, refusing to back down. "You know, don't you? You know what's going on."

Darryl looked down at the table and finally nodded.

Scott waited.

"It's the Society. They said the spirits or demons or whatever told them to hassle you."

"Why?"

Darryl shrugged. "I guess 'cause they're afraid of you."

"The demons?" Scott asked, a little surprised.

Again Darryl nodded.

The pieces slowly started to fit together. "So it's ..." Scott hesitated.

Darryl finished his thought. "It's the Society that's doing all the stuff to you, yeah."

"Not the Ouija board ... or something weird?"

Darryl nodded. "The way I hear it, the pitcher that beaned you yesterday is about twenty bucks richer."

Scott listened on. Part of him was relieved—no one likes to think there are spirits out to get him—but part of him was also growing angry.

Darryl continued. "They wanted to scare you, to make sure you wouldn't come back."

"No problem there," Scott said quietly.

"Yeah, but ..."

Scott looked up.

Darryl was doing his own bit of thinking. "If you're so much stronger, if you're that much of a threat—I mean, you could go in there and really show 'em your stuff, couldn't you?"

Scott was flattered and cautious at the same time. "Well, I uh ... I don't think—"

"Okay, guys." It was Mr. Lowry. "Your time's up. You're free to go home."

The boys looked at the clock in surprise. It was the fastest hour they'd ever spent.

"I trust you'll be a little more courteous the next time we have guests," he said.

The kids nodded as they gathered their stuff and headed toward the door. But the conversation wasn't over.

"The way I see it," Darryl gave another sniff, "either you're stronger than these demon guys or you're not."

"No question," Scott insisted. "Jesus said he gave us power and authority over all —"

"Then you need to prove it."

"What do you mean, 'prove it'?"

Darryl shoved open the library door, and they stepped into the hall. "Either Jesus is lying when he says you're stronger, or he's telling the truth. The only way to know for certain is by going back to the Society and proving it."

"Darryl, I don't think that's —"

"What's the matter? You're not chicken, are you?"

Scott bristled at the word. "No! It's not that ..." His mind raced, wondering how he got himself into this predicament and, more important, how he'd get himself out.

"Then I'll tell the rest of the kids, and we'll see if they want a showdown." Darryl nodded to himself as if the decision was made. He pushed open the outside doors, and they stepped into the late afternoon sun.

"Darryl," Scott said, "I don't think that's such a good —"

"It should be cool," Darryl interrupted. "Everybody will be there."

Before Scott could protest, a horn honked.

"That's my mom," Darryl said as he turned and started toward an approaching van. "I'll let you know what's happening as soon as I hear anything."

"Darryl, I don't think ..."

But Darryl wasn't listening.

"Darryl? ... Darryl!"

Darryl opened the van door, and immediately his mom began yelling at him for getting into trouble. He gave Scott a roll of the eyes — parents, sheesh! — and slammed the door.

Scott stared after the van as it sped off. Then he glanced down to his fingernails. He was gnawing on them again.

❧ ❧

"You shot off your big mouth again, didn't you, Scotty."

"Beck—"

"Some day that pride of yours is really going to get you in hot water."

"I think I'm already there."

Rebecca sank down on his bed. Cornelius hopped off his perch and started walking up her leg. "Doesn't the Bible say we're not supposed to test God and stuff?" she asked.

"Nobody's testing God," Scott said with a sigh. He snapped on the computer and went to his email. "But somebody's got to prove to those morons who's the strongest."

"And that somebody's going to be you."

Scott shrugged.

Rebecca rolled onto her back and stared at the ceiling. "Why wasn't I an only child?" she moaned.

"Hey, check it out," Scott said. "I got another message from Z." He brought it up onto the screen.

With the slightest sigh Becka sat up and read over Scott's shoulder:

> Another way of proving supernatural contact through the Ouija board is in the number of possession cases. Here's the rest of the information I promised: "Psychics and parapsychologists have received letters from hundreds of people who have experienced 'possession' (an invasion of their personalities). Rev. Donald Page, a well-known clairvoyant and exorcist of the Christian Spiritualist Church, is reported as saying that most of his possession cases 'are people who have used the Ouija board,' and that 'this is one of the easiest and quickest ways to become possessed.'"
> When a person is "possessed," a demon has come inside a

person and is controlling him or her. I warn you, this is not
something to play with. Exercise extreme caution.
    Z

Scott let out a low whistle, and he and Becka exchanged
looks.

"Who is this Z guy, again?"

"I–I'm not sure."

"Well, he's right about one thing. This is serious stuff."

"I know," Scott said with a heavy sigh. "But Christians still
have the power, right? I mean, I can still show them who's boss."

Rebecca looked to her little brother. Once again, she wasn't
sure what to say. All she was sure of was the uneasiness she felt
growing inside.

7

They hit you pretty hard, didn't they, son?"

It was another dream. Scott lay flat on his back in the middle of the football field. His dad was still in his suit of armor as he offered him his hand. Scott took it and slowly rose to his feet.

He knew he was dreaming, but with all this talk of spirits and demons and communicating with the dead, he still had to be sure. "You're not really my dad, are you?"

The man burst out laughing. "Of course not, Scotty. I'm a memory of your dad. Your dad's in heaven with the Lord. You know that."

Scott nodded.

"I'm just your imagination trying to get you to remember something."

"Well, for an imagination, you look pretty real."

"Thanks." The man smiled, wiping a smudge off his metal breastplate. "Now tell me, why didn't you use your shield? Or run one of our plays?"

"I don't ... I don't remember any plays." Scott sighed.

"Of course you remember." His dad chuckled. "We read from the Playbook every day."

Scott stared. "What plays are you talking about? What playbook?"

"The one your mother and I read to you and Becka at the breakfast table."

"We never read any playbook at any breakfast—"

"Sure we did."

"Dad, the only thing we ever read at the table was—" Suddenly Scott stopped. Wait a minute! They did read something at the table. Nearly every day. But it wasn't a football playbook.

Scott looked at his father. "Are you talking about the Bible? Is that what you're trying to get me to remember?"

The man grinned. "Bingo. Now, we haven't got much time, so let's get back in there."

They turned and started toward the line of scrimmage. Once again it was the two of them against an entire squad of shadowy giants. But as Scott looked up, the shadows suddenly disappeared. Now he clearly saw their faces—they were the kids from the Society! The chubby girl in black, the red-haired beauty, and the meaty guy in the tank top. They were all there in front of him. They were bigger—much, *much* bigger—but it was definitely them.

Scott's mind spun as he tried to figure out what was going on. Sure, their family read the Bible, but what did that have to do with football? Or with these kids who were looming over him like overfed gorillas ... gorillas waiting to turn him into human hamburger?

Dad took his position over the ball and waited for Scott's signal.

The Society dug in their cleats, waiting to make the kill.

Scott took a deep breath. *Oh well,* he thought, *it's only a dream, right?* He crouched behind his dad and yelled. "Ready!... Set!... HIKE!"

Dad snapped the ball. But it wasn't a ball. It wasn't a shield, either. Not this time. This time Scott was holding a sword. A sword with all sorts of words and letters on it.

The Society sprung toward him grunting and growling.

"Remember the Playbook!" Dad shouted. "Use your sword! Use your sword!"

Scott dropped back. The Society giants thundered toward him.

"Remember the Playbook! Use your sword!"

Scott was at a loss. He had no idea what to do.

The meaty guy was the first to hit him, knocking out all his wind.

"OOAAFF!" Scott gasped.

The others followed, one after another, leaping on top of him, stomping him ... crushing him.

Scott screamed, but nobody heard. Nobody cared. There was only his pain and the Society as they continued piling on top of him, one after another, grinding his body into the mud.

"Aughh!" he screamed again. "AUGHHHHHHHHH!"

"Scotty! Scotty, wake up." It was Mom. What was she doing on the field?

"Scotty, you're having a nightmare. Scott, wake up, wake up!"

Scott's eyes fluttered open. He was sweating and gasping, but at least the pain was gone and he was back in his room. At least he was no longer football road kill.

His mom was on the edge of his bed, holding his shoulders tightly, her eyes filled with concern. "Are you all right?" she asked gently. "I heard you screaming."

"Yeah," Scott said, trying to catch his breath. "I think so. I just ... it was a dream ... about Dad ..." His voice trailed off, and when tears jumped to his eyes, he was too tired to hold them back.

His mom pulled him close and held him. "I know, Scotty," she said. "I know. I miss him too."

Scott wasn't sure how long they sat holding each other. But he didn't care. All he knew was that he needed it.

They both did.

❧ ❧

The next morning, Scott was still trying to figure out the dream as he stood at his locker, dialing the combination.

"It's all set," Darryl's voice squeaked.

"What?" Scott glanced up. "Oh, hi, Darryl."

"The Society has agreed to meet you at the Bookshop after school."

"Today?"

"Of course today. You are ready, right?"

"Listen, Darryl, I don't—"

"You're not chickening out?"

"No, it's not that. It's—"

"Good. 'Cause they said you would. They said—"

"Hold it," Scott interrupted. "They said I'd chicken out?"

"Sure. They said you'd be afraid to take them on." Darryl gave a louder than normal sniff.

Scott could feel himself getting angry. Before he knew it, he shot back, "You tell them I'm not afraid of anybody." He slammed the locker shut. "You tell them I'll be there." With that, he turned and stormed off.

"Great!" Darryl called after him. "It's gonna be great!"

Scott slowly let out his breath. He wished he could agree. But he was already feeling lousy. Why couldn't he keep his big mouth shut?

❧ ❧

"Let me get this straight," Krissi said, almost letting a frown wrinkle the perfect skin of her perfect forehead. "You're saying if we keep wearing these things, we're all going to become like the girl in *The Exorcist?*"

Julie and the other kids at the lunch table snickered. Once again Julie had brought the subject up, and once again Becka was having to defend herself. "All I'm saying is that some witch doctors use those charms to control other people."

"What exactly do you mean by 'control'?" Ryan asked. His blue eyes looked at her intently. Becka was grateful that at least one person seemed to be taking her seriously.

"She means like demon possession," Philip explained.

Becka shook her head. "Not really. It's just a way witch doctors get people to depend on their charms instead of themselves ... or God."

"You, like, really know witch doctors?" Krissi asked.

"Wow!" Julie exclaimed.

Rebecca could tell they were getting off the subject. But before she could get them back on, she noticed Philip. His body was going rigid. He was becoming as stiff as a board.

Julie laughed and slapped him on the arm. "Knock it off, Philip."

But Philip didn't respond. For a moment, there was a look of panic on his face ... then it went totally blank. His eyes rolled up into his head, and he started choking.

"Philip ...," Krissi scolded. She was certain he was clowning. Well, almost certain.

But as the choking continued, Becka thought he might be having some sort of seizure. Maybe it was epilepsy or ...

She tried to push back the thought.

... something worse.

"Philip." Krissi was louder now. And frightened. "That's not very funny. Philip!"

The choking increased until it sounded inhuman — like some monster or alien. The kids from the surrounding tables stopped their conversations and turned to stare.

"Philip! Knock it off! Philip?!"

Ryan snickered. He still didn't believe it was true. But then

Philip spoke. Well, at least Philip's mouth spoke. His voice was different. Deeper. Sinister.

"Philip is no longer here—we have control now."

"Philip?" Krissi shook him, but he didn't react. "Philip, answer me!" Her voice grew louder. "What do you want with him? Who are you?"

"Our needs are simple."

"Who are you? Where's Philip?"

"Our needs are simple," the voice repeated.

"What do you want?!"

"Pass the salt, please—this hamburger casserole is gross."

There was a moment of stunned silence, then everyone broke into laughter. Philip, Ryan, Julie—everybody roared. Well, almost everybody. Krissi was too busy giving Philip a punch to the arm.

Then there was Becka. "Excuse me," she mumbled hoarsely as she rose and quickly dashed from the table.

"Becka," Ryan called. "Hey, Becka, it was just a joke. Come on back ..."

But Rebecca wasn't coming back. She wasn't mad. She just didn't want them to see the tears filling her eyes.

❧ · ❧

As they approached the Bookshop, Scott was nervous. Actually, scared spitless.

But not for long ...

The handsome, middle-aged woman was no longer there. She had been replaced by some pimply-faced, high school kid.

"Where's Priscilla?" Darryl asked.

"She, uh ... she said she had some errands to run. She'll be back after the, uh ..." He motioned to Scott. "You know, after you guys are through."

"She didn't want to be here?" Darryl squeaked in surprise. "She didn't want to see the fireworks?"

The guy shrugged. "I'm just telling you what she said."

"Cool." Darryl gave a loud sniff as they passed the counter and headed down the hall.

"What's cool?" Scott asked.

"She doesn't want to meet you."

"Who?"

"Priscilla, the lady who runs this place."

"Why not?"

"Sounds like she might be afraid."

"Yeah?" Scott could feel a twinge of the ol' pride returning.

Darryl sniffed again. "Maybe you have too much power for her to handle."

Suddenly Scott was feeling more confident. Somehow he seemed to be standing just a little bit taller, his chest swelling just a little bit bigger. Who knew — maybe he'd call fire down out of the sky to burn up the Ouija board (he'd read something like that in the Bible). Or maybe he'd make the kids unable to speak until they acknowledged God's power (he'd read that too). He wasn't sure. But whatever he did, it would be awesome.

They arrived at the door. It was closed.

Darryl turned to him and pushed up his glasses. "You sure you're ready?"

Scott nodded. "Let's do it."

Darryl sniffed and slowly opened the door.

Once again the room was dark, except for the dozen or so candles flickering. Once again the kids looked up — the chubby girl in black, the pretty redhead, and the meaty guy. There were plenty of other kids sitting around too. More than Scott remembered from the last time. But that was okay. Obviously they wanted to see the show.

"Come on in," Meaty Guy said, trying to sound casual. (He might have pulled it off if it wasn't for the way his voice quivered.)

Scott smiled. He strode confidently into the room, and for

good reason: The Ascension Lady had run off, the kids were shaking in their boots, and he, Scott Williams, had the power of God behind him. Not a bad combination.

This was going to be a piece of cake.

8

One, two, one, two, one, two ...
     One lap to go. Becka counted, she concentrated, she did everything Julie taught her. Everything to keep focused on the 1600 they were completing.

The Prelims were tomorrow. She and Julie would run the mile, the half mile, and probably a couple of the longer sprints. Who knows, if she did well, she might even help Julie beat Royal High.

But that wasn't the real reason she ran. Becka ran to forget the afternoon. She ran to forget the laughter, the snickers, the put-downs.

Ever since Philip's little possession routine at the lunch table, word had spread. Suddenly everyone knew her as the "Church Lady" — the superstitious Christian who believed the devil lurked behind every shadow.

One, two, one, two ...

Julie ran half a dozen steps ahead. As usual, her rhythms were smooth and flowing. It infuriated Becka. Not Julie's running, but that Julie hadn't stood up for her. In fact, Julie was the one who had started it. And she was still spreading it ... and enjoying it!

One, two, one, two, one, two ...

Once again Becka's lungs were on fire, but that was nothing compared to the anger smoldering in her heart. This was her reward for trying to help Julie? For trying to warn her? Total humiliation!

Half a lap to go.

What did Julie think? That because Becka was quiet, she didn't have feelings? That because they were friends, she could get away with that kind of junk?

She looked ahead to Julie. Miss Perfect, Miss "I've got the great looks and money and friends." Who did she think she was, anyway?

Becka's anger continued to burn—until an idea took root. She never thought she'd be able to take Julie. Julie was the expert, the teacher, the one destined to go to State. But there she was, not that far away ... and with no sprint to rely on for the end.

A strength surged through Rebecca—a strength connected with her anger. It started somewhere in her chest and flowed into her arms and legs. Her energy increased more than ever before. With two hundred meters to go, it was too soon to begin her sprint—way too soon. But it didn't matter. She started to count faster.

One, two, one, two, one, two ...

She began closing the gap.

Coach Simmons was the first to spot it. "What's Becka doing?"

Others looked up and watched. Becka continued to count, to dig in.

One hundred meters to go.

A couple of kids started to shout, to cheer her on. "All right, Becka! Go for it!"

One two one two one two ...

Inch by inch, she moved up until she finally pulled beside Julie. The look of astonishment on the girl's face almost brought enough satisfaction to Becka. Almost.

Who *did* she think she was, anyway?

Becka pushed harder.

Julie panicked. For a moment she lost her rhythm.

Perfect. Rebecca inched ahead.

Fifty meters to go.

Now it was an all-out race. Just the two of them. Becka was beyond exhaustion. Her lungs ached, but her rage was stronger than her pain.

One two one two one two . . .

Julie tried to keep up, but she had no sprint. She fell two strides behind, then three. Once again Becka heard the girl break her rhythm, but she didn't look back. She didn't have to.

Twenty meters.

"Atta girl, Becka!" kids shouted. "Kick it in, girl, kick it in!"

OneTwoOneTwoOneTwo . . .

Ten meters.

She could almost hear Julie's heart breaking.

Good.

Five meters.

Becka stretched and crossed the line — six strides ahead of Julie. She stumbled and practically fell as she came to a stop, but the team members were there to catch her and congratulate her.

"Way to go girl! 5:51!" Coach Simmons shouted. "That was incredible! You too, Julie." She turned to Julie who was standing behind her. "5:53! Your best time ever! You girls are going to stomp Royal tomorrow!"

Becka stayed hunched over, gulping air. She could hear Julie coughing and gasping beside her. But she didn't look. Instead, she rose, turned, and started for the showers.

A couple more kids congratulated her, but Becka paid little

attention. She had won. She had beaten Julie, and that was all that counted.

"Hey Becka ... Becka!" It was Julie's voice. But Becka ignored her as she continued toward the showers. Revenge was sweet. More than sweet. It was glorious.

And if she could do it today, she could do it tomorrow!

❧ ❧

Back at the Bookshop, Meaty Guy continued with the opening remarks. "So how do you want to do this?"

Scott shrugged. "It's your show."

The redhead stepped forward. "My name's Kara. This is James." She motioned to Meaty Guy. "And Brooke, here, she's our president."

The girl in black nodded. She was obviously the coolest and most collected of the group. At least that's how she looked on the outside. On the inside, Scott figured she was shaking like the others.

He approached the Ouija board, trying his best to appear calm. And why not? After all, he was holding all the cards. He glanced around the room, peering into the darkness. Then, motioning to the candles, he quipped, "So what's the deal? You guys forget to pay the electrical bill?"

No one laughed. Not even a smile. So they wanted to play hardball, did they? Fine. He could do that.

Brooke spoke next. "Darryl here says you think the Society is a hoax, that we have no power."

"Not exactly," Scott corrected. "I believe there's power here ... just the wrong type."

Brooke looked on, waiting.

Scott motioned to the Ouija board's pointer. "If you guys aren't moving that thing around, then something else is. And that something else is definitely unfriendly."

A brief silence hung over the room until Brooke finally answered. "Granted ... sometimes we wake a rather cranky spirit from the dead, but—"

"No way," Scott broke in. She glared at him over the interruption, but he continued. "Those aren't spirits of the dead you're talking to."

"If they're not spirits of the dead," she asked, "then who are they?"

Scott shrugged. "Just your average, run-of-the-mill demons."

"And by demons you mean ...?"

"The bad guys. The angels that got kicked out of heaven with Satan."

Brooke looked at him a moment. "Interesting," was all she said.

"Truth," was all he said.

After another pause, she continued. "Yes, well, we'll see, won't we?" With that she placed her fingertips on the plastic pointer and nodded to Meaty Guy to do the same. There was a slight shuffling in the room as the kids moved in for a better view.

Brooke threw back her head and closed her eyes. "So tell me," she said, still speaking to Scott, "who would you like to talk to?"

"Got me," Scott forced a grin. "How 'bout Fred Flintstone."

A couple kids chuckled.

"Get real," Meaty Guy scowled. "It has to be somebody dead. You know, like—"

But that was as far as he got. Suddenly the pointer began to move. Meaty Guy's eyes shot down to it as it scooted across the board.

Scott swallowed a wave of uneasiness. The chill was back—licking up his spine, crawling over his skin.

The pointer continued to move, momentarily stopping over each letter until it spelled out the name:

H-A-R-R-Y P-O-T-T-E-R

Meaty Guy stared at the board. "I don't get it. Harry Potter isn't real. He's a cartoon character just like Fred—"

"It's a joke, stupid," Brooke said, pretending to laugh. Then, looking back to the board, she asked, "Helen, is that you? Helen of Troy, are you here?"

Immediately the pointer shot to the word *Yes*.

"That's Helen of Troy," Brooke explained. "She's got a great sense of humor."

"A regular comedian." Scott smirked.

There were a couple more chuckles from the back, but Brooke ignored them. "Helen," she called, "we have an unbeliever in our midst. Is there someone he can talk to—one of your friends who can help him achieve greater enlightenment?"

The pointer rested silently.

"Helen? Are you still here?"

Again no movement. Nothing.

"Helen?" Brooke repeated. "Is there someone here who can make him a believer? Please, tell us. Anybody?"

Then, ever so slowly, the pointer began to move. All eyes watched as it gradually spelled out the letters:

H-I-S

Then it stopped.

Brooke looked at Scott. "'His'?" she asked. "Do you know anyone who calls himself 'His'?"

Scott shook his head, trying not to smile. Things were already falling apart, and they'd barely started. This was easier than he'd thought it would be.

"Maybe they're initials," the redhead offered. "You know, somebody with the initials H. I.—" She stopped as the pointer started moving again. The letters came much faster this time:

F-A-T-H-E-R

" 'Father,' " Meaty Guy exclaimed. "His father?"

Brooke looked up to Scott. "Is that true? Is your father dead?"

Scott felt the chill spread across his shoulder blades and into his chest. He gave a little shudder. "Well, yeah, sure, but anybody could know that."

Brooke nodded and closed her eyes again. "Helen … Helen, will his father speak to us?"

Scott shifted uneasily. Somewhere, in the back of his neck, a dull ache began.

But there was no answer.

"Helen?"

The pointer started to move again. All eyes watched as it spelled out the letters:

H-E-L-L-O S-O-N

Scott took another swallow. "You're going to have to do better than that." He tried to smile, but he couldn't quite pull it off.

"What was his name?" Brooke asked.

"Uh, Hubert," Scott lied. Actually his dad was named after the apostle Paul.

Brooke turned back to the board and closed her eyes. "Hubert, tell us, what —"

Before she could finish, the pointer moved again.

P-A-U-L

Scott sucked his breath in as though he'd been punched in the gut.

Brooke opened her eyes. "Your dad's name isn't Hubert. It's Paul."

Scott's heart started to pound in his ears. The ache in his neck crept into his head and up to his temples. He took a deep breath and tried to relax. "Yeah, I, uh, I guess it is."

For the first time since they met, the slightest trace of a smile formed on Brooke's lips. "You still don't believe, do you?"

Scott searched for a snappy comeback but couldn't seem to find one.

"Ask him a question," the redhead said to Scott. "Ask him something only the two of you would know."

Scott's heart pounded louder in his ears. His head throbbed. It was getting hard to think. He knew he had authority over these guys, he knew he could win ... but how, where to start?

"Go ahead," Darryl spoke up. "Ask him something."

"Okay," Scott said, nervously clearing his throat, "All right ..." Everyone waited as he thought. Finally he had it. "If you're really my father ..." He took another breath. "If you're really my father, tell me what happened to my Swiss army knife."

It was a trick question. The Swiss army knife was actually his dad's. Scott had bought it for him last Father's Day, but Scott fell so in love with it that he constantly borrowed it from his dad. It had become a joke between the two of them ... until his father's death.

The pointer went into action and quickly replied:

N-O-T Y-O-U-R-S ...

Scott's jaw dropped as the answer continued to form:

M-I-N-E

A lump grew in his throat. Before he knew it, Scott's eyes began to burn. Could it be ...? No one else would have known. Not Mom. Not Becka. No one. Was it possible?

For the past six months, he had longed for his father ... but it was more than a longing. It was an ache. An ache that went all the way into his gut. And nothing, absolutely nothing could ease it. Oh sure, he made his little jokes and pretended to have a good time, but underneath, the pain was always there. The man he adored, the man who had been the center of his life, had been suddenly and violently ripped away from him. And for six months, the pain had been unbearable.

But now ...

At last Scott spoke. His voice was thick, barely audible. "Dad?" He reached out to the table to steady himself. "Dad ... is it ... is it you?"

The pointer quickly spelled:

T-E-L-L M-O-M A-N-D B-E-C-K-A ...

The letters continued to form, but Scott's eyes were filling with moisture so quickly that it was hard to see. He tried to blink back the tears, but they only came faster. By now his heart thundered in his ears. His head throbbed unbearably. His father was there, somewhere in the room, trying to communicate. His father, the one he thought he'd never ever see again, was right there ... spelling out the words:

I M-I-S-S Y-O-U G-U-Y-S

"Oh, Dad — " The phrase caught in Scott's throat. He choked back a quiet sob. He couldn't help himself. He tried to speak again, his voice hoarse with emotion, just above a whisper. "I miss you, too ... so much ..."

And then, ever so gently, the pointer came to a stop.

Scott looked on, waiting for more.

But there was nothing.

"Dad." His voice carried a trace of panic. "Dad, don't go."

No answer.

"Dad ... Dad, come back!" He was much louder. Practically shouting. "There's so much we don't know ... Dad!"

Brooke turned to him. Her own eyes had a glint of moisture in them. "I'm sorry, Scott. He's gone."

"Dad," Scott desperately scanned the room, "Dad! Dad, don't go! Dad! Please come back! *Daaad!*"

But there was no answer. No movement on the board, no sound in the room. Only the uneasy cough of one or two kids. Everyone felt for him. Some looked to the ground in embarrassment. It's true, they'd won. They'd proven the board's power. But at the moment, no one felt like celebrating.

Scott's voice was fainter now, weaker. "Dad ..." He angrily wiped at the tears spilling onto his cheeks.

But there was no answer.

9

I can't believe you thought it was Dad!" Rebecca said as she paced back and forth in Scott's room. Mom had gone to bed hours ago, but they hadn't. The day had been brutal for both of them, and they were still up in his room comparing notes.

Cornelius sat on his perch, sound asleep.

"You had to be there," Scott insisted. "The Ouija board knew things."

"Like?"

"Like Dad's name, like that he died, like—"

"Scotty, anybody could have known—"

"Like the Swiss army knife I gave him for Father's Day."

Becka slowed her pacing and turned to him. "It knew that?"

Scott nodded. He slumped down in front of the computer. After a lengthy silence, he went to his email. Maybe Z had sent him another message. The guy seemed to have pretty good timing.

Becka also had to sit. Slowly she eased herself onto the bed. She missed Dad as much as Scott did. She still cried, usually at the most inconvenient times. It didn't take much to set her off, just some little memory or some little phrase Dad had used, and suddenly, against her will, there were the tears. "How ..." She cleared the thickness in her voice. "How could it be Dad when the Bible says ..." Her voice trailed off.

"I know," Scott sighed. "The Bible says we die one time, then go to face God. No dead souls haunting houses, no dropping in for late-night seances. But it also says we're supposed to beat the bad guys." He hesitated a moment, then continued. "I gotta tell you, Beck, after today I'm not sure what I believe."

Becka threw him a look. What was he saying? That the Bible was wrong? That he didn't trust it?

Feeling her eyes on him, he shrugged. "I call them like I see them. You get clobbered. I get clobbered. Then I wind up talking to Dad. Doesn't sound like what we've been told is all that accurate, does it?"

Rebecca took a long, deep breath and slowly let it out. All of their lives they'd been taught the Bible was true ... but that was before Dad had died, before Becka had become the laughingstock of the school, before Scotty started getting beat up, before Dad started talking through Ouija boards. Maybe they were wrong, maybe the Bible wasn't—

NO! Becka pushed the thought out of her mind. Impossible. She refused to think it.

"Nothing from Z tonight," Scott said as he shut down the computer. "Well, I guess we'd better hit the hay."

Becka nodded and rose from the bed. "Sweet dreams," she said half sarcastically.

"Yeah, maybe I'll have another crazy one about Dad and his suit of armor."

Becka stopped at the door. "You've been dreaming about Dad?"

Scott nodded. "We're always playing football. And he's always wearing this suit of armor."

"Armor?"

"Weird, huh?"

"Not for you, Scotty." She sighed. "Nothing's too weird for you."

He nodded. "See you in the morning."

She stepped into the hall, hesitated, then turned back. "You know, Dad used to talk about armor."

Scott looked to her.

"Yeah," she continued. "Remember? 'Put on the whole armor of God.' He used to tell us that, remember?"

A scowl crossed Scott's face. "He did, didn't he?" He walked over to the shelf near the door and picked up his Bible. "Do you remember where that was?"

"Here let me." She took the book from his hands and quickly riffled through the pages. "Ephesians something . . ."

Scott's mind churned. Wasn't that what the dreams kept saying? "Put on the armor, put on the armor"?

"Ah, here we go." Becka finally found it. "Ephesians six, verse eleven. Listen: 'Put on all of God's armor so that you can take your stand against the devil's schemes.'"

Scott nodded. Satan was definitely pulling some tricks, all right. But what kind of armor was it talking about? "Is there more?" he asked.

She continued: "'For our struggle is not against flesh and blood, but against . . . the powers of this dark world . . .'" Rebecca quietly groaned.

"What's wrong?" Scott asked.

"It's the way I treated Julie, like she was the enemy. But she's not. She's the one I'm trying to *save* from the enemy."

Scott nodded, but his mind was already on something else. "Read that last part again."

Becka backed up and repeated: "'For our struggle is not against flesh and blood, but against the rulers, against the authorities, against the powers of this dark world and against the spiritual forces of evil in the heavenly realms.'"

"Of course," Scott quietly whispered. "Why didn't I see it?"

Becka looked to him, not understanding.

He talked slowly, piecing it together as he spoke. "If we're fighting against all these evil spirits ... and if they're all around ... don't you think at least one of them would have known about that army knife?"

Becka frowned. "Run that past me again?"

"If these demons are everywhere, then one of them must have heard me and Dad joking about the knife back in Brazil, back when he was alive."

Rebecca began to nod. "Then it wasn't Dad talking through the board."

Scott nodded. "It was a demon, just like we thought ... just like the Bible says."

They looked at each other a long moment before Rebecca turned back to the page and continued reading: "'Therefore put on the full armor of God, so that when the day of evil comes, you may be able to stand your ground.'"

"We know that." Scott sighed impatiently. "But what does it mean by armor? What type of armor?"

"Hold it," Becka called as she silently read ahead, "there's more. Listen to this: 'Take up the shield of faith, with which you can extinguish all the flaming arrows of the evil one.'"

"Shield?" Scott nearly shouted. "You said 'shield'!"

"Yeah—" Becka nodded toward the verse. "—'shield of faith.'"

"That's it!"

"What's it?"

"Just like in the dream," he continued. "I didn't have my shield in that bookshop, so I got clobbered, just like in the dream!"

"What are you talking about?" Becka demanded. "You have faith; you have a shield."

"No." Scott spun around to her. "I put my faith in what that Ouija board said. When I was there, the board convinced me I was talking to Dad. I believed what the board said instead of what the Bible said. I let down my faith—I dropped my shield."

"And got clobbered."

"Exactly," Scott exclaimed. "In the dream, it was physical with the football players, but in the Bookshop, it was spiritual."

Becka began to nod.

"Go ahead," he said, motioning toward the Bible. "Is there more? Anything else about armor or shields or anything?"

She read on. "'Take the helmet of salvation and the sword of the Spirit, which is the word of God.'"

"Yes!" Scott could barely contain himself. "Just like in the dream!"

Becka looked back at him.

"Don't you get it?" Scott grabbed the book out of her hands. "This is our sword. This is what we fight with. We don't just win 'cause we're Christians. I strolled in there like some hot shot, thinking 'cause I was a Christian everything would go my way. But we have to use our shield and our sword. We have to believe God—that's our shield—and we have to use his Word," he said, waving the Bible, "our sword!"

Rebecca nodded, then she smiled. He was right.

"Isn't that incredible!" Scott cried. "It was all right here, right here! All we had to do was read it!"

👁 👁

Again Scott lay flat on his back in the middle of the football field. It was another dream, only this time he was wearing armor—just like his father's.

"Glad you finally suited up." His dad chuckled as he reached down and pulled him back to his feet.

"It took me a while to catch on." Scott grinned. "I tell you, for my imagination, you were sure vague about all this."

"Not really." His dad slapped him on the shoulder plate. "It's right there in the Playbook; you just had to be reminded." With that, the man turned and headed toward the locker room.

"Hey," Scott called after him, "where you going?"

"The game's over. You learned your lessons."

"But what about those kids?" Scott motioned toward the other team. "What about the members of the Society?"

"What do you care? You've got the truth now; that's all that counts."

The man had a point. Why should Scott care? He'd learned his lesson. He'd learned the truth. What difference did it make what they thought? After all, these were the kids responsible for locking him in the locker, for hitting him in the head with the baseball. If they wanted to fool around with fire, let 'em get burned. What did he—

And suddenly he saw them, over at the line of scrimmage. But this time the shadows were gone, and they were no longer giants. Now they looked like frightened kids—Meaty Guy, the redhead, even Brooke, the leader. They were all huddled together and seemed to be searching the field for someone ... for anyone.

Suddenly the words Becka spoke earlier rang in his ears. *"They're not the enemy ... they're victims of the enemy."*

He tried to ignore the thought; he tried to look away. But for some reason he couldn't. Then slowly, one after another, the faces turned toward him. Meaty Guy, Brooke, the redhead. Soon all their eyes were locked on his. They almost seemed to be pleading, to be begging. They didn't want to play anymore. It was obvious. They wanted to stop the game; they wanted to go home.

"Dad," Scott called, unable to take his eyes from the kids. "Dad ... someone needs to tell them. They need help."

"You just want to show off again." His dad laughed lightly.

"No, I'm serious."

The man continued walking away.

"Please! I want to help. I mean that."

The man came to a stop, but he did not turn to face his son.

"They need someone to tell them," Scott repeated. "I know I was all full of pride, I know I was showing off before, but ... just look at them."

The man still did not turn.

A tightness formed in Scott's throat. He wasn't sure if it was anger at his dad or pity for the kids. Maybe it was both. "Will you look at them!" he shouted. "They've got to be warned!"

The man still did not move.

"Aren't you listening?!" Scott cried. "Don't you care?!"

And then, ever so slowly, the man turned. There was a faint twinkle in his eyes. He began to nod. Scott wasn't sure, but somehow it felt like he'd just gone through another test—only this time he had passed.

"How?" Scott stammered. "What can I do? How can I help?"

The man looked on saying nothing.

"Please," Scott said, "tell me straight, no riddles, this time, just ... tell me."

His father opened his mouth. He said only one word. But it was enough. "Prayer."

Scott shot up in bed—wide-awake. He wasn't covered in sweat this time, but he was filled with determination.

👁 👁

"Becka, Becka wake up."

"Umph rommle raaur sa mophma ...," she mumbled. She was trying to say, "It's 4:30 in the morning—leave me alone, jerkface," but at the moment, "Umph rommle raaur sa mophma" was the best her mouth could come up with.

Twenty minutes later, the two of them were in her room with their Bibles open and were poring over every verse they could find about prayer.

"This is it!" Scott finally cried. "I knew it was here." He began to read: "'And I tell you that ... whatever you bind on earth will be bound in heaven, and whatever you free on earth will be freed in heaven.'"

"'Bind,'" Rebecca repeated, "like tie up?"

"Yeah." Scott nodded. "Like demons or spirits."

"And whatever we free?"

"Probably like angels and God's power and stuff."

Rebecca nodded.

"There's more. Listen: 'Again, I tell you that if two of you on earth agree about anything you ask for, it will be done for you by my Father in heaven.'"

Rebecca shook her head.

"What's wrong?"

"How could we have been so stupid ... to try and do all this stuff without even praying?"

"Well we're not stupid anymore. What time do you have?" Scott asked.

"Almost six."

"Then let's get to it."

"To what?"

"There's two of us, right?"

"Right."

"And it says, 'if two of you agree on anything ...'"

"You want to start praying for the Society?" Rebecca asked incredulously.

Scott nodded. "The Society, Julie, your friends, everybody —binding the spirits that are trying to hurt them and loosing God's power to protect them."

Rebecca gave him a look. "That's a lot of praying."

"You read it yourself. That's where the power is."

Becka hated admitting when Scott was right, but the guy had a point. A major point. "Well," she said, taking a deep breath, "let's get started."

10

Things turned for the worse. All day Julie avoided Becka. Word quickly spread around school that the two friends had become enemies … that Becka had used Julie, that she had become a traitor, that she had taken everything Julie had taught her in track and was planning to turn it against her that afternoon at the big meet.

So much for answered prayer, Becka thought. She almost wondered if it would have been better not to pray.

Almost, but not quite.

It seemed those verses about believing and not dropping her shield of faith kept rattling inside her head. So she kept praying. She prayed for Julie when the girl ignored her in the hall. She prayed when Julie's lunch table was suddenly "filled up." And now she said a silent prayer as she sat on the ground stretching and warming up for the 1600 meter race.

"Lord, please help Julie … show her your love, help her understand that—"

"All right, Becka, where is it?"

Rebecca glanced up. Julie hovered over her with her hands on her hips.

"Where's what?"

"Don't play innocent with me," Julie said with a scowl. "What did you do with my good luck charm?"

"What did I—"

"I put it in my basket when I suited up, and now I can't find it. Where is it?"

"Julie," Becka rose to her feet. "I haven't seen it."

"Don't lie to me!"

"All right ladies," said the woman at the check-in table. "Let's head on up to the starting line."

All the girls rose from the nearby benches and began to pull off their warm-ups. All the girls, including the three from Royal High ... the three who swept the long distant events. Julie glanced over at them and swallowed hard. These were the people she wanted to beat. These were the people she *had* to beat.

They moved upfield toward the starting line—but Julie wasn't done with Becka. Not by a long shot. "Everybody knows you have it in for me, that you want to bump me out of getting to State."

Becka started to argue, but Julie would not be interrupted. "Where is my charm?" There was no missing the tremor in her voice.

"I haven't seen it," Becka insisted. "Honest."

Julie searched her face. "Becka, if you're lying ..."

"I'm *not* lying. Could you have dropped it? Did you leave it with your sweats?"

"I've checked—I've checked everywhere!" Julie was starting to panic. "I need that charm."

"Julie, you're a better runner than me; you're better than all of us. You don't need some stupid—"

"You don't understand; I've never run without it!"

Becka looked at her, surprised.

Julie shrugged. "It sounds dumb, I know, but I need it. Becka, I ..." She searched for the words. "I just need it!"

Becka felt herself growing angry, but not at Julie. She was angry at the charm. She was angry because it was turning her gifted friend into a quivering pile of self-doubt. There was nothing magical about that charm. It had no power. Becka looked at Julie again, and her eyes narrowed. Then again, in one sense, maybe it did. In one sense, Julie had given it so much control over her life that she might actually lose the race without it.

They approached the line. The starter—a man in a red and white tracksuit—motioned them forward. The best runners from five different schools, including the dreaded trio from Royal, stepped onto the track.

"All right ladies, listen carefully, because I'm only going to explain this once…"

As the starter gave last-minute instructions, Becka shot a glance at Julie. The poor girl's eyes darted nervously about. No way was she concentrating. No way was her mind on the race. It was on that stupid charm. Finally Becka leaned over and whispered, "Focus."

Julie took a deep breath and nodded, but Becka could tell when her friend looked over to the runners from Royal her mind resumed spinning.

"You can do it," Becka whispered. "Focus, just like you told me. You and me, Numero Uno, all you have to do is—"

"Excuse me, miss?"

Becka looked up. The man was glaring directly at her. "Am I interrupting anything?" he asked.

Becka shook her head and croaked, "Sorry."

"All right, let's get going then. Any questions?"

There were none.

The starter crossed to the end of the line and cleared his throat. "Runners to your mark."

Everyone stepped up to the line, taking last-minute breaths, shaking out last-minute tensions. Everyone but Julie. She was as tight as a fiddle string.

The man raised his pistol.

Becka caught Julie's eye. She mouthed the word, "Focus."

Once again Julie nodded and took a breath.

"Runners set ..."

Everyone crouched, preparing.

Please, Jesus, Becka prayed.

And the pistol fired.

👁 👁

Scott stood all alone in the hallway of the Bookshop. He had not told Darryl. He had not told anyone. All he had were the words of Scripture, the prayers he and Becka had prayed that morning, and his faith. Was that enough? He'd soon find out.

He reached out and knocked on the door.

There was no answer.

He knocked again, louder.

Still no answer.

Fighting off another shiver, he asked God to be with him, to protect him. Then he took the knob, turned it, and quietly pushed open the door.

There was the usual darkness, the usual candles, the usual kids sitting around—half a dozen on the sofa, four or five around the Ouija board. They glanced up as he entered. A few started murmuring.

Meaty Guy scoffed. "Well, look who's back. Didn't you get enough yesterday?"

There were a few chuckles.

"No." Scott cleared his throat. "I mean, yes. I mean—" He took a breath and started over. "Look, I just want to let you know that what you're doing here, well, it's pretty dangerous."

"For who?" the redhead teased.

Scott let the dig go. "All I'm saying is that these demons are—"

"Spirits," Meaty Guy corrected. "Departed spirits."

Scott continued. "These demons are playing for keeps. You think you're using them, but they're really using you. They want to hurt you; they want to—"

"And you've come to save us?" Meaty Guy asked in mock seriousness. "To show us the light?"

Suddenly Scott remembered how much he disliked this guy. Suddenly he wanted to yell, "That's right, loser! I have the light! I have the power! Stand back and let your puny brain be amazed!" But he pushed the urge aside. He remembered the faces on the football field; he remembered why he came.

To help.

"No." Scott shook his head. "I just came to tell you that what you're doing is—"

Suddenly he stopped. Something was happening. Brooke, the leader, hadn't said a word since he'd entered the room. In fact, she'd sat there the whole time, patiently waiting, with her eyes closed. But not anymore ...

At first her movement was slight, like gentle swaying. But now her entire body started to shake.

"Uh-oh," Meaty Guy said, "here we go again."

Tension swept through the group. Suddenly Brooke's eyes flew open. She looked directly at Scott, but not with her usual self-assured arrogance. She was looking at him with desperation ... and terror.

The shaking increased. Her hands slid off the table, and she knocked the pointer to the floor.

"Somebody give me a hand," Meaty Guy shouted as he rose and crossed to her. He grabbed her by the shoulders and tried to hold her down in the chair.

"Brooke!" he shouted. "Brooke, can you hear me?!"

She didn't answer.

Other kids were on their feet, quickly moving to help.

"What's going on?" Scott called.

"It's Joan!" Meaty Guy yelled. He did his best to hold Brooke down, but she grew more violent by the second.

"Who?"

"Joan of Arc," the redhead shouted. "She doesn't come often, but when she does, look out!"

Scott started forward then hesitated. He had to be certain.

The redhead continued to explain. "Joan is so powerful she doesn't use the Ouija board to communicate. She talks right through Brooke."

That was it! Now Scott was sure. He'd seen this sort of thing before, back in Brazil, when the natives took their drugs, when they called on the demons to enter their bodies and take control.

The shaking had turned to violent lungings and lurchings. Sometimes Brooke would pull the entire chair into the air with her. They could no longer hold her. She was too wild. Too strong. She twisted and squirmed until she broke from their grasp and crashed to the floor.

"Brooke!" they shouted, "Brooke, can you hear us!?"

But if Brooke heard, she could not answer. Faint cries came from her mouth, but they were unintelligible, more like muffled screams. She writhed and thrashed and rolled on the floor like a madwoman.

"Stand back!" Meaty Guy yelled. "Let her go!"

Everyone stepped back. They yanked the chairs and table away so she wouldn't bang into them.

Scott had seen enough. "No!" he shouted. "Stop it!"

Everyone looked up startled. But he wasn't shouting at them. He was shouting at Brooke.

"Don't worry," Meaty Guy yelled. "It'll be over in a minute."

"No!" Scott repeated to Brooke. "Stop it!" But nothing happened. "I said stop it!"

Still nothing.

"In the name of Jesus, stop!"

Immediately the thrashing slowed. Not a lot, but enough. If Scott had had time to think, he probably would have stopped. After all, shouting this sort of stuff wasn't the coolest thing in the world. Fortunately, he didn't have the time to think about being cool. "In the name of Jesus Christ," he repeated, "I command you to stop! Leave her alone!"

Meaty Guy started to protest, but there was something about the look in Scott's eyes that told him it wouldn't be smart to try and stop him. Scott stood directly over the girl and shouted, "In the name of Jesus Christ, I bind you! I command you to leave her. Now!"

No response.

"NOW!"

The writhing stopped. Instantly. One minute Brooke was a wild animal, the next she was totally normal — well, except for the heavy breathing, the sweat-drenched body, and the exhaustion. Her dyed black hair was thrown in all directions. Her cheeks and chin were wet with saliva. But she was back in control. Slowly she raised herself up to all fours, still panting.

Scott gently knelt at her side. Her hair hung over her face so he couldn't see it. He wasn't sure what to say, what to do, but he knew he had to explain it to her, he had to offer some comfort. He stretched out his hand to brush her hair aside, when suddenly she sprang at him, snarling like a wounded animal.

Kids screamed, and Scott jumped back. Brooke missed him by an inch. She hit the ground hard and resumed rolling and squirming and thrashing.

Scott sat on the floor, looking on in disbelief.

"See what you're doing!" Meaty Guy shouted at him. "You're making it worse!"

Scott looked up to him. For a moment he almost believed the guy. Then he remembered his dream. He remembered the

Scriptures. He would not drop his shield. He would not put his faith in this kid or in what he saw on the floor in front of him. He would put his faith in God's Word.

Whatever you bind on earth is bound in heaven.

Scott jumped back to his feet and raced to Brooke. He stood over her and pointed. "I command you to leave her alone!"

Brooke's body tensed.

"In the name of Jesus Christ, I command you to leave!"

Suddenly a long, shrieking cry came from the girl's mouth. When it was over she collapsed, all her energy gone.

Scott stood over her, panting, catching his own breath. He sensed it was real this time. Whatever had taken control of Brooke had left. The room was silent.

Finally one of the girls approached Brooke. She knelt down and helped her sit up. Another joined them. Carefully they wiped her mouth and helped her over to the sofa. No one spoke. The only sound was Scott's and Brooke's labored breathing.

Nearly a minute passed before Scott spoke. "Look ... I wasn't trying to show off here. But ... well, you can see for yourself how dangerous — "

"Leave."

All eyes turned back to Brooke. "I'm sorry?" Scott looked at her, puzzled. It was her voice and she was back in control, but she didn't seem to be making any sense. "What did you say?" he asked.

"You are not welcome here," she answered hoarsely.

"I'm only trying to help."

"We don't need your help."

Scott stared at her in amazement. "What are you talking about? Don't you know what happened? Don't you know how that thing took control and threw you all over the — "

Brooke interrupted. Her voice was weak, but it was determined. "The greater the power I have, the greater the price I must pay. Now go."

Was she serious? After all that had happened? Scott glanced at the other kids. Most would not look at him. None would speak.

He turned back to Brooke. "You can't be serious."

Brooke nodded to Meaty Guy. "Show him to the door."

Meaty Guy hesitated.

"Now."

Scott held up his hand. "No. If you want me to go, I'll go. But you've got to see that—"

"We see more than you think, Scott Williams," Brooke said. "You are not welcome. Now go."

Again Scott looked at the faces of the group. They were kids, lots of them younger than he was. He wanted to help. He wanted to show them the dangers. But now ... after all they'd seen, after all they'd experienced, and they still wanted to continue? Yet if this was what they wanted, there was nothing he could do. Demons he could command. But not people. People could do what they wanted.

Sadly, Scott turned and headed toward the door. When he arrived, he looked back at the group one last time. They were as helpless and pitiful as in his dream. There was so much more he wanted to say, so much more he wanted to do. But they'd made their decision.

Scott turned and stepped into the hallway. They shut the door behind him.

11

Halfway through the first lap, Becka knew her friend was in trouble. Like always, Julie pulled away from the group of runners early.

But this time there was a problem.

This time the trio from Royal had also pulled away from the pack. And now they were pulling away from Julie. With every stride they took, they moved farther and farther ahead of her. The reason was obvious. Even from Becka's position, back in the pack, she could see that Julie's concentration was gone. Totally. Instead of her easy, graceful strides, Julie was pumping and fighting and struggling. Instead of a fluid body that glided across the track, she was all elbows and knees.

Come on, Julie, Becka thought, *Concentrate... Focus.*

By the end of the first lap, it was worse. Julie was a dozen meters ahead of Becka and the pack, but she was over a dozen meters behind the kids from Royal. Even with three laps to go, it appeared the race was over. Once again Royal High would take the 1600. Once again Julie would be bumped out of a chance to go to State. Everyone knew it.

Everyone but Rebecca.

As they started the second lap, Becka clenched her jaws in steeled determination. She took several deep breaths. And then, to everyone's amazement, Rebecca Williams began to sprint.

Coach Simmons looked on in disbelief. "Not now!" she yelled. "It's too early! What are you doing?"

But Becka knew exactly what she was doing. She knew that if she started her sprint this early, she'd be too exhausted to finish. She knew that if she killed herself on this race, she'd have nothing left for the other races—she wouldn't qualify for anything. And yet, despite all of that, she still dug her cleats in and pushed harder.

She moved through the pack, passing one runner after another. At last she pulled to the front. Julie was still fifteen meters ahead; the three girls from Royal were thirty.

As they passed Coach Simmons, the woman shouted at Becka. "You're too early! You'll have nothing left!"

Becka paid no attention. She pressed on.

They finished the second lap. Julie's strides were as unfocused and clumsy as ever. Meanwhile, Becka methodically closed the gap between them, from ten meters, to eight, to five.

Up in the stands, Krissi sat with fifty or so other students, watching. "Look at that," she cried. "Becka's challenging her, just like at practice. I told you she was a user."

Philip, her boyfriend, nodded, but Ryan wasn't so sure. "I don't think so, Krissi," he said. "Look ..."

Gradually Becka eased up beside Julie. Now they ran side by side. Becka's lungs were beginning to hurt again. She could never go the remaining two laps at this pace, but that didn't matter.

Julie glanced at her. There was no missing the fear in her eyes. But Becka was not challenging her. She neither pulled ahead of Julie nor dropped behind her. Instead she stayed right at her side.

Coach Simmons looked on in astonishment. She shook her

head. Could it be? Was Becka doing what she thought she was doing?

Rebecca stayed glued to Julie's side. And then, through labored breathing, she began to shout:

"One! Two! One! Two!"

Her rhythm was rock steady, like a metronome.

"One, two, one, two ..."

Back in the stands, Krissi demanded, "What's going on? What's she trying to prove?"

"I'm not sure," Ryan said, "but I think ... I think Rebecca's pacing her."

"She's what?"

"She's giving her a count, a rhythm to follow."

Becka continued. Running at Julie's pace was hard enough. But to use up her air by counting out loud made it even harder.

"One, two, one, two ..."

Gradually Julie fell into the rhythm. She began running with Becka, stride for stride. Her concentration returned. Her fighting and struggling smoothed into the ease and grace for which she was known.

Becka continued counting, fighting for breath, "One, two, one, two ..."

They moved ahead, the two of them together, gaining on the Royal runners.

"Atta girl!" Coach Simmons shouted. "Keep her steady, keep her steady!"

"One, two, one, two ..."

They finished the third lap. One more to go.

Becka's throat was raw, like she'd worn a groove in her windpipe. Her lungs screamed for more air. She had never run at this pace for this long. Her arms were becoming dead weight, her legs were turning to rubber. She could not go another lap. And still she counted:

"One, two, one, two ..."

They passed the first runner from Royal. The girl looked up in shock and surprise. But there were still two more to go. It was time to pick up the pace. Becka knew Julie couldn't sprint, but they'd still have to move faster. Somehow, somewhere, Becka found the strength to push them ahead:

"One-two-one-two ..."

They passed the second runner.

Becka stumbled, regained her balance, and continued. Her head was light, her legs almost useless. She was losing control and she knew it. But she kept pushing.

Half a lap. Two runners down, one to go.

Becka stumbled again. Julie glanced at her in concern.

"Go!" Becka gasped. "Keep counting ... faster!"

Julie picked up the cadence. "One-two-one-two ..."

But it was over for Becka. Her legs had no feeling, no control. She had pushed them too far, and now, finally, they gave out.

She stumbled and lunged face first toward the track.

The crowd gasped as she hit the cinders and slid, as the red stones dug and slashed into her knees and arms. It was almost a repeat performance of her first day at practice.

Almost, but not quite.

She quickly staggered to her feet, gasping for air, looking toward the finish line. "Focus!" she shouted with her last ounce of energy. "Focus!"

It was doubtful Julie heard. She was concentrating too hard on the runner ahead. Inch by inch, she closed the gap. Thanks to Becka, she had found her rhythm. But more important, she had found the inspiration. After all Becka had done, after all she had sacrificed for her, how could Julie let her down?

She couldn't. She wouldn't.

For the first time in her life, Julie reached deep into herself. And for the first time in her life, she found a sprint. It wasn't much ... but it was enough.

OneTwoOneTwo ...

Faster and faster she ran.

Ten meters to go.

Julie crept forward until she pulled alongside the final Royal runner. The girl was so startled that her own concentration faltered.

That was all it took. Julie stretched out the last few strides.

Five meters ... Two meters.

She stuck out her chest, and with one final push, she hit the tape a fraction of a second before the girl from Royal.

The crowd went wild. They ran, shouting, onto the field. Julie staggered to a stop in their arms. She bent over, trying to catch her breath as the PA blasted out the time and announced the news, "That's a new District record, ladies and gentlemen. Julie Mitchell has just set a new District record!"

Spectators cheered. Team members hugged her and slapped her on the back. But Julie barely noticed. She was too busy looking through the crowd to the other side of the field.

There, Rebecca stood all alone—her hair messed, her knees raw and bleeding. The old Becka would have been embarrassed beyond belief. But, at least for now, this new Becka didn't care. For now, it was just the two of them on the field—no people shouting praises, no PA announcing records. Just two friends.

Slowly Becka raised her hand. Blood ran down her arm as she lifted her index finger. The gesture was simple, but Julie immediately knew what it meant.

"Numero Uno."

Julie returned the salute, raising her own hand, pointing her own finger. And as she did, her eyes filled with moisture. Tears spilled onto her cheeks. But they weren't tears of sadness or even tears of joy.

They were for Becka. They were tears of gratitude.

12

"WE'RE NOT IN KANSAS ANYMORE! *SQUAWK!* WE'RE NOT IN KANSAS ANYMORE!"

Cornelius waddled across the desk as Darryl and Scott stared at the computer screen. The bird picked up a pencil in his mouth and began bobbing up and down with it, but no one paid attention.

"I'm still mad you didn't tell me you were going to the Bookshop," Darryl squeaked in his usual high-pitched voice. "I wanted to see you do your stuff."

"I told you," Scott repeated, "I didn't go to put on a show."

"Just the same, everybody in the Society is pretty steamed."

Scott shrugged as he entered the chat room. "I was only trying to help."

As they looked at the screen, Darryl gave an unusually loud sniff. Scott threw him a look. By now the sniffing had really gotten on his nerves. He was thinking about giving the guy a gift certificate for tissues or maybe a lifetime supply of Sudafed, when an email popped up.

"Another message from Z," Scott said.

"This is that guy you were telling me about?" Darryl asked.

Scott nodded and clicked on the message. "I'm not sure who he is. But he's, like, this expert on—"

The two boys were silent as they read Z's latest message. It was short but definitely carried a punch:

> Congratulations on your victory. But remember, it is only the first battle. The war has just begun.
> Z

Both boys stared at the screen. Darryl was the first to speak. His voice was higher and even more unsteady than usual. "How'd he know? It was just a few hours ago ... how'd he know?"

Scott slowly shook his head. There was a lot about Z he didn't know. And what did he mean, "The war has just begun"?

"*SQUAWK*, MAKE MY DAY, MAKE MY DAY ..."

Cornelius was now jabbing at Scott's shoulder with a pencil he held in his beak. Scott reached over and scratched the nape of the little fellow's neck. The bird stretched his head in ecstasy, but Scott barely noticed. He was too busy staring at the screen, wondering.

👁 👁

"That's enough for now," Mom said, as they dumped the contents of another box from the garage into a plastic garbage can. "If we just do one or two of these a day, we'll get through them in no time," she said, wiping her hands.

Since they were together and since there was still some daylight, neither of them felt too uneasy about being in the garage. If they did, they didn't show it—except, of course, for their frequent glances toward the boxes at the far wall.

Becka hated the idea of being afraid of her own garage. It ticked her off. She was determined to get to the bottom of the mysterious light and sounds. And she would. Soon. Count on it.

But not tonight. Tonight she was too wiped. The track meet had taken too much out of her.

Instead, she followed Mom into the kitchen, grabbed the garbage under the sink, and went back out to dump it into the second plastic garbage can. Then, with more than the usual grunts and groans, she dragged the two cans down the drive to the curb. Tomorrow was pickup day, and putting out the trash was one of her chores. She'd flipped Scott for that or for cleaning Cornelius's cage. And for once in her life she won.

Or so she thought ...

"Need a hand with that?"

Becka looked up with a start. It was Ryan. Once again he had caught her hauling trash. Once again she was an unkempt sweatball.

"Oh, uh ... hi, Ryan," she stammered as she instinctively straightened her hair (as if it would do any good).

He waited.

Remembering he'd asked a question, she frantically searched her mind. *What did he say? Something about helping? Oh, yeah.* "No, thanks," she replied. "I'm just setting these two garbage cans out on the curb."

He nodded.

What a stupid answer! she thought. *Of course I'm setting the cans out on the curb. Anybody can see that.* But Ryan didn't seem to notice her lapse of intelligence.

"Listen ..." He coughed slightly. "I saw what you did out on the track this afternoon. It was pretty impressive." Becka started to protest, but he continued. "No, it was cool. And, uh ... well, I'm sorry if we, you know, gave you a rough time or anything."

Becka shrugged. "It wasn't that bad," she lied.

He looked at her. Was it her imagination or were those blue eyes sparkling slightly?

Suddenly Ryan remembered something. He reached into his pocket and pulled out Julie's leather pouch. "She said it was in her gym basket all along—guess she just didn't see it." He held out the pouch to Becka. "It almost cost her the race, so she figures it's not so lucky after all. She said you'd know what to do with it."

Becka reached out and took the pouch into her hand. She wanted to say something, but once again her voice was on vacation ... along with her mind. It was the same trip they always took whenever this guy was around.

The silence grew. They both shifted slightly.

"Well, I, uh ... I guess we'll see you tomorrow," he finally said.

"Yeah," Becka croaked. "Tomorrow."

Ryan turned and sauntered on up the street. Rebecca glanced back down at the charm in her hand. The charm. All that trouble over a leather pouch with a bunch of stupid rocks and stuff inside. Well, it was over now.

Without a further thought, she dropped it into the garbage.

"Oh, hey?" Ryan turned back to her. "I got tickets to this cool speaker coming to the library next week. The Ascension Lady gave them to me."

Becka looked at him.

He shrugged. "It's some reincarnation guy claiming to be Napoleon in some past life. Guess he's going to give a demonstration. Want to come?"

Rebecca continued to stare. She knew her mouth was hanging open, but there wasn't much she could do about it.

Ryan waited another second before continuing. "Well, think about it. Maybe you can let me know tomorrow." With that he turned and headed back up the street.

Becka closed her eyes. Could it be? Could this whole thing be starting all over? The Ascension Lady ...? Reincarnation ...?

Oh brother, Rebecca thought, taking a deep breath and slowly letting it out. *Here we go again.*

Discussion questions for *The Society:*

1. Scott sensed something was wrong when he entered the bookshop. Have you ever sensed evil in a particular place or in a particular person? What did it feel like?

2. What would you have done after you entered the back room of the bookstore? Or if you heard a familiar voice come from a Ouija board?

3. Julie carried a good luck charm, which Becka first believed was harmless. Do you think good luck charms are harmless? Why or why not?

4. What could Becka have said to warn Julie about the good luck charm? Have you ever warned someone about something you thought was dangerous? If so, how did they respond?

5. Scott had a dream where he was wearing armor. Look up and read Ephesians 6:10–17. What does this passage tell us about the Armor of God?

6. The Society claimed to be communicating with the spirits of dead people—or ghosts. Who does the Bible say these spirits are?

7. Priscilla, the "Ascension Lady," claimed to be a good witch. Is there such a thing as "good" witch? Why or why not?

8. Was it a bad idea for Scott to challenge the Society to a contest of power? How was he misusing the authority he had in Christ? What could he have done instead?

9. How can believers defeat demons?

10. Imagine you are Becka or Scott. What would you have thought after encountering the supernatural forces in your new town? Or encountering Z?

THE DECEIVED

Just as man is destined to die once, and after that to face judgment ...

Hebrews 9:27

1

Where are we going?" Rebecca half croaked, half squeaked. "This isn't the way to the library." She wished her voice was strong and in control, like one of those recording stars. But since this was her first date with Ryan and since her stomach still did little flip-flops every time he smiled at her ... well, that meant major dry-mouth ... which meant major no-voice ... which meant sounding more like Miss Piggy than Beyoncé.

Ryan broke into another one of his easy grins—the type Becka had fallen for the first day they met. "I have a little friend who wants to meet you," he said. "It'll only take a minute."

Becka tried to swallow, but of course, there was nothing left in her mouth to swallow. She looked out the window of the white vintage Mustang and gave a tug at her denim skirt. It was shorter than she felt comfortable with—actually any skirt would have been shorter than she felt comfortable with—but Mom thought it looked "adorable." And since wearing sweats probably wasn't the best choice for a first date, there she was, stuck in a skirt, having to do her best imitation of being a lady.

Ryan glanced at the clock on the dashboard. "The guy doesn't start speaking till seven. We've got plenty of time." He turned left off the main road and bounced onto a bumpy side street full of potholes.

Becka wasn't crazy about going to the library to hear the guest speaker. He was one of those New Age fruitcakes who claimed to have been Napoleon or somebody in a past life. The fact that his talk was sponsored by the Ascension Bookshop didn't add to her enthusiasm — not since her little brother's run-in with the Bookshop's "Society" last week. But that was old news. Ancient history.

At least she hoped it was.

Unfortunately, Ryan *was* interested in the guy, Ryan already had tickets, and, most important, Ryan had asked her to go with him. So ... here she was.

She still couldn't figure out why he had asked her. It certainly wasn't her sparkling personality. As far as she could tell, anytime he was around she had none. And it certainly wasn't her looks. Let's face it, being a five-foot-six bean pole with thin, mousy-brown hair wouldn't exactly get you in the swimsuit issue of *Sports Illustrated*. So what was someone as gorgeous as Ryan doing with someone as ungorgeous as her?

She continued pondering the question as she stared out the car window. Outside, the houses were becoming more and more run-down. Ryan made another turn and then another. They followed the street as it dipped under a low, rusty train trestle and then rose back up. He slowed the car and pulled it over to a stop.

The houses were the worst here. They either needed big-time repairs or a bulldozer; Becka wasn't sure which. One thing was certain — they hadn't seen a coat of paint in years. Most of the yards were nothing but dirt with a few clumps of grass here and there that posed as lawns. Half a dozen junk cars were parked in the driveways, in the yards, or beside the curbs — all in various degrees of renovation or dilapidation.

Becka grew uneasy. Poverty was nothing new to her. Growing up in the jungles of Brazil, she'd seen it most of her life. But why had Ryan brought her to this place? What was he up to?

He turned off the car's ignition. "Here we are," he said. Without another word he opened his door and crossed around to her side.

Becka's mind raced. *Is this how it happens? Is this how nice girls wind up on those missing persons posters? They travel to places like this with people they think they can trust, and then . . .* She panicked. *What should I do!?* She glanced to the door locks. *I could lock them. I could lock them, hop behind the wheel, take off, and leave Ryan in the dust to walk home. Yes!*

Her hand started toward the lock, then paused. *What if I'm wrong? I'll be the laughingstock of the school . . . But which is worse? Being the laughingstock of school or guest starring on the side of some milk carton?*

She watched as Ryan approached, brushing the jet-black hair out of his eyes and breaking into another grin. Becka's stomach flipped again and she shook her head. She could trust Ryan Riordan. She knew it.

"Where are we?" she asked as he opened her door.

"Definitely on the wrong side of the tracks." His deep blue eyes sparkled as he held out his hand to help her from the car. Becka could easily get out on her own, but the guy was sweet to offer, so she took his hand and let him help.

The sun had already set, leaving just a few bands of red and violet across the horizon. As usual for this time of year, the fog was billowing in from the beach. Becka pulled her jacket closer and folded her arms to hold back the chill.

"Hey, Riordan! You're late!"

They turned to see a skinny kid, nine or ten years old, scamper down the grade of the train tracks behind them.

"Pepe," Ryan called, "what's up?"

The kid wore a dirty T-shirt, torn pants, and no socks. Immediately Becka's heart went out to him. How could she have been so stupid? Poverty didn't mean people were bad. It meant they were struggling to keep up, struggling against hunger, ignorance, disease—the very things her folks had fought against in South America ... before her dad died.

Once again she looked over the neighborhood—at the sagging houses, the ragged kids playing in a vacant lot—and this time she saw them for what they were: people. Like herself. But in need.

As Pepe arrived and high-fived Ryan, he gave Becka the once-over. "¡Qué bien!" he said with a mischievous grin, winking at Ryan.

Ryan laughed. "English, my man. Talk English."

Pepe turned to Becka. "I said the pretty lady is almost as beautiful as what he's been bragging about."

Rebecca felt her ears grow hot from the compliment. She threw a glance to Ryan. He seemed as calm and unflustered as ever.

"How's your mom?" Ryan asked.

Pepe shrugged.

"No change?"

Another shrug. "The doctors, they say if she doesn't keep taking her medicine, she'll get a sickness they can't cure."

Ryan frowned. "You tell your mom the doctor's right. TB's a tricky thing. Even if she thinks she's getting better, she still has to keep taking the medicine."

Pepe shrugged again. Then, turning to Becka, he grinned. "So, the pretty lady's come to see the Death Bridge?" he asked, motioning to the train trestle behind them.

"Death Bridge?" Becka asked.

Pepe turned to Ryan. "You didn't tell her about our Death Bridge? Doesn't she want to see it?"

"Next time," Ryan said. "We need to get going."

Pepe gave another mischievous grin. "Got other plans, huh?"

Ryan tousled the boy's hair. "Not what you're thinking, amigo."

Becka looked to the ground as her ears grew hotter.

"Listen," Ryan continued, "you'd better be heading home. Your momma's probably worried." He turned back to the car to open the door for Becka, but Pepe quickly stepped in and beat him to it.

"It was a pleasure finally meeting you," he said as he held open the door.

"Thanks," Rebecca said, smiling. She stepped inside, but Pepe did not shut the door. Instead, he hung on it and continued talking. "I've heard soooo much about you." He flashed another smile.

The heat from Becka's ears spread to her face.

"Pepe," Ryan scolded as he crossed to his own side of the car.

Pepe shrugged and pushed her door shut, but he kept right on smiling.

Ryan climbed in and fired up the car. Becka reached for the seat belt. Fastening it would give her something to do to cover her embarrassment. "Cute kid," she heard herself say. "How'd you two meet?"

"I'm in the Big Brother program," Ryan answered as he pulled the car onto the road and made a U-turn. "He doesn't have a dad, so I come down a couple of times a week, you know, just to hang out."

Becka's heart swelled. Imagine a high school guy taking time from his busy schedule to help someone like Pepe. She stole another look in Ryan's direction. What other secrets lay behind that heartbreaker grin of his?

They passed Pepe and gave a final wave. The boy returned it and shouted, "¡Salud, amor, y mucha familia!"

"What'd he say?" Becka asked.

Ryan gave a self-conscious smile. "Nothing."

"No," Becka insisted. She was pleased to see that Ryan could also be embarrassed. "What did he say?"

Ryan pushed the hair out of his eyes.

"Tell me," she prodded.

"He wished us health, love … and many children."

Rebecca giggled. It was either that or die of embarrassment. Ryan laughed too, and she liked that. In fact, she was liking everything about this guy.

As they approached the train trestle, she looked up at the brown, rusting girders. The tracks were about twenty feet above. "Why do they call this the Death Bridge?" she asked.

Ryan gave no answer.

Still smiling, she turned to him, but his grin was already gone. "Ryan?" she repeated. "Why do they call this the Death Bridge?"

They were directly under the trestle when Ryan finally answered. There was no humor in his voice. Not even a trace of a smile. "Every year … one or two kids … they die up there."

❧ ❧

"BEAM ME UP, SCOTTY, BEAM ME UP!"

"Not now," Scott muttered as he remained hunched over the open encyclopedia. He had the same brown hair and thin frame as his "big" sister, Rebecca. Fortunately his arms were starting to thicken and his shoulders were starting to widen. That, along with his cracking voice, were sure signs of manhood sneaking up just around the corner. But as far as Scott was concerned, it was sneaking way too slowly.

At the moment he was reading a section on rain forest butterflies—but for all he knew it could have been on Mickey Mouse. His eyes had quit focusing quite a while back. Now he just hoped that by staring at the words, the information would somehow sink in.

"TO INFINITY AND BEYOND! *SQUAWK!* TO INFINITY AND BEYOND!"

"Cornelius, I said not—"

Suddenly his face was full of green and red feathers. One thing you could say about the family parrot, he never took no for an answer. Another thing you could say is that he hated being ignored. The bird began prancing back and forth across the pages of the book, bobbing his head up and down, making it impossible for Scott to read.

Scott let out a heavy sigh, reached for his pencil, and began scratching under Cornelius's chin with the eraser. The bird scrunched and craned his neck until the pencil hit the perfect spot.

It was quarter to eight. Darryl would be there any minute to help work on their rain forest report. And since Scott still had nothing prepared, and since he was still clueless about their topic, he did the only thing he could do ... he closed the book and checked his email. As he hoped, he had a message. This one from the mysterious Z.

The guy never revealed information about himself, but he always seemed to know what was going on—especially when it came to stuff about the occult and the supernatural. In fact, if it hadn't been for Z's help last week, Scott could have been seriously hurt by his "little encounter" with the Society.

He opened the message and read:

> It has been several days since we last spoke. Have you had any more problems with the Society? If you wish to talk, I will be back online around 9:00. We can IM. Say hello to Rebecca for me.
>
> Z

A chill swept across Scott's shoulders. He had never told Z he had a sister. And he had definitely never mentioned her name.

Becka and Ryan were a few minutes late when they entered the auditorium and took their seats toward the back. The lecture had already started, but Becka barely noticed. Her mind was still on the conversation she and Ryan had had back at the train trestle.

"You mean they just stand up on that bridge and wait for the train to come?" she had asked.

"It's a courage thing," Ryan had explained. "A power trip. They wait in the middle till the train comes, then they race it back to the end of the bridge and jump out of the way."

"And the last one to jump …?"

"Wins," Ryan had answered. "Unless he doesn't jump fast enough. Then he loses. Big-time."

Rebecca shuddered. Even here, in the warmth of the library, the thought gave her the creeps. She wanted to ask more, but she knew she'd have to wait until after the lecture.

She turned her attention to the speaker. Maxwell Hunter was good-looking with a tan face, a distinguished beard, thick silver hair, and an expensive suit. But what really caught Becka's attention were his eyes. They didn't just scan back and forth across the audience; they seemed to probe people, locking onto them, connecting with each of them as if they really mattered.

"You see," he was saying, "reincarnation is the perfect answer to the age old question, 'If there's a loving God, why is there suffering?'" He paused to take a drink of water, then continued. Once again his eyes swept the room, looking at members of the audience. "Stop and think about it. Is it fair that some people are mentally retarded and others are geniuses? Is it fair that some are physically handicapped and others are Olympic athletes? Is it fair that some starve to death in garbage dumps and others live in palaces? Of course not."

At last Maxwell's eyes connected with Becka's. The effect was startling—as though he had peered into her soul. It only lasted a second, but she was certain he had learned something about her. And then he was gone, peering into someone else.

"Life is completely unfair, unless—" he lowered his voice and continued with quiet intensity—"unless people are suffering now for the evil they have performed in the past … unless people are rewarded in this life for the good they've performed in past lives. You see, if we truly believe in a loving God, a compassionate 'Force,' then reincarnation is certainly a viable possibility."

Becka had never given much thought to reincarnation. As far as she figured, it was just another one of those weird Eastern religions where people were afraid to kill a cow because it might wind up being their great-grandmother or something. But Maxwell's idea was intriguing. Reincarnation, the way he described it, *would* explain why some people suffer and others have it so good. Becka frowned and bit her lip. That idea sure beat the thought that God was up there playing games with people's lives and destinies.

"But don't just take my word for it," he continued. "Reincarnation can be proven. That's right. It can be proven absolutely and scientifically."

Becka leaned forward. The man definitely had her attention.

Maxwell stepped down from the stage and walked into the audience as he went on. "Every day thousands of people are remembering their past lives—either on their own or through hypnotic regression." He looked at the audience. "People like you and me. People who recall historical times, dates, facts … down to the tiniest detail. Not because they read about them, but because they lived them. Some people can even speak in foreign languages. Not because they've learned them in the here and now, but because they spoke them in the past."

He paused to let his words sink in. There was a shuffling of feet and some quiet murmurings. After a moment, he resumed. "These just aren't folks with overactive imaginations. These are people who seem to have firsthand experience with things they have never seen, who know things they have never learned—impressions, events, foreign languages—all verified by historians as one hundred percent accurate!"

The murmuring increased.

Maxwell smiled. "But, as I said, don't take my word for it. Let's find out for ourselves." He stopped and carefully looked over the audience. "May I have some volunteers? Are there a dozen or so people courageous enough to go up on that stage and let me prove my point?"

A few hands shot up immediately. Becka glanced around and wondered how many of the willing volunteers belonged to the Society. Other hands rose a little more tentatively.

Maxwell started to move through the room, nodding and pointing. "You sir, yes you ... and you ma'am. Just go up on the stage and have a seat. I'll be there in a minute." He continued through the crowd. "And you ... and you ..."

Others started to rise and move toward the stage.

"And you ..." He drifted in Becka's and Ryan's direction. "And you ma'am ... yes, and you." He paused to scan the room. "I still need half a dozen more."

A few other hands slowly rose. He continued moving toward the back of the room. "And you sir ... and you ..."

Now he was less than ten feet away from Becka. "And you, yes ..." His eyes scanned across Becka, then he nodded to Ryan. "And you son."

Becka looked to Ryan with a start, surprised to see his hand raised.

"And your friend too."

Becka spun back to the man. "Me?" But he'd already moved past them and across the aisle. Ryan rose to his feet, taking Becka's hand. She held back.

Ryan smiled down at her and gave a little tug. "Come on," he whispered. "It should be fun."

Rebecca shook her head. Being on stage in front of everyone was not her idea of fun. But Ryan kept insisting.

"Come on," he coaxed.

A few looked in their direction, and Becka could feel her ears start to burn. Ryan flashed her another one of his smiles. She felt herself weakening. Other people turned in their direction to check out the commotion. By the look in Ryan's eyes, Becka could tell he wasn't going to take no for an answer. She realized she'd be making more of a scene by staying than by following.

Ryan gave another tug on her hand, his smile breaking into a grin.

Reluctantly, Becka allowed herself to be pulled from the seat. They headed down to the platform, hand in hand.

"Don't worry," Ryan whispered as they stepped up onto the platform. "I won't let anything happen to you."

Becka wished he was right. Unfortunately, wishes don't always come true ...

2

Becka continued to fall ... backwards ... slowly ... softly ... as in a dream—gently drifting, lower and lower. At first the sensation frightened her, but soon she gave in to it. Soon she was feeling a strange and wonderful sense of detachment and a peace that said everything would work out—that someone or something far greater than she was taking control.

"That's it," Maxwell's voice continued to soothe, "concentrate on your breathing ... just your breathing. In ... and out ... in ... and out ..."

With her eyes closed, everything around Becka was cotton-soft, velvety-still. She had no idea how long she had been sitting on the stage. She no longer cared. Earlier, she'd felt the sweaty palms and the embarrassment of everyone staring. Out of pure desperation she had focused on Maxwell's voice, his softly spoken commands. And now, as she concentrated on her breathing, as she kept her eyes closed and remained focused, she no longer cared about the audience. She no longer cared about anything, except—

The falling. The gentle, peaceful falling.

Suddenly she was six years old again, floating on her back in a lake. She even recognized the lake. It was one she'd gone swimming in when she was a kid. She could feel the water lapping in her ears, closing around her face, but never quite reaching her mouth. She knew as long as she stayed relaxed, as long as she concentrated on her breathing, she would stay afloat.

Maxwell's voice echoed around her, soft and calming. "Listen to your breath; it is your life force ... Keep emptying your mind ... letting go ... drifting backward ..."

The lake around Becka slowly dissolved. The water became layers of color. Soft reds, burgundies, purples. She was falling again, but now she was falling through the layers of color. One after another. But they weren't just layers of color. They were layers of emotions ... and memories.

A tender face looked down at her through the colors. *Daddy!* Sudden feelings choked Becka. How she missed him! Six months had passed since he had died, and she still ached to be with him, to hear his voice, to feel him holding her. It was an ache she knew would never leave—a pain deep inside, that no one could ever remove.

And yet—there he was, looking at her, his face gentle and loving. He was younger than she remembered, except from photographs. He still had his beard—the one Mom had made him shave off after Scotty was born. She could feel his big hands wrap around her as he scooped her into his arms.

He began to sing. At first she couldn't hear the words, but the voice grew louder. They were lyrics she had forgotten—lyrics from long ago. As she listened, a tight knot of emotion formed in the back of her throat.

Ride a little horsey, to town, to town,
Ride a little horsey, to town, to town,
Careful, Becky, don't fall ...
down.

With the last word, he pretended to drop her just a few

inches. She heard herself gurgle in delight. How she loved the feel of those hands wrapped around her, holding her. She wanted to touch him, to reach out and stroke his beard. But as her hand rose, his face faded.

Again she was falling backward.

Soon she was someplace even warmer, even more secure — surrounded by soft reds and pinks ... and lots of warm, soothing liquid. She looked at her hands — and her eyes widened in surprise: They were the hands of an unborn baby! She'd seen pictures of babies in the womb in science class, and their hands were just like this, pink and translucent. The fingers were nearly formed, but not quite.

I'm — I'm not even born yet! I'm still inside Mom! she thought. *This is too weird!* But Becka wasn't afraid. In fact, she had never felt so protected. So tranquil.

And still she fell. Farther and farther back ...

Then she heard voices, faint at first, but growing louder. Harsh voices. Mocking voices. She tried to make out the words, but they were gibberish.

She tried to move, to see who was there, but she was suddenly struck in the back, and she fell to her knees. Momentarily stunned, she struggled to catch her breath and slowly realized she was kneeling on a bloody, wooden platform.

It was night. The voices were much louder now. Glancing cautiously around, Becka saw people carrying torches and dressed in clothes she had only seen in movies and history books. They shoved and pushed at each other, trying to break past the guards who surrounded the platform. Becka stared in confusion at the guards' weapons: ancient rifles and bayonets. The people shouted, they screamed, they jeered. Suddenly it struck her: They were shouting and screaming and jeering at her!

She tried again to lift her head and was struck again. She tried to move her hands, but they were tied behind her back.

Where am I?

Suddenly hands grabbed her by the hair, dragging her onto a small table, forcing her onto her stomach, and shoving her head down onto a bloody wooden block.

To her right she could just see a wooden pillar. Beyond that and below was the screaming mob. She looked to the left. Another wooden pillar. And beside that a fat, muscular man. She looked to his face and gasped. He wore a black hood with two holes cut out for eyes.

"Where am I?" she cried. "What's going on?!"

He paid no attention.

Somewhere, a group of drums began to roll and then stop. They rolled again, then stopped. They started a third time. Only now they did not stop but kept rolling and rolling and rolling. The crowd yelled louder, working themselves into a frenzy.

Becka squirmed and strained. With great effort she turned her head to follow one of the wooden pillars as it reached skyward. And then she saw it. A giant blade—ten, maybe fifteen feet above her head. Its sharpened edge glistened in the light of the torches.

A guillotine! she thought. *I'm in a guillotine!*

The drums continued to roll. Becka turned back to the hooded man. He was holding the rope taut, keeping the blade suspended above her.

"No!" she cried. "It's a mistake! NO!"

She twisted her head back up to the steel blade just as the man released the rope. The blade fell, plummeting toward her.

"NOOOO ... !"

❧ ❧

"Miss, come out of it. You're back with us, now ... Miss ... Miss ..."

Someone was shaking her.

"Becka, it's okay! I'm here. I'm here ..."

Her eyes fluttered, then opened. She was back on the stage in the library—covered in sweat and gasping for breath.

"It's okay," Ryan repeated. He had dropped to his knees and was holding her. "Becka, I'm here, it's okay, it's okay ..."

She clung to him fiercely. Her eyes darted wildly to the audience staring up at her.

"It's okay, it's okay ..."

She continued fighting for breath, her chest heaving. But she was safe. She was back home. She was in Ryan's arms.

👁 👁

"And you're sure this Z fellow is a good guy?" Darryl asked, his voice high and squeaky. Scott grimaced. As the "all-school nerd," Darryl's voice was supposed to squeak. It was expected. Just like it was expected that he would be half a foot shorter than anybody else, dress in last year's hand-me-downs, and have a haircut that ... well, let's just say he was one missed haircut short of a mullet, and not the cool rock star kind.

For some reason the little guy had picked Scott out as his best friend. Of course Scott had tried to get out of the deal, but he was just too nice. Besides, as the new kid in town, Scott really couldn't be that picky. He'd take whatever friends he could get.

Darryl plopped onto Scott's bed and bit into one of the apples they'd just scored from the downstairs fridge. Like Scott, he knew they had to prepare a major report on the rain forest. And, like Scott, he knew it was the last thing in the world he wanted to do. That was okay, though. With any luck, they could stretch this Z mystery out all night so they'd never have to crack a book.

Scott answered Darryl's question. "As far as I can tell, he's okay. I mean, he sure helped me out with the Society and all that Ouija board junk."

Darryl took another bite of apple. "And you're positive you never talked to him about your sister?"

Scott nodded and motioned toward the computer. "I save all the messages. I went through them before you got here."

"And?"

"I never mentioned Becka—not once."

Darryl toyed with the stem of his apple, thinking. "I have this computer-hacker friend—well, actually he's a cousin—anyway, he's got this computer program that can track cell phones."

"Is that legal?" Scott asked. He glanced at the time on his cell phone: 8:58. Z would be available to chat in a couple of minutes.

Darryl shrugged and gave a loud sniff. (Besides a squeaky voice, he was always giving his nose a workout—sniffing and snorting and sometimes spitting. It drove Scott crazy, but outside of slipping a cold capsule into the kid's drink every twelve hours, there wasn't much he could do.) "If you really want to find out who this Z guy is, my cousin can track his cell phone and get an address."

"Really?" Scott asked.

"No sweat."

Scott started gnawing on his left thumbnail. He always chewed his nails when he thought over stuff. Finally he shook his head. "Nah, that's invading his privacy. He'll tell me who he is eventually."

Darryl pushed up his glasses and gave another sniff. Scott brought up his email. A chat window popped up:

Hello.

"It's him," Scott half-whispered.

Darryl sat up on the bed and watched as more words formed.

How are you and your sister adjusting to Crescent Bay?

Scott exchanged glances with Darryl. Then, with a deep breath, he typed:

How do you know about my sister?

There was no answer. Scott waited tensely. Still nothing. Finally he typed:

> *Are you there? Z?*

The pause continued. Then letters slowly appeared:

> There are some things you must not know. In time, perhaps, but not now.

Scott and Darryl looked at each other. But Z wasn't finished.

> How is Rebecca?

> *Are you changing the subject?*

> Yes.

"Well," Scott sighed, "at least the guy's honest." He leaned back over the keyboard.

> *Becka's at a lecture at the library. Some New Age hypnotist guy.*
> *Z?*

> Tell her to be careful.

> *Why?*

> Hypnotism can be tricky.

Scott gave a snort.

> *Are you telling me hypnotism isn't good?*

Another pause, another answer.

> Opinion is divided. Some feel hypnotism is helpful for patients in clinical situations. Others feel the hypnotic trance is the exact state that mediums and witches have been using for thousands of years to communicate with spirits.

Scott and Darryl stared at the screen. Scott typed:

How do you know all this stuff?
Z?

Finally the words appeared:

I know.

But how? How do you know?

Good night.

Z. Don't go. Wait a minute! Z!

But Z had signed off. Scott angrily shut the chat box and turned away from the computer.

There was a long moment of silence. Darryl sniffed. More silence. Then a louder snort. Finally Darryl asked the question running through both of their minds. "So you really think you can trust him?"

Scott turned to look at his friend.

"Just say the word," Darryl said with a shrug. "We can find out who he is and he'll never know. Just say the word."

Scott took a deep breath and slowly let it out. "Okay," he finally said. "As long as he won't know."

❧   ❧

Rebecca's head ached.

"Are you certain you're all right?" Maxwell asked.

She rubbed the back of her neck. "Yes," she answered for the hundredth time. "I'm okay."

By now most of the crowd had left. There were still a few hangers-on scattered around the stage — mostly the weirdo fringe who wanted to talk to Maxwell about weirdo fringe stuff. But he showed no interest in them. All of his attention was focused on Becka and Ryan.

"That was one of the most intense experiences I've ever witnessed," he said as he walked with them toward the side exit. "Especially for a first timer. Are you certain you've never practiced hypnotic regression before?"

"Not in this lifetime." Becka tried to laugh at her little joke. It only made her head throb worse.

Maxwell smiled. He turned to Ryan. "Take her straight home."

Ryan nodded.

Turning back to Becka, Maxwell continued, "You'll need plenty of rest. Take some aspirin. Oh, and chamomile tea; that is always good. It will help you relax."

Becka nodded. "Thanks."

They arrived at the door.

"Rebecca ..."

It was the first time the man had used her name. It was just as startling and unnerving as the first time his eyes had connected with hers. She hesitated, then looked up to meet his eyes. Once again she felt him entering her soul, uncovering her thoughts. He held the gaze a long moment before finally speaking. "There is a greatness about you. You don't fully understand your power yet, but if you listen to your past, if you let the power emerge, it will unlock remarkable talents within you."

Becka swallowed and continued staring. She wasn't sure she could look away, even if she wanted to.

"Would it be possible ..." He chose his words carefully. "Would you mind if I visited you and your parents sometime this week?"

Becka's eyes widened in surprise.

Immediately, Maxwell apologized. "I am sorry. After all you have been through ... that was terribly insensitive. I do apologize." He reached into his suit pocket and pulled out a business card. "I will be in town for five more days." He began writing a phone number on the back. "If for any reason you wish to talk with me about your experience or if you have any questions, please call this number."

He handed her the card. She looked down at it a long moment.

"Becka?"

Rebecca looked up. Ryan held open the door for her, waiting for her to pass.

"Thanks," she mumbled as she stepped into the foggy night of the parking lot.

"It was a pleasure meeting you," Ryan called over his shoulder.

"Yes," Becka said, remembering her manners. "It was a—"

"No, Rebecca," Maxwell spoke with such authority that both Becka and Ryan stopped and turned. Maxwell remained at the door, smiling broadly. "The pleasure was mine."

3

The following morning Rebecca stumbled to the breakfast table half asleep. She hadn't told Scott what had happened in the library auditorium. Somehow, she knew he wouldn't approve — especially after his little run-in with the Society the week before. And if she hadn't told him about being hypnotized, she definitely wasn't going to tell him about her dreams.

The dreams. Talk about weird. All night they'd come at her: screaming mobs, guillotines, little Pepe, the Death Bridge — and a few dozen thundering trains thrown in just to keep things lively. Everything was jumbled together. Nothing made sense. But that didn't stop them from coming again and again ... and again. By morning Becka was more exhausted than when she'd gone to bed.

Mom flitted about the kitchen, eating dry toast and asking if her sleeveless dress made her look too heavy for her upcoming job interview. Of course, she also wanted to know every detail of Becka's date.

Unfortunately, the word *fine* was about all she could get out of Becka that morning.

"How was your date?"

"Fine."

"How was the lecture?"

"Fine."

"How was Ryan?"

"Fine."

Usually the two shared everything. Clothes, shoes, girl talk. They had always been close, and now that Dad was gone, they were even closer ... when they weren't fighting about the usual mom/daughter stuff. Becka knew her mom wasn't happy with her answers, but for this morning, "fine" would have to do—at least till Scott wasn't around.

Becka and Scott were also good friends ... when they weren't fighting about the usual brother/sister stuff. But there was something about her experience at the library that she knew he wouldn't like. And she definitely wasn't in the mood for an argument—not this morning.

At the moment Scott was plowing through his second or third bowl of Kix and chattering on about uncovering Z's true identity. Becka pretended to listen, but she barely heard. Her mind still churned over her experience at the library. And over her dreams.

What had Maxwell said? *"There is greatness about you. Listen to your past ... Let your powers emerge"*?

What kind of greatness? What kind of powers? Becka sighed. The guy was probably just making it all up. But the image of the guillotine suddenly flashed through her mind. That had certainly been real enough. And what about those crazy dreams?

Maybe there's something to all this after all ...

⊕ ⊕

Forty-five minutes later, Becka entered Crescent Bay High. As far as schools go, it was pretty cool. Unfortunately that was her problem. The school was cool, but she wasn't. Something about growing up in the jungles of Brazil keeps you a little out of touch with the latest California fashions and trends. But through trial and error (mostly error), she was learning.

Becka had barely entered the hallway when Julie Mitchell joined her. As usual, Julie wore the perfect clothes — loose shorts, a designer t-shirt, killer shoes — all coordinated to look perfectly casual while, at the same time, calculated to show off her perfect body and her perfect, thick, blonde hair. Normally Becka totally avoided spoiled rich kids. But Julie was different. She didn't have the ego or the attitude. She was actually nice. She'd been friendly to Becka the first day they met. And as they worked out together in track and hung out together at lunch, their friendship grew.

"So how's Super Celeb?" Julie asked as they headed down the hall.

"Super what?"

"Hey, Becka, how's it going?" a voice called.

Rebecca looked over to see a couple of jocks in letterman jackets. They leaned against the lockers, grinning. She wasn't sure which one had spoken, but it didn't matter. Twenty-four hours ago neither of them had known she existed. She glanced down to make sure she hadn't put her pants on backwards or made some other tactical mistake in wardrobe. Nope, as far as she could tell, everything was normal — just your basic, average clothes on your basic, ho-hum body.

Others kids passed, also smiling, also nodding.

"Hey, Beck."

"How's it going, Becka?"

She looked to Julie and whispered, "What's going on?"

"Everybody's talking about last night. I guess you put on quite a show."

"Tell me about it," she muttered, feeling her face start to flush.

"Don't be so gloomy." Julie chuckled. "Everyone thinks it's

cool. They say Maxwell spent all sorts of time with you afterward. Even gave you his phone number."

"Hey, Becka." A couple of freshmen girls passed and giggled, obviously showing off for the others around them.

"So, when you calling him?" Julie lowered her voice, pretending to sound ominous. "When's he going to tell you your mysterious past?"

Rebecca took a deep breath. All morning she had been struggling with that same question. What she had experienced up on the stage was real; there was no doubt about it. But remembering it still gave her the creeps. "I don't know," she sighed. "I mean, he seemed nice and everything, but—"

"But what?" Julie prodded.

"Isn't he friends with the kids in the Society and with the Ascension Lady from the Bookshop? I mean, didn't she, like, sponsor his talk?"

"So?" Julie asked. "Look, I know she messed me up with those charms and stuff, but that doesn't mean everything she does is bad."

Becka took another breath.

Julie continued. "You're the one that had the vision or whatever it was. You're the one who's supposed to have all of this untapped power. Not the Ascension Lady and not that Maxwell guy. It's you. And if you ask me, you'd be pretty stupid not to at least check it out."

They arrived at Julie's locker, and she dialed up her combination.

"Hey, Rebecca." A couple of senior guys approached. Cute. Very cute. They nodded and ambled past without another word.

Julie and Becka turned to watch. Yes, very cute indeed. "Go for it," Julie giggled. "What do you have to lose?"

Julie was right. What did she have to lose? It was just your basic hypnotism, the same stuff doctors and psychiatrists used every day. And Julie was right about another thing. If she *had* been someone great in a previous life, if she *did* hold some kind of secret powers, wasn't it her responsibility to find out?

By two-thirty Rebecca had made up her mind. It wasn't just the attention she received—although being looked upon as someone with super, hidden powers didn't hurt. And it wasn't just the expectations Julie, Ryan, Krissi, and the other kids at the lunch table seemed to have of her. It was also the expectations she had of herself. All of her life she had lived in the background. Scotty was the star of the family; she was the "nonperson," the nobody no one ever noticed. But now ... now she had a chance to be a somebody everybody would notice. Didn't she owe it to herself to at least find out?

All it would take was one little phone call.

A little later, with Ryan at her side, Becka pulled her cell phone out of her bag. But even as she placed her hand on it, she found herself slowing.

"Go ahead," Ryan urged. "It's just a call." Rebecca looked at him. He gave her another one of his heartbreaker smiles. "I'm right here ... What can happen?"

He was right, of course. It was just a call. And with him at her side, what could happen?

With a nervous smile, she punched in the number on the back of Maxwell Hunter's business card.

👁 👁

Scott stood beside Darryl as the kid knocked on the blistered and peeling front door. But it wasn't just the front door that was blistered and peeling—the whole house was that way. Then there were the added attractions of broken shutters, a crumbling chimney, and a rotting porch. The place looked like it belonged in some sort of horror flick.

"You sure Gomez and Morticia are expecting us?" Scott quipped, trying to fight off the jitters.

"Don't be fooled," Darryl squeaked. "On the outside Hubert is a slob, but on the inside he's a genius."

A voice barked through the intercom near the door. "Who is it?"

Darryl tilted his head toward a surveillance camera mounted on the porch roof.

"It's me. Darryl." He pushed up his glasses and gave a sniff.

"What do you want?" the voice demanded.

"I brought a friend. We need your help."

"Not interested! Go away."

"See," Darryl said as he turned to Scott. "I told you he couldn't help us."

Before Scott could respond, the voice interrupted. "What's that?"

Darryl gave Scott a wink and turned back to the camera. "I told my friend our problem was too hard for you, that you'd never be able to solve it."

"Says who?"

Darryl just shrugged.

"Why'd you come here if you didn't think I could solve it?"

"My mistake," Darryl said as he turned to leave.

"Hold it. Wait a minute."

"No, you're right." Darryl started down the steps. "We'll find somebody else."

"Hold it, I said!" The voice paused. "All right, come on up—but just for a minute."

Darryl grinned slyly as the door buzzed and they pushed it open. "It works every time," he whispered.

The first thing Scott noticed when he entered was the smell. It was like a giant cat box that hadn't been emptied in weeks. Make that months. Then he saw the reason. Cats. Dozens of them, lying on the floor, curled up on dusty furniture, and spread out on the stairway that lay in front of them.

"Come on." Darryl headed for the stairs and motioned for Scott to follow. "Just don't step on the cats. He's kind of partial to them."

"I noticed."

They made their way up the stairs, threading around the cats, ducking the cobwebs, and sidestepping more Domino's Pizza boxes than Scott could count.

"He likes pizza too," Darryl explained.

Upstairs was just as cluttered. Computer junk was scattered everywhere — monitors, speakers, web cams, modems, and connector cables. The place looked like a tech store gone berserk.

"Over here," a voice called from a room to the right. They turned to see a skinny guy with no shirt. He was hunched over a table piled high with gutted printers, computers, telephones, modems, and whatnots. The guy's hair was frizzy, his face unshaven, and his glasses were held together with masking tape. At the moment he was messing around with a computer hard drive in one hand and wiping his nose with the back of the other.

"Scott — " Darryl beamed as they approached the room and entered — "I want you to meet my cousin Hubert."

Both Darryl and Hubert sniffed in perfect unison. Somehow Scott wasn't surprised they were related.

Hubert never looked up. He stayed hunched over the hard drive. "So what's this unsolvable problem?" he asked.

"We gotta get the address of somebody who's been texting Scott."

"Easy " Hubert sniffed.

Darryl grinned. "I told you."

The two boys stood in silence. Scott cleared his throat. "So, uh, how're you going to do it?"

"Simple," was the answer.

More silence. More fidgeting.

Another question from Scott. "How?"

"Multilateration."

"Multi-what?"

Hubert rolled his eyes. I compute the TDOA of his roaming signal to three or more cell towers."

"TDOA?" Darryl asked the question this time.

"Time difference of arrival," Hubert said flatly. "I zero in on the location where the phone is more often at rest and you've got your boy's address. All I need is his cell number."

Hubert gave another loud sniff to indicate the problem was solved.

Darryl sniffed back in confirmation.

Hubert sniffed one last time as if to have the last word.

"And he'll have no idea you're doing this?" Scott asked.

"Nada."

❧ ❧

Meanwhile, back at the house, Mom was exhausted. The last few weeks had been rough on her. Real rough. Besides helping the kids adjust to their new surroundings (Crescent Bay, California, was just a little different from Jungleland, Brazil), she was also pounding the pavement, looking for work. It had been another long day of driving, filling out applications, and hearing the all-too-familiar "Sorry, no openings. Why don't you try again next month?"

She had barely dragged herself up the porch steps and entered the door when Becka grabbed her, sat her down on the sofa, and explained that they'd be having company any minute. Mom wasn't thrilled about the idea of a strange man coming into the house. She was even less pleased after Rebecca told her all that had happened at the library the night before. Granted, Mom didn't know much about reincarnation, but what she did know made her nervous. As she listened to Becka, little alarms began to go off inside her head. The same alarms she'd heard whenever villagers back in Brazil shared stories about witch doctors and black magic.

But those alarms were interrupted by another sound: the doorbell.

"It's him!" Becka exclaimed as she jumped up and dashed out of the room.

"Where are you going?"

"I gotta brush my hair!"

Mom shook her head as she wearily rose and crossed to the door. When she opened it, she was caught completely off guard. She had expected some sort of strange and eccentric-looking weirdo. What she saw was a tall, handsome man with thick silver hair, who was dressed in stylish khaki slacks, a crisp button-up shirt, and a blazer.

He looked positively respectable. And gorgeous.

"Mrs. Williams?"

"Y-yes?" Mom stuttered.

"I'm Maxwell Hunter."

"Yes, uh, we were expecting you." It wasn't until she looked into his warm, masculine eyes that Mom realized she hadn't changed or freshened up or even combed her hair. She looked exactly like she felt ... a mess. But there was something in the way Maxwell held her gaze that said he saw past the mess, that he understood her day's trials, and, as amazing as it may seem, that he was actually attracted to the person underneath the frazzled exterior.

She liked him instantly. And with that liking came guilt. After all, the man wasn't here for her. He was here to talk about Becka. Besides, how could she be feeling such things for another man? Her husband had been dead only six months.

Yet wasn't she human? Wasn't she at least entitled to appreciate another man's company?

As though understanding her struggle, Hunter smiled gently. "May I come in?"

"Oh yes, of course." Mom blushed slightly and opened the door for him. As he entered she found herself smoothing the wrinkles in her dress.

"What a lovely home you have, Mrs. Williams."

"Oh, well thank you, but it still needs, well, it needs lots of work. The tenants who used to live here were ..." Her voice trailed off.

"Strange?" he finished for her with an amused twinkle in his eyes.

"Well yes, how did you know?"

He slowly surveyed the room. "Sometimes ... I just sense these things." He turned back to Mom and smiled warmly. "I sense lots of things."

She glanced away. Had he "sensed" what she was thinking about him? Or was he just flirting? Whatever the case, for the first time in a long time, she suddenly felt attractive, flattered, and nervous all at once.

"Ah," he said, turning toward the kitchen, "there she is."

Becka had just entered the room. She was carefully eyeing her mother. Again Mom flushed. Had Becka also read her mind?

"Your mother and I were just discussing the past tenants of this house."

"Yeah," Becka agreed. "You should see the stuff out in the garage."

Maxwell turned in the direction of the garage and paused as if listening to something. Becka and Mom glanced at each other.

"There's something out there that disturbs you?" It was part question, part statement.

Becka and Mom looked at each other again. Each knew the other was thinking about the strange noises and the dancing light Becka had seen in the garage last week.

"Yes, well." Mom tried to change the subject. "I'm sure it's nothing. Won't you have a seat?"

He nodded and eased himself onto the sofa. "I am certain you have many questions and are probably more than a little skeptical." He turned to Becka. "But may I ask one question first?"

Becka shrugged. "Sure."

"Your dreams last night, were they disturbing?" Once again his eyes locked onto hers, and once again, they seemed to be looking inside her.

"Well ... yes." She fidgeted. "They were a little weird."

He smiled. "I thought as much. Let me come straight to the point." He turned to Mom. "I believe your daughter—in fact, your entire family—has some very unique gifts. And I believe many of these gifts come from past lives, from who you were in other eras."

Mom looked down and cleared her throat.

"Please." He smiled. "Don't be embarrassed. I know you don't believe me. I'd recognize that tone of throat-clearing anywhere."

They chuckled lightly.

"It's not that." Mom paused, looking for a diplomatic way out. "It's just ... well, we're both Christians and—"

"So am I," he broke in with a grin. "I knew we shared common ground. I sensed it."

"You're a Christian?" Becka asked.

"Absolutely. I believe Jesus was the Christ prophesied throughout all of Scripture."

"So you believe in the Bible?" Mom asked.

"Certainly. It is one of the most holy books we have."

A wave of relief swept over the two women. "Good," Mom said. "I'm glad we have that cleared up."

"Yes indeed." Maxwell nodded. "That is very important. You see, what I am proposing is not contradictory to Scripture. Not at all."

Mom continued to watch him. If what he said was true, then her concerns should be calmed. But the alarms were still ringing in her head. He leaned forward and touched her arm gently, growing more sincere. "I know it all seems strange. The truth often sounds outrageous. Just look at how the disciples reacted to Jesus when he told them things they didn't expect. They also were confused. It took them a long time to really understand what he was saying."

The man seemed so sincere, so genuine, that Mom found herself wanting to believe him. He smiled, and as he looked at her, Mom could swear there was a real honesty in his eyes.

"I understand your hesitation. You're a good mother, and you're just protecting your daughter."

His words continued to comfort her ... no, it wasn't just comfort she felt. There was something else. What was it about this man that made her feel so ... good?

"Mrs. Williams, I want to protect Rebecca too. Believe me, I don't want to harm her in any way. But I believe your daughter has led a powerful life in the past, and with your permission, I would like to help her unlock that power to assist her in this present. Not to hurt her but to help her. Isn't that what we both want? To help her?"

Mom held his gaze. The alarms were growing quieter. "How?" she asked.

He leaned back. "Hypnotism. Nothing strange. No hocus-pocus. Just the simple clearing of your daughter's mind—helping her push aside distracting thoughts so her past memories may surface."

Mom hesitated. "I don't know ..."

"I understand your concern. That is why I felt it would be best to do it here in your own home, under your supervision."

"You want to do it here? Now?"

"Only with your permission." His voice remained calm and reassuring. "And under your careful scrutiny. If for any reason you feel the slightest bit uncomfortable, we will stop immediately. You need simply say the word."

Mom continued to hesitate. "I'm not sure …" She looked at Becka.

"Of course," he added, "we will pray together before we begin and ask God to guide us."

A wave of relief swept over Mom. If he was willing to pray with them, wasn't that proof that he was genuine in his faith? She paused, then looked again at Becka. "Sweetheart, what do you say?"

Becka swallowed. "Will it be scary … you know, like the last time?"

"No." He shook his head firmly. "That was your death. We will skip past that and go directly to earlier years. We will discover your powers of the past, which will allow you to utilize them in the present."

Mom shifted slightly as she watched Becka thinking it over. Despite Maxwell's calm words, she still felt a little anxious. She wished her husband were here. He had always been able to see things more clearly, to see past the surface to the truth. But he wasn't here. He would never be here again.

At last Becka spoke. "I think … it would be okay." She turned to Mom. "I mean, you'll be right here to watch." She looked to Maxwell. "And she can stop it any time?"

Maxwell nodded. "Any time."

Mom turned to her daughter. "Are you sure?"

Becka slowly nodded.

"It's really that important to you?"

Becka shrugged. "I don't know if it's important. But it would be kinda neat, don't you think?"

Mom looked at her daughter a long moment. Finally she nodded. "Okay, sweetheart … if it's what you want."

"Good." Maxwell clasped his hands together in approval. "You won't regret this, Mrs. Williams. I assure you."

Mom tried to smile, hoping he was right. "So, what exactly do we do?"

"Do you have a candle and some matches?" he asked.

"Yes, in the kitchen."

"If you would bring them in."

"Certainly." Mom rose and headed into the kitchen, once again straightening her dress and, this time, also smoothing her hair.

"And Becka, if you will just get comfortable in that chair over there." He pointed to the overstuffed chair near the window. "We will set the lighted candle on this coffee table, here, and get started."

Mom entered with the matches and candle.

"Thank you," he said. As he took them, their hands brushed slightly and their eyes met. He held her gaze for a moment, and Mom glanced to the carpet, once again feeling her face flush.

Maxwell positioned the candle and its holder on the table. He smiled at them reassuringly. "Let's all pray now, quietly, and ask God to guide us." They bowed their heads.

"O high god," he said, "we ask you to help us—to show us the perfect path to greater enlightenment."

There was a moment's pause, and then the sound of a match being struck. Mom and Becka opened their eyes. Apparently the prayer was over, for as they looked up they saw Maxwell touch the flame to the candle. It flared brightly, and their gazes locked onto his. He smiled.

"Let us begin."

4

Becka concentrated on the candle's flame, on seeing nothing but its pure, white light and hearing nothing but Maxwell's soothing, calm voice.

"Put aside your thoughts. Think only of your breathing. In … and out … in … and out … in and out …"

Gradually her eyes closed. She focused on her breathing, listening to it, feeling it, making it her only thought. Once again she began to float … to fall gently. Once again there was that strange feeling of detachment as she drifted backward through layers of burgundy reds.

"What do you see?" Maxwell's voice was far away. "Do you see any light?"

Becka began searching the colors.

"No, don't look," Maxwell ordered. "Don't force it to appear. Let the light emerge on its own."

She relaxed. Gradually, it appeared directly in front of and slightly above her.

"Yes," she whispered, "I see it. It looks like … it looks like a star."

"Excellent," Maxwell's voice cooed. "Let it approach, let it draw you in."

It came closer and closer. Becka noticed a tiny, pinpoint hole in the center. As the star approached, the hole grew larger. Soon she saw that it was an opening, a type of doorway. It drew closer, continuing to grow. But as it did so, Becka began to feel uncomfortable. A cold fear stirred somewhere inside her.

"Let go, Rebecca," Maxwell's voice encouraged, "let it approach."

As the hole grew, so did her fear. "I—I can't ..."

"Let go, Rebecca. Let it have its way ..."

"I—" She tried to relax, but the fear was just too great.

"It's okay, then," Maxwell soothed. "Another time ... another time ..."

The opening and its surrounding light faded as quickly as they had appeared.

Instantly Becka heard sounds. Human voices screaming and shouting in French. Once again the shapes and shadows of the platform, the soldiers, and the crowd appeared.

"No!" Becka gasped. "I'm back at the guillotine!"

She heard her mother's voice but couldn't make out the words. Then Maxwell broke in, peaceful, in control. "Let them go. Let those images wash over you. Go back farther, go deeper."

Rebecca forced herself to relax, and sure enough, the images shifted and flickered. The screaming mob and surrounding soldiers shimmered and waved until they became towering trees.

"I'm in some sort of forest," she whispered.

"Good, good," Maxwell said. "Look around you. Tell me what you see, what you feel."

"I feel movement. The ground is shak—no, wait. It's not the ground. I'm on a horse. I'm on a horse, and we're trotting through woods. I hear men talking and dogs barking. I think ... it looks like a hunting party."

"That is marvelous, Rebecca, just marvelous. Look down at yourself. Tell me what you are wearing."

Becka looked to her hands. She could see them holding the horse's reins. She was surprised at all the rings she wore—there must have been half a dozen. She was also surprised to see the silks, lace, and the white furs draped across her arms. But what really shocked Becka were the hands. They were strong and large . . .

Becka gasped. "I'm a man!"

She heard Maxwell chuckle. "I suspected as much. Look about you, what else do you see?"

Becka looked around the forest. There were men on horses ahead of her and behind her. Their clothes were nice but not nearly as elegant as hers.

And then she saw them. On the ground. A handful of peasants dressed in rags dropping to their knees and bowing their heads as she passed.

"They're bowing—people are bowing. Maxwell, am I, like . . . royalty?"

"Look back to your hands. Do you see any rings?"

"Yeah, plenty."

"On your right hand—do you see one large ring with letters on it?"

Becka looked to her right hand and saw a large gold ring with writing. "Yes, it has letters and numbers—Roman numerals."

"Read them!" Even though his voice was far away, she could hear his excitement. "Read the numbers. What do they say?"

She obeyed. "There's an *X* and a *V* and an *I*."

"That's sixteen! Are you sure you're reading a sixteen?"

"Well, yeah. What's that supposed to mean?"

"Are you sure it's sixteen?"

"Yes. Why is that such a big—"

But her question was cut off by another voice, a different one than Maxwell's—a voice filled with alarm.

"Becka!" It was Scott. "What are you doing to her!"

Now she felt somebody shaking her.

"Becka, wake up! Becka!"

The ring started to fade, and then the hand.

"No," she whispered, "not yet. Not—"

More shaking. Harder. "Becka, wake up! Come out of it! Wake up!" Scott's voice was much louder.

"Scotty . . ."—that was Mom—"You don't underst—"

Becka felt herself returning to the overstuffed chair in the living room.

"Becka . . . BECKA!"

Her eyes fluttered open. There was Scott, shouting into her face. Behind him stood Mom. Then Maxwell.

"What do you think you're doing?" Becka croaked. Her voice was dry and raspy. And angry. Very, very angry.

☉ ☉

Half an hour later, Scott sat up in his room, steaming. How was he supposed to know what they were doing? When he had entered the living room, all he saw was some gray-haired goon leaning over his sister, getting all excited about the number sixteen. How could he know this was something Becka wanted to do? How could he know this was something she had *already* done?

Hypnotism . . . reincarnation . . . Scott shook his head. What was going on?

He was mad. No doubt about it. Mad that Becka hadn't told him about last night. Mad that she was mad at him. And mad at the gray-haired creep. Maxwell.

Besides giving Scott the scare of his life, the guy claimed Becka might have been some sort of powerful king in some sort of past life.

Puh-leeze, Scott thought. *Past life? King? Give me a major break!*

And if that wasn't enough, ol' Maxy boy had asked Mom if he could call her sometime. Call her? *His mom?* The guy was practically asking for a date right there in front of her own kids! What a jerk!

Scott didn't like him. Not one bit. And this whole thing about reincarnation. How could his sister believe that? Wasn't reincarnation some sort of Hindu thing? And weren't the three of them supposed to be Christians? Christians didn't believe in reincarnation ... did they?

Scott's phone vibrated on the table beside his bed. He picked it up. He had a text message from Z.

I heard what happened to Rebecca last night at the library.

Great! Scott thought. *Everyone heard about it but me!* His thumbs tapped out his response:

So what do you know about reincarnation?

A moment later the answer came:

Go to your computer, I'll IM you.

Scott plopped down in front of his computer and a few keystrokes later, he was chatting with Z.

So is reincarnation a Christian thing?

If you are Christian, reincarnation is directly opposed to what you believe.

How?

Reincarnation teaches that you die again and again and keep coming back until you are finally good enough to enter heaven. Your Bible clearly states that people are destined to die once and after that to face judgment. That's in a book of the Bible called Hebrews, chapter 9, verse 27.

"I knew there was something fishy about it," Scott muttered. But deep inside he was a little disappointed. He was hoping for more than just one Bible verse. He typed:

Is that it? Isn't there anything else?

Reincarnation teaches that the only way to get rid of your sins is to live several lifetimes until you work them out. Christ teaches that he paid the price for your sins when he died on the cross.

So?

So ... those who believe in reincarnation are saying they don't need Christ. They believe they can work their way into heaven on their own.

Scott mulled this over a moment. Z was right. It didn't get any more basic than Jesus dying on the cross. But what about Rebecca's experiences? What about seeing herself as some king?

What about all the stuff Becka is seeing when she is hypnotized?

Good night.

And, just like that he was offline.

Scott stared at the screen and blinked. He had a lot more questions but he also had something to think about.

👁 👁

"*A mighty king ... incredible greatness ... Unlock your secret powers ...*"

Maxwell's words tumbled through Becka's mind as she lay in bed, trying to sleep. What type of powers? What type of greatness? And what about that star with the opening inside—why was that so frightening? Maxwell wouldn't say. No matter how much she pleaded, he would not tell her. As he'd left the house that evening, his only words were that she should keep listening to her dreams, that the power would eventually reveal itself.

Becka wasn't sure when she finally drifted to sleep — or when all the tumbling words and thoughts finally solidified into a dream. She only knew it was night ... and that she was standing on some sort of hill or ridge. There were no stars, no wind, no sounds.

She glanced down. Once again she was robed in the silks and furs of royalty. Twenty or so feet below the ridge was a path where she saw the students from her school. Like the peasants in her vision, they were all kneeling on the ground, bowing before her. Julie, Ryan, friends from the lunch table — even the two seniors who had passed her in the hall — they all had their heads lowered in honor and respect.

Becka shifted, embarrassed over the attention. She wanted to call down to them, to tell them to get up, to stop making such a fuss. But then she saw it, directly ahead. She sucked in her breath. It was the star from her vision. And it was moving quickly along the ridge, coming directly at her!

With its approach came a low rumbling that grew louder and louder — a thundering so powerful that it shook the ground beneath her feet.

Becka looked back down to her friends. They began rising, concern filling their faces.

She turned back to the approaching star. It was growing into a blazing light, brighter than the sun. The thundering had turned into a roar that filled her ears.

"Run!" the kids shouted. "Get out of the way!" Ryan started scrambling up the ridge. "Becka!" he screamed. "BECKA!" But his friends pulled him back.

The light was practically on top of her now. She could feel its power surging against her, pulsating, beckoning her. Again she saw the dark hole in the center, and again she felt the icy fear as the opening grew. She tried to push the fear aside. There was power here, waiting for her. Why should she be afraid of it? But as the hole grew, her fear increased. Now the hole was the size of a small tunnel, a passageway that led to the very center of the light. She saw nothing else. Just the blinding light of the star — and the darkness of the tunnel.

Fear turned to panic. Light was everywhere, enveloping her, enfolding her, sucking her into the tunnel, its center. But the more it pulled, the more she struggled, until finally, gasping for breath...

Becka awoke.

She lay in bed, staring at the ceiling, chest still heaving ... and felt outrage at her cowardice. Twice now she had refused the light. Twice now her fear of the unknown had prevented her from entering the tunnel, kept her from experiencing its power. And it *was* a power. She knew it. She had felt it.

She glanced at the clock radio: 5:07.

She still had a good couple of hours before school, but that was okay. She reached over and snapped on the bedside lamp. Becka Williams didn't plan on going back to sleep.

5

It felt kinda weird for Rebecca to be at the breakfast table before Scott. After all, he was the morning person. The Mr. In-Your-Face-with-the-Jokes-before-You-Had-the-Chance-to-Wake-Up. But there she was, on her prehistoric laptop, reading away. When you're a missionary kid, people give you stuff like their old computers. But Becka was thankful to have it.

"How long have you been up?" Scott asked as he shuffled into the room. He crossed to the cupboard and grabbed his faithful box of Kix. Next stop was the refrigerator for milk and then the dishwasher for a clean bowl and spoon. It was the same routine every morning. He could do it in his sleep. Sometimes he did.

"I've been up 'bout an hour," Becka answered as she continued reading.

Scott plopped down at the table. "What are you doing?"

Becka knew he wouldn't like the answer, but she also knew she couldn't hide it from him. "I'm reading up on reincarnation."

"Don't tell me you buy that garbage."

His attitude irritated her, but she pretended not to notice.

"I'm not buying into anything. I'm just checking on a few facts, that's all."

Scott snorted in disgust and poured his cereal.

She continued, trying to be casual. "Did you know that over half of the world believes in reincarnation? And so does one out of every four Americans?"

"So?"

"So it's considered to be the fairest and most just belief system in the world."

He looked up. "What?"

She read from the website, " 'Reincarnation teaches that each individual is punished or rewarded for their deeds. If one is evil in a past life, he will suffer in the next. If he is good, he will be rewarded.' "

"Tell that to Z."

She glanced up from the screen. "You talked to him?"

Scott poured the milk over his cereal. "Last night. He says reincarnation is a total joke."

Another wave of resentment washed over Becka. "Maybe Z isn't an expert in everything."

"I'm just telling you what he said."

"He can say whatever he wants, but he can't say I didn't see what I saw."

Scott shrugged. "He also said you can't believe in reincarnation and be a Christian."

That was it. Becka had had enough. "That's exactly what I'm talking about—he doesn't know everything. Mom and I asked Maxwell if he believed in the Bible, and the guy said yes, absolutely, one hundred percent. He believes in Jesus, and he even prayed with us before the hypnotism. Got that, Scotty? The man prayed with us."

Scott stared. For once in his life, he had no comeback.

"Morning, guys." Mom breezed into the kitchen. Her tone was so cheery that both kids looked over at her. She opened the bread, pulled out a couple of slices, and dropped them into the toaster. Was it their imagination, or was she humming? Then there were her clothes. She wore her navy, floral print dress, one of her favorites. And her hair — it had been months since either of them had seen it so carefully brushed and sprayed.

"What are you all dressed up for?" Scott asked.

Mom stood at the sink, filling a coffee mug with water. She crossed over to the microwave and set it inside. "Not a thing," she answered as she punched in the time and hit Start. The oven gave a little beep and began to whir.

Becka broke into a mischievous smile. "Wouldn't have anything to do with Maxwell Hunter, would it?"

"Of course not," Mom said, catching her own reflection in the window and adjusting her bangs.

"Oh, please," Scott moaned.

"What's your problem?" Mom asked.

"I think he's just jealous," Becka offered. "He doesn't like you dating good-looking guys."

"If he calls up, you're not really going to go out with him, are you?" Scott whined.

"Knock it off," Mom chided, "both of you. Just because a person takes a little care in their looks doesn't mean they're suddenly jumping into the dating scene."

"You didn't answer my question," Scott said.

Mom put the loaf of bread away and resumed humming.

Becka looked back at the screen with a knowing smile.

"If you ask me," Scott said as he shoved another spoonful of cereal into his mouth, "I think the guy's totally bogus."

"Really?" Becka pretended to question.

"Oh, yeah, you read about those type of fakes all the time."

Perfect. He'd set himself up. Becka went in for the kill. "Well, it just might interest you to know that that 'fake' knew all about the noises and light in the garage."

Scott stopped chewing. The noise in the garage had been a

mystery to the three of them ever since they moved in. They figured it was somehow connected to the weird boxes the last renters had left behind, but they couldn't be sure. It was an eerie screeching sound that came at the most unpredictable times. And to top it off, just last week, when Becka was investigating it, she'd thrown open the door connecting the kitchen and the garage and had seen a mysterious light flit across the room.

Of course, none of them believed the sound and light were supernatural or anything, but for some reason they'd been keeping the door to the garage locked ... and for some other reason they only went out there when they absolutely had to.

Becka felt calm and reassured. Twice she had been able to shut down Scotty's arguments. Maybe this was part of the power Maxwell had promised—the "unlocking of secret talents." She didn't know, but it felt great. It was time to change the subject. "Can Ryan pick me up after track practice?" she asked.

"Will you come straight home?"

"We might swing by the east side. He's a big brother to one of the kids over there."

The microwave chimed. Mom removed the mug of hot water and headed for the cupboard to dump in a teaspoon of instant coffee. "Ryan seems like a nice boy."

"He's better than nice, Mom. Even you would approve."

Mom smiled. "I'd better."

Becka continued, "The guy's so sweet, you wouldn't believe it."

"Oh, *please!*" Scott groaned for the second time. He rose, crossed to the sink, and rinsed his bowl. He didn't say another word. He just headed out of the room and back upstairs to get ready for school.

Becka watched. She wasn't entirely sure what his problem was, but she expected it had to do with Maxwell. Why? What about Maxwell Hunter made Scott so angry?

"We got him." Darryl scooted beside Scott at the cafeteria table.

"Got who?" Scott asked.

"Z. His cell phone was in the same location from about 5:30 to 9:30 last night and then again from 11:00 until this morning."

"That sounds about right," Scott said. "He said he had to take care of something around 9:30."

Darryl pushed up his glasses and gave a heartier-than-usual sniff.

Scott looked on with distaste as the kid swallowed. He was getting pretty used to the sniffs and snorts. But not the real loud ones ... and not while he was eating. He glanced at the vanilla pudding cup in his hands and thought he'd wait a minute before digging in.

Darryl hadn't noticed a thing. "My cousin called up with his address this morning."

"You're kidding! That fast?"

Darryl reached into his shirt pocket and pulled out a folded piece of paper. "I told you he was good." He handed the paper to Scott. Now, at last, they could discover who Z was. Maybe uncover how he knew so much. And most important, maybe they could find out why he had taken such an interest in Scott's family.

And yet, with all of those possibilities, Scott hesitated. He could not unfold the paper.

"What's wrong?" Darryl asked.

"I don't know ..."

Darryl gave his glasses another push.

"I just feel like what we're doing is wrong—you know, invading the guy's privacy."

"What's that got to do with anything? He'll never know we know."

Scott nodded. "But, still ..."

"Hey, Williams."

He turned to see one of the members of the Society passing by the table. It was the big, meaty guy in the tank top—the same tank top he wore nearly every day. Luckily he wasn't looking for a fight. In fact, he almost sounded friendly. "I heard about your sister," he called as he moved toward the exit. "Pretty cool. Let her know we're rooting for her."

Scott nodded but did not smile. The fact that the Society thought Rebecca's experiences were "cool" didn't exactly thrill him. And what did the guy mean, they were "rooting for her"?

"Are you going to open it or what?" Darryl asked.

Scott was still thinking about his sister.

"Scott." Darryl sniffed again, loud enough to bring Scott back to reality. "If you want, we can track him down and pay him a visit as early as tonight."

Scott looked back to the folded paper in his hand. "Tonight?" his voice croaked.

"Sure." Darryl shrugged. "Why not?"

Scott raised a finger to his mouth and began chewing a nail. Why not, indeed?

☜ ☜

At track practice Becka's mind was barely on her running. In fact, Coach Simmons had shouted at her more times than she could count. "Come on, Williams. Focus! FOCUS!"

Becka tried, but there were just too many things on her mind. Funny, a week ago running was all she thought about. But now ... well, now things were changing.

"Everything okay?" Julie asked as they toweled off in the locker room after their showers.

"Huh?" Becka looked up a little startled.

"Are you all right?"

"Oh, yeah ... sure." Becka forced a smile and reached for her sweatshirt.

Julie watched her carefully. "Ryan's waiting outside."

"Great!" Becka said as she finished dressing, grabbed her things, and headed off. "We'll see you tomorrow."

"Yeah …," Julie said slowly. "Tomorrow." She watched as Becka disappeared around the lockers. There was no missing the concern on her face.

❧ ❧

"Come on, pretty lady, it's 8:08. Hurry up!" Pepe tugged at Becka's hand as they scrambled up the grade toward the train trestle. The loose gravel slipped under her feet, slowing her progress, but at Pepe's insistence, she pressed on.

Ryan was right behind them. "You sure this is safe?" he asked.

"Sure I'm sure," Pepe said. "I do it all the time. We won't even be on the tracks, I promise."

Ryan had made it clear that he wasn't crazy about visiting the Death Bridge. But ever since they'd arrived, it was all Pepe had talked about. And he assured them again and again it would be perfectly safe.

The thought of being this close to the spot where so many kids had been killed should have given Becka the creeps. But, for some reason, she felt a faint attraction toward the place. It probably was just morbid curiosity. But Becka sensed there was more to it than that.

At last they reached the top of the grade. Becka let out a gasp. She had been here before! Last night … this was the ridge she'd stood on in her dream! Only now there was a train trestle just ahead and tracks that continued another hundred yards before disappearing around the bend. Other than that, it was identical to her dream. Becka was certain of it.

For a moment all three stood looking on in silence. And, for a moment, all three thought of the crazy, half-drunk teenagers who had been batted off of the trestle like flies or crushed under the train's merciless wheels.

"Come on." Pepe tugged at Becka's hand, urging them to follow him onto the trestle.

"No way, amigo," Ryan said. "This is far enough."

"I don't mean we stand on the tracks. I mean we stand over there." Pepe pointed to the outside girder of the trestle, a steel beam with plenty of room to walk.

"Pass," was all Ryan said.

Pepe shrugged and looked to Becka. She also shook her head. He let go of her hand and started toward the trestle.

"Pepe!" Ryan warned.

"I do it all the time, *mi hijo.* Don't worry." He reached the trestle and stepped onto the steel girder.

"But—"

"You're sounding like my mother." He grinned. "Don't worry."

Becka and Ryan watched as Pepe tightrope-walked the steel beam—effortlessly working his way along the outside of the bridge. From his position it was clear there was no way a train could hit him. Of course if he slipped and fell, he could bash his brains out on the road twenty feet below. But with all the handgrips and footholds, that didn't seem likely.

"Be careful," Ryan warned.

"Relax," Pepe called. "It's no biggie."

"Just be careful."

As Rebecca watched she felt a strange detachment creep over her. The same detachment she felt when she was being hypnotized. Suddenly it was as if things weren't completely real. As if they weren't that important. If Pepe remained safe on the trestle, fine, he deserved it. If he slipped and fell, that would be okay too, because he probably deserved that. It was as if everything was part of a plan ... the workings of a "fair and just universe."

She turned and looked out over the neighborhood. Here,

high atop the grade, she could see everything. The pathetic houses, the broken-down cars, the ragged children playing in the street. But this time she felt no heaviness. This time she felt very little pity or compassion. Only detachment. All this poverty, did it really matter? If reincarnation was true, then this was justice — people simply paying for how they had lived in the past. Why should she feel sorry for them if they were getting what they deserved?

The thought struck her as strange and yet perfectly logical. But before she could think it through, she heard a faint rumbling.

"What's that?" Ryan asked.

"It's the train!" Pepe called over his shoulder. By now he was halfway across the steel beam. "It's the 8:10 — right on time."

"Get off there!" Ryan's voice was sharp and full of concern. "Come on! Get off there!"

Pepe laughed.

"Pepe!"

"Don't worry, amigo! I do this all the time!"

"Get off there now!"

"I'm perfectly safe!" Pepe called. "But you two, you'd better climb down."

Becka and Ryan looked up the tracks to the bend. They saw nothing, but they could feel the ground vibrate as the rumbling grew louder.

"PEPE!" Ryan cried.

"Go on!" Pepe shouted. "Get down. It will be here any second!"

Ryan stood frozen, unsure whether to go out and try to get the boy or to head down the grade with Becka.

"Come on," Becka said. "He'll be okay."

Ryan looked to her. How could she be so sure? Granted, Pepe was on the outside of the bridge, far from the train, but still ... how could she be so sure?

"It'll be okay," she repeated and took his hand. "Come on."

At last the train rounded the bend. Its bright headlamp cut through the night fog, flooding their faces, forcing them to squint. Its rumbling grew louder. Suddenly it blew its whistle—a shrill and piercing warning.

"Come on!" Becka pulled at Ryan and, at last, he followed. They slid down the steep gravel grade. The rumbling had turned to a roar—a roar so powerful it filled their ears and vibrated their bodies.

They did not look back but continued sliding down the grade.

By now the roar was deafening. Halfway down, safely out of reach, Becka suddenly released Ryan's hand and spun back to the train ... just in time to see the locomotive thunder past. The wind hit her face and blew her hair. The ground pounded. The roar filled her body.

Over on the trestle, Pepe clung to the outside beam, laughing and shouting.

Becka didn't notice. She closed her eyes to savor the moment—the pounding, the thundering, the roaring. It was here. The same power she had experienced in the dream. It was exhilarating. Overpowering. Before she knew it, she also began to laugh. Like Pepe. Only harder. She gulped in the air, reveling in the power. A power she could practically taste. A power she knew would be hers.

6

So how do I look?" Mom asked Becka for the twentieth time.
"You look great."

"You sure?"

"Trust me."

Becka wiped down the kitchen counter while Mom loaded
stray cups and dishes into the dishwasher. Scott was out with
Darryl, tracking down Z, and that was just fine with Becka and
Mom. They were about to receive a guest—a guest they both
knew Scott wasn't crazy about. Maxwell Hunter had just finished another lecture and would be arriving any minute to pick
up Mom for a late-night dinner.

"What if we don't have anything to talk about?" Mom asked
as she poured the soap into the dishwasher and closed it.

"Ask him about himself—guys always like that."

"How do you know?"

"That's what you always told me!" Becka laughed.

"Oh, right," Mom chuckled. "That's how I caught your
father." Suddenly she turned to Becka. "You don't think I'm
betraying him, do you—your father, I mean?"

The question brought Becka up short. Not because she hadn't

thought of it, but because ever since she learned Maxwell had called, it was all she had thought of. Becka missed her father. Desperately. People had said the pain would go away, but they were wrong. It had been six months since his plane had crashed in the deep jungles of Brazil, but sometimes it felt like six minutes. The ache would never leave. She knew it.

But she knew something else too. She knew Mom could not go on living life alone. Oh sure, she was a strong lady and could make it on her own—with God's help, of course. She'd been doing just that for a lot of months now. But Becka could see how much Mom missed the sharing, the support, the closeness she and Dad had always had. Mom needed someone she could love—and someone who would love her—the way she and Dad had loved each other. And as much as it hurt Becka to think of another man married to her mother, she was pretty sure someday it would happen.

"I think it's great!" she lied. "I'm sure Daddy would think so too."

Mom searched Becka's eyes, grateful for the words but somehow sensing the lie.

The doorbell rang.

"It's him!" Another wave of panic hit Mom, which of course led to more dress smoothing and hair adjusting.

Becka grabbed the coat on the chair and slipped it over Mom's shoulders. "You look great. Stop worrying." She turned her mother toward the door and gave a little push. "Go."

With the added momentum, Mom headed for the entrance hall. She checked herself in the mirror one last time, then opened the door.

Maxwell stood on the porch. He wore tailored black slacks and an expensive-looking blue sweater that heightened the intensity of his eyes. In his hands were a dozen roses. "Hello, Mrs. Williams."

Mom stood speechless.

Becka waited for her to say something, but nothing was coming from Mom's mouth. Finally the word *hi* squeaked out—a little too loud, a little too hoarse.

Becka winced. Suddenly she understood where her own clumsiness with boys came from. It was hereditary. Like varicose veins.

Maxwell handed Mom the roses, and she gave the obligatory "Oh . . . they're beautiful."

Maxwell smiled, then spotted Becka standing in the background. "Good evening, Rebecca."

"Hi." She smiled.

"How are your dreams?"

Her smile faded. She tried to answer but only managed to give a shrug.

"Listen to them very carefully. They will unlock your power."

"You know, don't you?" Becka asked. "You know who I was, and you know about this power." She hadn't planned to bring up the subject—this was Mom's night. But the guy had started it. "Why can't you just tell me?"

Maxwell's smile broadened.

Becka continued. "When I saw the number sixteen on my ring, you got all excited. You know who I was."

"Listen to your dreams," Maxwell repeated. "Once you know your past, it will unlock the power of your future."

"Why won't you just tell me?"

"When the time is right, you will know."

Rebecca sighed in frustration.

"Becky," Mom said, trying to change the subject, "would you put these in some water for me? There's a vase up in the—"

"If you don't mind," Maxwell interrupted. "I would prefer you to keep these this evening."

Mom looked at him a little surprised.

He explained. "Their beauty only reflects the greater depth of your own."

Becka had never seen Mom blush, but there was no missing the color running to her cheeks. "Well ... all right," she fumbled. "If that's what you want."

Becka smiled. It was kind of cute.

"Our reservations are at nine," Maxwell said, reaching for the door. "I am afraid we must be on our way." He opened the door and allowed Mom to pass.

"Have a good time," Becka said.

"Thanks," Mom called back.

Maxwell hesitated, then slowly turned to Becka. "You too, Rebecca Williams. This evening will have surprises. Be sure to enjoy them." He gave her a knowing smile, then stepped outside and shut the door.

Becka stared at the closed door. A little puzzled ... and a lot unnerved.

👁 👁

Scott and Darryl rode their bikes down the secluded road. It was another foggy evening. There were no lights except for a soft moon whose edges were blurred by the fog. The dampness collected on Scott's handlebars and seeped through his jacket.

It had been half an hour since they rode out of town. Oh sure, there was still the occasional house and barking dog, but on the whole, things were definitely getting on the deserted side.

"You sure you know where we're going?" Scott asked.

"Absolutely." Darryl gave a loud sniff. The moisture didn't help his sinuses much. "Potrero Road. It's just around this corner, up here."

"That's what you said for the last three corners," Scott complained.

"Then we must be getting close."

Finally a tract of half-built houses appeared to the left in the moonlight. They were constructed back when everybody was moving to California and buying new homes. But now they just sat there, month after month—bare wood frames waiting to be completed.

As the guys approached a street leading into the complex, Darryl read the sign. "Potrero Road. See, I told you," he squeaked.

They turned off the pavement and onto a dirt road. It was strange. Everywhere they looked, they were surrounded by the bare skeleton houses. Stranger still was the fact that Z would choose to live in a place like this.

"Ohhh Darryllllll ...," Scott goaded.

Darryl pulled the paper from his pocket and read. " 'Potrero Road.' It says right here, '1750 Potrero Road.' "

"Right," Scott nodded. "I see two basic problems: One, nobody lives here. Two, there aren't even addresses on the houses. Now, call it a wild guess, but maybe, just maybe, your cousin screwed up."

Darryl scowled, then sniffed. "I don't get it," he squeaked. "Hubert never makes mistakes ... not like this. Maybe there's—"

Suddenly a security patrol car pulled around the corner and approached them. In a true, hospitable fashion, the driver snapped on his searchlight and shone it directly into their eyes, purposely blinding them.

"Hey!" Darryl shouted. "Turn that off!"

Scott said nothing as he tried to shield his own eyes.

The car pulled beside them and stopped. But the light never left their faces. It remained directly on them, so bright they were unable to see the driver.

"What are you kids doing out here?" The voice was coarse and gruff—anything but friendly.

"We're looking for somebody," Darryl answered with a definite attitude.

"You're what?" the voice sounded even tougher.

Scott stepped in. One of his specialties was diplomacy, defusing tense situations. He cranked up his smile to about 9.9 and did his best to sound friendly. "We're looking for 1750 Potrero Roa—"

"Nobody lives out here," the voice snapped. So much for diplomacy. "These houses are all vacant."

"But we have the address right here," Darryl protested. "It says—"

"This here's private property, kid. So get your rear ends outta here 'fore I have you arrested."

"Nobody lives out here at all?" Scott asked, giving diplomacy one last shot while trying to see past the light to the driver.

"Does it look like it? Now, move it."

Darryl argued, "Hey, it's a free—"

"Get outta here 'fore I throw you out!"

"Yeah," Darryl demanded. "You and who—"

Scott interrupted. "We're on our way, mister. Sorry to bother you." He gave Darryl a look that said, "I'm not in the mood to have my face turned into pizza topping by some gorilla security guard."

Darryl took the cue. Reluctantly he followed Scott as they turned their bikes around and headed back toward the main road. Unable to resist, Darryl shouted over his shoulder, "Have a nice day!"

The driver said nothing. He remained at the curb and followed them with the searchlight until they were out of sight.

☜ ☞

Rebecca was obsessed.

No matter how hard she tried to concentrate on her homework, her thoughts kept drifting back to Maxwell's words. They weren't idle chatter—she knew that. And he wasn't a fake—she knew that too. Her visions had been real. So was the power she had experienced in her dream—and the power she'd felt beside that train. She was somebody great. She knew it. Somebody with extraordinary powers and talents that were trying to surface from within.

But who? Who had she been?

She'd tried praying about it, but her prayer had felt strange, empty ... like there was no one at the other end. So once again she was on the computer.

First she had tried to search *guillotine*. That was her original vission, back on the stage in the library when she was about to have her head cut off. But she wasn't sure how to spell it and typed it in half a dozen different ways before finally giving up.

She padded over to the bookshelf and reached for the dictionary. Maybe that would be easier. As she flipped through the pages she thought of the age-old question: *If I knew how to spell it, why would I have to look it up?*

After another half-dozen tries, she finally found the word.

guillotine: a machine for beheading by means of a heavy blade that slides down in vertical guides

"Wonderful," she sighed. "I've already figured that out." But at least she had the spelling. Back on the computer, she searched *guillotine* adn read the description:

GUILLOTINE, French method of beheading; a blade between two posts falls, when a supporting cord is released, onto the victim's neck below. The guillotine came into use in response to J. I. Guillotin's call for a more humane form of execution. Last known public use: in France in 1977.

"More humane?" Becka mumbled. "They've got to be kidding!"

Well, all that told her was that her vision could have taken place anytime before 1977. With a frustrated sigh, Becka set the book aside.

Now what?

She remembered the soldiers with the long bayonets. But they used those things just about everywhere in the seventeen or eighteen hundreds.

Okay, what about the screaming mob?

Again, no clues. *If I could only make out what they were saying,* she thought. But since it was in French, she had no idea what they—

"Wait a minute!" she exclaimed. "French! Of course!" If they were speaking French, chances are it happened in France. And if it was a French guillotine . . .

She struck her forehead, once again astounded by her incredible lack of intelligence.

She typed in "French History." If she were a great king of France, she would surely be mentioned somewhere. The search produced about a billion results.

"Great . . . I'll be here all night." She clicked on a link and started scrolling down the page, scanning pictures, captions and headings. Then she saw it. A sketch of a guillotine! Her eyes shot to the caption, which read: "Method of execution used during the French Revolution."

Becka's heart started pounding. She searched "French Revolution," clicked on a link and started reading—dates, leaders, key events. It wasn't until she'd scrolled through five or six pages that she saw it. Then she could only stare.

There, in front of her, was a portrait of a man. A man dressed in the same flowing materials she had worn—the same silks, the same furs, the same lace.

She looked to his face. It was heavier than hers, but there was no missing the eyes. They were *her* eyes. She was certain of it. She was looking at herself!

Finally, she glanced to the caption. It simply read: "Louis XVI, king of France."

Becka closed her eyes. She could feel the power tugging at her—washing over her. It was all there ... a king, France, and the Roman numeral sixteen. Rebecca Williams had been Louis XVI!

She took a deep breath and opened her eyes. She clicked on the link to Louis XVI and read on.

She read how Louis ... no, how *she* had tried to be a good king, how she was compassionate toward the poor peasants, how she loved hunting (which explained her vision on horseback with the dogs). She read how she was well-meaning but too trusting—too kind and inexperienced. And she read how those latter qualities led her to make wrong decisions, which eventually led her to be executed. By the guillotine.

Everything was there ... Becka Williams ... compassionate, kind, trusting to a fault. And, most importantly, king of the most powerful nation on earth.

She took another trembling breath. But she wasn't shaking with fear. She was shaking with excitement. And power. She had been a king. A great king. True, she had had one weakness. Her kindness and gullibility. But now she knew. And with that knowledge and the power of her past, imagine what she could become today!

❧ ❧

Scott entered his room and peeled off his jacket. Cornelius was dozing on his perch, so the kid didn't bother turning on the light.

It was late and he was tired. As far as he could tell, Mom and Becka had both gone to bed early. At least their lights were off.

He undressed, switched on his computer and went to his email.

There was one message.

He clicked on it and read:

> I heard you stopped by. Sorry to miss you. How about
> tomorrow night, 7:00, same place?
> Z

Scott shuddered and stared at the screen. How could Z have known?

7

It had been a long time since Mom had felt so protected, so secure, so ... *cared for.* Ever since her husband had died, she'd been the one who had to take control. The one forced to run the show. Of course, the kids did their part, but the final responsibility always rested on her shoulders.

Until tonight. Because tonight, Maxwell Hunter was in charge.

From the flowers to the Italian restaurant (complete with a violin player) to the maître d' who doted on her slightest whim — every detail of the evening had been taken care of. And it felt wonderful.

Maxwell Hunter radiated power — and tonight, that power seemed absolutely devoted to her. As the evening progressed, Mom found herself growing more and more attracted ... but at the same time, there was still the slightest trace of caution. It was a strange yet pleasant mixture of emotions: attraction and caution.

It took nearly an hour for the small talk to drift to Maxwell's faith. "So, when exactly did you become a Christian?" Mom asked.

Maxwell smiled as he poured the remainder of the wine from the bottle into his glass. He wasn't drunk, but he was definitely relaxed. Very, very relaxed. Once again he offered some to Mom, and once again she politely refused.

"When did I become a Christian? Well now, that's difficult to say. I think I first became aware of the Christ within sometime during my sophomore or junior year of college."

"I'm sorry?" Mom asked, "'the Christ within'?... You mean, that's when you received Christ?"

Maxwell smiled. "Yes and no. You see, he's always been inside. I just didn't experience him until then."

Mom was confused. "What do you mean, 'He's always been inside'?"

"I mean, each of us have the Christ living inside—" he took another sip of wine and continued—"from the moment we are first born."

Ever so faintly, the alarms Mom had heard when they first met began to sound again. "You mean," she gently corrected, "Christ comes inside, once we ask him to forgive us of our sins."

Maxwell chuckled. His eyes were growing moist, taking on the dull sheen of someone who was slowly but steadily getting drunk. "Sin. Now there's a quaint notion. Sin is a state of mind. We all have the Christ inside. We're all sons of the most high. It just takes some of us longer to tap into that power than others."

"Power?" Mom shifted slightly. The alarms grew louder.

"Yes." Maxwell nodded. "We are all Christ. We all have his power." Before Mom could respond, he glanced around the restaurant and lowered his voice. "Would you like to see that power?"

Mom simply looked at him.

"Watch." He fumbled with a spoon beside his plate. It may have been the wine or just a little clumsiness, but it seemed to take him a while to pick up the spoon and set it on the white tablecloth between them. When he had, he stretched out his index fingers and placed one at each end of the spoon—not touching it, but very, very close.

Mom watched uneasily. When she glanced up at Maxwell, he was grinning—like a schoolboy about to play a prank. Ever so slowly, he raised his index fingers. They never touched the spoon. But as he raised his hands, the spoon followed, lifting off the table ... one, two, four inches high.

Mom continued to stare. Her uneasiness had turned to fear. The alarms were going off strongly now. Full volume. Whatever power this man had was definitely not from the Lord. "I ... uh," she pulled the napkin from her lap and stood. "I think we'd better call it an evening."

Maxwell looked up at her in surprise, and the spoon suddenly fell to the table with a loud clatter. He looked at it, startled, and then back at her with an almost hurt expression. "Why did you do that?"

Mom shifted uneasily. "I think you'd better take me home."

Three minutes later, Mom strode as fast as she could along the outside of the building toward the back parking lot. Maxwell was several yards behind, shouting, "Will you please wait up!"

As she passed the garbage bin, she noticed a black and brown stray dog. He was so busy scrounging for food that he didn't see her, but for some reason, as Maxwell passed, the dog suddenly lifted his head, his ears pricked. He spun around, letting out a harsh growl.

Maxwell looked at the animal, surprised.

Mom glanced over her shoulder.

The dog drew back his upper lip, snarling—the deep, guttural growl coming from deep inside his chest.

Maxwell slowed to a stop.

Mom also slowed. As much as she wanted to avoid this man,

she didn't want to see him hurt. "Just keep walking," she called. "He won't attack if you let him be."

But Maxwell didn't seem to hear her. He was concentrating on the dog.

"Maxwell?"

As Mom watched, the man's stare seemed to intensify, until it became a menacing glare—a glare as fierce as the dog's.

Mom felt a cold shiver spread over her. It was unnerving, as if the man and dog were entering some sort of unspoken, but formidable, standoff. Mom heard another growl—but this time she could swear it came from Maxwell.

"Maxwell?"

He still didn't seem to hear. His gaze was fixed on the dog.

"Maxwell."

Finally the dog made his move. He crouched down, taking two tentative steps, preparing to attack.

Mom stepped forward in alarm. "Maxwell, look out! He's—" But she never finished the sentence, for suddenly Maxwell pointed his arm directly at the dog and shouted in some unintelligible language.

The dog yelped and was thrown to the pavement, whimpering in pain.

"Maxwell! What are you doing?"

As she watched Maxwell with growing alarm, it seemed as if someone or something had taken control of him. He continued glaring at the dog, which seemed to increase its pain, making it writhe in agony. The beast's whining was only interrupted by an occasional pain-filled howl.

"Stop it!" Mom shouted. "You're hurting him!"

"Wrong, my dear," Maxwell mumbled in a strange, flat tone as he continued glaring at the pathetic animal. "I'm not hurting him. Not at all." A faint smile crossed his face. "I'm killing him."

The dog lay on his side now, his tongue rolling out, the panting and whining growing weaker, more pathetic.

Horrified at what she was seeing, Mom screamed at Maxwell. "Stop it!"

But Maxwell would not listen. He actually seemed to take pleasure in the creature's pain.

Without thinking, Mom rushed at him, hitting him with her small purse. "Stop it! I said, stop it!"

The unearthly glare suddenly vanished from Maxwell's face. He glanced around, confused, disoriented. Immediately the dog's whimperings stopped, and it struggled shakily to its feet. Mom wasn't sure who looked more baffled by what had just happened, the dog or Maxwell. The pitiful animal licked his chops, gave a final uncertain whine, then quickly slinked away, stealing into the dark shadows of the alley.

Maxwell turned to Mom. "What ... what happened?" He sounded lost, almost helpless.

Mom stepped back. She wasn't sure what she had witnessed, but she was sure she had seen enough.

Maxwell saw the fear in her eyes and forced a smile. "It's all right," he said, trying to sound in control. "I can explain. I can explain everything."

But Mom was in no mood for an explanation. Any more than she was in the mood to be anywhere near this man. She turned and started to run.

"Wait! Please, I can explain!"

But Mom did not wait. She did not reply. She just kept running. All she wanted was to get away—from Maxwell, from whatever evil this was—and to get home so she could warn her little girl.

❧ ❧

Rebecca dreamed.

She had shut the laptop and gone to bed early for that specific purpose. Maxwell had said the evening would hold surprises. He had been right so far. Maybe there were more.

Soon she was standing on the train trestle. Again everything was still. No wind. No stars. Just a thick fog. Below her, the loyal friends and subjects were on their knees, bowing their faces to the ground.

Becka adjusted her fur robe and straightened the lace of her sleeves. This time she was not embarrassed. This time she knew why they bowed. It was her birthright. Her destiny.

The ground under her feet began to vibrate. She looked toward the bend up ahead and waited. Any second, the star would appear. And with it, the power. She was frightened, but she was also excited. She had failed twice—but this time she would not back down. She would let the power have its way.

A faint rumbling began ... and grew.

The students below looked at each other. Some began rising to their feet in alarm, but Becka was not worried. She knew their minds could not understand what was happening; they could not comprehend the power she was about to experience.

The rumbling expanded into a roar. Suddenly the star pierced the darkness. But this time it was more than a star. It was also the headlight of the train.

The crowd panicked, but Becka wasn't surprised. The train, the star, the power ... somehow they were all connected. Soon she would be a part of that connection.

The train thundered toward her. She could feel its energy. Its whistle cut through the night, but she did not move. This time she would not back down.

"Becka!" Ryan shouted. "Becka, run!"

Becka barely heard. She looked into the approaching light. It blazed brighter and brighter, filling more and more of her vision. And with it, directly in the center, was the tunnel ... the passageway. Again her fear rose, but this time she was able to push it aside, for, as the light continued its approach, its energy began flowing into her, filling her, empowering her.

Then she saw him ... inside the tunnel. In the center of the power stood Maxwell Hunter. It was impossible to see his face, but there was no mistaking his blazer and distinct jaw line.

The power roared in her ears, filling her head, flooding her body. The tunnel grew wider—wide enough to enter.

Fear tried to stir within her. *"Be careful,"* it whispered. But as Maxwell reached out his hand to her, motioning for her to join him, the whisper faded away.

She saw no train now—only light. Finally she understood. The *light* held the power. And if she could feel this much power outside of the light, imagine what intensity awaited her inside.

She raised her arms toward Maxwell. He continued holding his hand out to her as they drew closer and closer. Their hands were just a few yards apart now, when suddenly—

Becka awoke.

Once again she was breathing hard. Once again she was covered with sweat. And once again she was angry that she could not go further. Why? What was preventing her from entering the light?

She rolled over and looked at her clock: 11:33.

Then she heard a muffled noise. Straining to listen, she realized it was footsteps. Up and down the hall they paced. Back and forth. And murmurings. Quiet but anxious murmurings.

Still angry at being awakened and still feeling the power of the light, Becka threw her feet over the side of the bed and went to investigate. She had no fear as she crossed to the door and threw it open.

A shadowed form turned to confront her.

"Mom?"

Her mother was pacing back and forth, head bowed. She still wore her evening dress and coat.

"Mom, what are you doing?"

The woman looked up, startled. "Oh, Becky." She ran to her daughter and threw her arms around her.

"What's wrong?" Becka asked. "What are you doing?"

"He's evil, Becka. Whatever he's doing, we must stay away from him."

"Who is? What are you talking about?"

"Maxwell Hunter!"

Becka felt herself stiffen. She was not prepared to hear this. Not from her mother. Not after all the power she had just experienced. "Why? What happened? Did he make a pass at you?"

"No, it's more than that." Her voice shook slightly, and she drew a deep breath. "Becky, he's involved in the occult. I'm sure of that much now."

Becka grew defensive. Maxwell was a good man. She knew it. Look at the power he had unlocked inside her, the power that was just waiting to be hers. She started to speak, but one look at Mom told her she was too worked up to reason with—at least for now. So Becka tried to change the subject. "What are you doing out here, pacing back and forth?"

Her mother held her look for a long moment. Finally she answered. "I was praying, Becky. I was praying that whatever we got ourselves into, God would forgive us. That whatever influence Maxwell may have over you would be broken."

Rebecca's anger flared. How could her mother be so ignorant? Just because she didn't understand Maxwell's powers didn't make him evil! Mysterious, yes. But not evil!

And Becka was angry for another reason. Suddenly she knew, without a doubt, that it had not been her mother's pacing that had awakened her. She knew it had been her mother's prayers. That's what had stopped the dream. That's what had prevented her from stepping into the tunnel of light.

It was her mother's careless, superstitious prayers that had prevented her from experiencing the power that was waiting for her.

👁 👁

At school the following day, Rebecca's attitude was no different. Finally she knew who she was and the power that would soon be hers. All she had to do was endure the ignorance of those surrounding her.

She was sitting at a table in the library, poring over a book when she heard, "Missed you at lunch."

She glanced up. "Oh, hi, Julie."

Julie pulled out a chair and sat. "Can I talk to you a sec?"

"Well, I'm kinda busy—"

"What are you reading?" Before Becka could answer, Julie spun the book around on the table and read, *"Modern Day Hinduism.* What's that about?"

Becka turned the book back and said, "I'm afraid it's too complicated for you to understand." She hadn't intended to hurt Julie's feelings, but she had succeeded all the same.

Julie scowled slightly. "Beck, can I be honest?"

"Sure."

"Some of the kids are saying—not me, of course—but the others, they say you're getting, like, a major attitude."

"What do you mean?"

"Well, after that hypnotism thing … it's like, I don't know … it's like these last couple of days you're thinking you're better than the rest of us."

Becka just stared. How immature. How petty. Of *course* she was better. She had been a king, a powerful ruler. But that was only the beginning. Soon she would be experiencing even greater powers. Becka wanted to explain all this, but she knew it would be pointless. So, instead of explaining, she played dumb. "What do you mean?"

Julie took a deep breath. But before she could answer, Ryan strolled in. "Hey, Beck." He gave his usual grin. "We missed you at lunch."

"Yeah, well I had a little research to do."

"You going with me to Pepe's after track practice?"

"Uh … I don't think …" Becka hesitated. She knew they

wouldn't understand, but she had to tell them. "I won't be staying for track tonight."

"You what?" Julie asked in surprise. "Beck, we have the state meet coming up."

"I know, it's just—well, I have some other more important things to do."

"More important than State?"

Becka looked down at the table and shrugged. She'd known it would be pointless.

Julie and Ryan exchanged glances.

"Well, uh … " Ryan cleared his throat. "Maybe I could pick you up later, at home, and we could swing by Pepe's this evening." He forced a gentle laugh. "If you ask me, I think he's really got a crush on you."

"Maybe I'll go," Becka said as she glanced at her watch. There were only a few minutes left of lunch. Funny, a week ago she would have died for the opportunity to go to the state meet or to spend any time with Ryan. But now … now she just wished they'd both leave so she could get back to work.

"I can't explain it …" Apparently Ryan was still talking about Pepe. "But when we hang around him, it kinda gives him hope—like maybe he can get out of there someday."

Becka hesitated, wondering if her friends could understand what she was about to say. There was only one way to find out. "Ryan, have you ever thought that … well, that maybe Pepe is living where he is for a reason?"

"What do you mean?"

"There's this thing called karma." She nodded toward the book on the table. "It's like the justice you create for yourself, and then you carry it around wherever you go. If you've been good in the past, if you have good karma, you'll be rewarded, like in future lives. If you've been bad, then your karma will be bad and you will be punished."

"What's that got to do with helping Pepe?"

She tried again. "What if by helping Pepe, you're really hurting him? What if you're just messing up the justice of the universe so he has to come back and suffer all over again?"

Ryan frowned. "Run that past me again?"

Becka glanced to Julie. She looked equally confused. Becka had been right. Her friends wouldn't understand. But then how could she expect them to? After all, they hadn't experienced what she had. She tried one last time. "What I'm saying is—"

The bell rang to end lunch. Becka felt a wave of relief. "Oh well." She smiled. "It's just a theory." She closed the book and started to rise. "Maybe we'll get into it again some time." She gathered her stuff and headed for the desk to check out the book.

Of course she knew Julie and Ryan were staring after her, but she didn't hold it against them. It wasn't their fault they didn't know. It wasn't their fault they didn't understand. Nobody understood. Not Scott, not Mom, not her friends. Nobody.

Nobody but she herself. And, of course, Maxwell.

<❧ ❧>

The skeleton houses loomed on both sides as Scott and Darryl pedaled down Potrero Road. It was 7 p.m.—the time Z had asked for the meeting.

Though neither boy would admit it, their hearts both pounded.

Ever since Scott and Becka had moved to Crescent Bay, Z had been a mystery. He seemed to know everything about them … and he seemed to know everything about the occult. Why? Was it the occult that gave him his powers? Was it the occult that told him Becka's name and the other half-dozen things he knew but had never been told? Perhaps. But if he was involved in the occult, then why would he spend so much time warning them about it? None of it made sense.

But it would. Soon. Very soon.

A set of car headlights rounded the corner. Scott and Darryl recognized them instantly.

"Uh-oh," Scott groaned. "It's Mr. Hospitality."

The security patrol car headed directly toward them.

"Here we go again," Darryl muttered.

But this time there was no bright light glaring in their eyes. This time they were able to clearly see the driver. He was a plump man in his sixties. He pulled up alongside them and rolled down his window. Reluctantly Scott and Darryl slowed to a stop.

His voice was no more friendly than the night before. "You're late."

Suddenly Scott's heart sank. Could this be him—could this be Z?

Before either boy had a chance to respond, the driver continued. "Follow this road for two more blocks. After the second cross street, it's the fourth house on your right."

Scott's mouth dropped open. He thought he heard himself saying, "Thanks," but he wasn't sure. In any case, the guard didn't answer. He simply rolled up his window, pulled away, and continued down the street.

Scott and Darryl looked at each other in amazement. But they didn't say a word. What could they say? As always, whenever they dealt with Z, there was a surprise.

They pedaled down the road of deserted structures in total silence. At last the house came into view. It had to be the one. No question. It was the only house with a car parked in front. A white Jaguar.

They slowed, hopped their bikes over the curb, and stopped on what would someday be the front lawn. Like all the other houses, this one only had bare studs for walls and bare rafters for a roof.

Scott and Darryl glanced at each other one final time. Silently they set their bikes down and started toward the house. They could see nobody inside. There was no light, no movement.

They stopped at what was supposed to be the front entrance.

"Hello?" Scott called.

No answer.

"Hello?" he repeated. "Anybody home?"

"Knock, knock," Darryl called.

Suddenly, deep inside the house, an orange light flared. Someone had struck a match. For the briefest second they saw the glow of a man's face lighting a cigarette. He was small and had long dark hair.

"Hi, there," Scott called, trying his best to sound casual. He might have succeeded if his voice hadn't cracked. But it always tended to do that when he was scared out of his mind.

"Over here," the voice called. Scott and Darryl froze in astonishment. It was the voice of a woman!

She was only a shadow among the other shadows. A shadow ... and a faint glow of a cigarette.

Darryl and Scott stepped into the house and headed toward her.

8

"**Z**? Is that you?" Scott called as they moved through the house toward the shadowy form.

There was no answer. Only the brightened glow of the cigarette as the woman took another long drag. She tilted her head back and blew the smoke out impatiently.

The guys continued forward. "Are you Z?" Scott repeated.

"Don't be ridiculous." Her voice was thick and raspy.

As they approached, they could see she was seated on a wooden sawhorse. She was small, almost tiny, and her feet barely touched the ground. She kept her head in the shadows so it was impossible to make out any detail of her face. But the moonlight struck the cloud of smoke behind her, making it glow, creating an eerie silhouette of her nose, chin, and hair.

They slowed to a stop. Once again the cigarette grew brighter as she took a long drag. Scott cleared his throat. "We were supposed to meet somebody here. His name is—"

"I know," the voice cut him off. She leaned forward, momentarily bringing her face out of the shadows. She was dark complexioned, maybe Hispanic. "Z could not come. I am a friend of his. I owe him a great deal." Her accent was not Spanish but Asian. Maybe from India.

"So you've met him." Scott stepped a little closer.

The woman chuckled. "Yes, I have met him."

"Well, could you ... I mean, who is he? Could you tell us how he knows so much about—"

"There are some things that are better for you not to know." She took a final drag from the cigarette, dropped it to the floor, and crushed it out. Scott's mind raced. He had heard that exact phrase from Z just the other day.

"There are some things that are better for you not to know."

"But who—"

"It is your sister that should be your concern."

Scott tensed. "How do you know about my sister?"

"I know nothing about your sister except that she is dabbling in something about which she is ignorant."

"Dabbling? In what?"

"Reincarnation."

"Hold it." Darryl sniffed a little irritably. "Are you telling me Z brought us all the way out here just so you could tell us about his sister?"

Scott agreed. "I know Becka's reading up on all that junk, but it's really not that big of a—"

"Maxwell Hunter is a well-known proponent of hypnotic regression and channeling." She paused, then continued. "His methods can be most dangerous."

"Dangerous?" Scott repeated. "What do you mean?"

The woman gave no answer.

Scott continued. "Reincarnation is—well, just a belief. Of course it's not true, but there's nothing wrong with believing in something, just because it's not tr—"

The woman interrupted. "I am a victim of that belief."

The answer brought Scott up short. "Victim?"

"My name is Nagaina. I was born in Nepal, a mountainous

country north of India. My parents were killed in an earthquake when I was only seven."

"I'm sorry. But what's that got to do with—"

"My village was Hindu, which meant we believed in reincarnation. Because my parents were killed, I was thought to be cursed by the gods. I was believed to have been an evil person in my former life."

"That stinks," Darryl offered.

The woman nodded. "For my own good, I was cast out of my village and left to die. They believed the more quickly I died and paid for my past evil, the more quickly I would be reincarnated into a better life."

"You mean nobody would help you?" Scott asked.

"They were afraid to interfere with my karma, to incur the wrath of our gods."

"So ...," Scott said slowly, "you not only lost your parents, but you were thrown out of your village and left to die."

The woman nodded. "When your—" she stopped and started again. "When Z found me, I was dying in the woods, so starved that I was eating dirt to fill my stomach."

"All because your village believed in reincarnation?"

She nodded. "On the surface it seems innocent, almost plausible. But as you follow reincarnation to its logical conclusion, you will see inhuman treatment, indifference to suffering, and little respect for human life."

There was a long pause as Scott and Darryl digested the facts. Finally Scott spoke. "And you're telling us all this because ...?"

"Z is greatly concerned for your sister."

"Because she's playing with reincarnation?"

"And because she is associating with Maxwell Hunter, who is an acclaimed Eastern mystic. A man who uses the forces of hell to ensnare his victims."

Scott gave an involuntary shudder. "'Forces of hell'? Those are some pretty strong words."

"They are truth." The woman glanced at her watch and rose to her feet. "It is late. I must go."

"Wait a minute, where are you going? How can we get in touch with you if we need—"

"You will not see me again." She produced another cigarette and struck another match.

"But ... what if, what if we need to get a hold of you or something?"

She drew the smoke in deeply, then blew out the match as she exhaled. "I have done this as a favor for Z. He is a great man. I owe him much. But I think we shall not meet again, Scott Williams." She dropped the match to the floor and moved through the skeleton house toward her car.

❧ ❧

Becka didn't know how long she sat on the bed in her room. All she knew was that she was getting sick of fighting with Scott and Mom about Maxwell Hunter. Of course, she knew they were under a lot of pressure—especially Mom, what with moving into a new town, getting everyone situated, having to be both mother and father. Of course, she didn't want to add to that pressure. But that didn't give Mom the right to try and stop something she knew nothing about.

Maxwell Hunter was a good man. In just a few short days, he had given Becka the self-confidence she had always lacked. He had freed her from the old Rebecca Williams—the shy, self-conscious little loser who always blended into the background. That Rebecca was dead. And with the help of Maxwell, the new Rebecca was being born. Soon she would be leaving obscurity and rising toward the greatness destined to be hers.

It might have been easier if Maxwell wasn't friends with the folks at the Ascension Bookshop. And it didn't help that he sometimes acted a little weird. But that couldn't dismiss Becka's experiences or the revelation of who she was or the incredible power beckoning to her.

Mom had said she would not let Becka see Maxwell again. She had made that crystal clear as they fought and argued over their dinner of macaroni and cheese. But no more Maxwell meant no more hypnotism. Which meant no more clues. Becka sat in silent frustration. Then, slowly, gently, a thought crept into her mind.

Maybe ... maybe Becka didn't really need him. The book she had checked out of the school library—and that she'd been reading all evening—said she could obtain the same state of "higher consciousness" she'd experienced in hypnotism on her own. It was just a matter of relaxing and "clearing one's mind."

Weren't those the exact same words Maxwell had used?

She flipped to the page of a woman practicing this "higher state." Following the example of the picture, she crossed her legs, sat up straight, and touched the middle finger of each hand to its opposing thumb. So far so good. Now it was just a matter of relaxing and "clearing her mind."

Easier said than done. It seemed every time she closed her eyes, a thousand thoughts tumbled in. Without someone like Maxwell to direct her, it would be very difficult.

Difficult but not impossible. It could be done. The book said so. She sat there, trying again and again until, gradually, she was able to push aside her thoughts and concentrate only on her breathing ...

In ... and out ... in ... and out ...

Slowly she emptied her mind.

In ... and out ... in ... and out ...

Until every thought was gone. Now her mind was empty, a blank slate. There was only her breathing.

In ... and out ... in ... and out ... and the now-familiar sensation of falling backward through layer after layer of color.

It could have been minutes; it could have been hours. She wasn't sure. But, slowly, the light appeared. It hovered in front of her and above. When she looked at it, it would fade. But when she stared straight ahead, keeping her mind empty and not forcing it, the energy grew brighter and brighter until it was finally so strong she knew it was no longer just inside her head. She knew the light had somehow entered the room!

She opened her eyes.

Yes! There it was! Just above the foot of her bed. It continued to brighten. As its energy increased, so did its power. Becka could feel it blowing against her face. But it did more than blow. As it touched her face, she could feel it saturate her body.

Once again a dark passageway formed in the center. And once again she saw a man.

Maxwell.

He turned to her and smiled. She smiled back.

The light grew. It filled the entire room. She could feel the power invading her, surging through her body. She started to laugh. She couldn't help herself. The feeling was too pure, too intense.

Maxwell laughed too.

From inside the tunnel, he reached his hand out to her. This time there would be no interruptions. This time she would take his hand and the power would finally be hers ... she would be absorbed into it, and it would be absorbed into her. The two would become one. And with that oneness would come such energy, such strength, that no one would ever doubt her again. She would belong to power, and the power would belong to her.

Becka raised her arm toward Maxwell. The energy surged. It had a sound. A roar. Like the train. She could feel and hear it thundering inside her.

Their hands drew closer, fingers nearly touching. She was losing control. Good. Finally, she would be able to give herself over to the power. Completely. Without reservation.

But something stopped her. A noise. A . . . knocking. Banging.

"Becka! Becka! Open up!" More pounding. "Becka, open up!" It was her mother.

No! Not again!

She threw a quick glance at the door. The light dimmed.

No! Don't go! She focused back on it.

"Beck!" A different voice. "Beck, it's Scott. We gotta talk!"

She felt Maxwell's irritation, his displeasure. He began to withdraw his hand.

"No!" Becka cried.

He hesitated.

She reached out both of her hands. *"Please?"* she begged. "Please!"

There were a series of crashes at the door. Scotty was obviously trying to break in.

"Please," Becka repeated, rising to her knees, reaching toward the light.

It grew brighter. Maxwell began to smile.

"Becky! *Becky!*"

She barely heard.

Maxwell reached out his hand.

"BECK!"

Closer and closer they came.

"BECKY!!"

At last they touched. The power swept into her, enveloping her. She gasped. Her eyes fluttered. She was losing consciousness, being pulled into the center.

Suddenly the door exploded open.

9

B eck!" Scott raced into the room. Mom was right behind.
The light disappeared. The power vanished.

Becka turned on them furiously. "I was there! I had it!"

"Had what?" Mom asked. Her eyes fearfully searched Becka's.

Rebecca glared at her in contempt. The woman was so ignorant, so superstitious. But before she could answer, Scott jumped in. "I just talked to a friend of Z's. Mom's right about this reincarnation stuff. It's wrong—real wrong. And this Maxwell guy, he's like some sort of—"

"I know exactly who he is," Rebecca snapped. "He's a man with more power than your little mind can possibly understand."

"Becka!" Mom scolded.

"Well, it's true. Just because you don't understand something doesn't make it wrong."

"Maybe so …," Scott agreed, "but this guy's bad news, Becka. And his power's flat-out wrong."

She rose from her bed and stepped to the other side, keeping it between them. "What do you know about power?" she demanded. "Have you ever felt it? Have you ever experienced it?"

"Becka." Her mother took a step forward. "It's not just the—"

"I was king! King of France!"

"Becka—"

"And that's only the beginning. There's more for me—more than you can comprehend!"

"But it's counterfeit!" Scott was practically shouting.

The phrase struck Becka in the chest. She turned on him. "It's what?"

"Maxwell Hunter's into the occult. He's a major-league player in Eastern mysticism."

Becka started to tremble. Not with fear but with rage. Why were they doing this to her? She'd finally found something, a way to be somebody, and now they were trying to take it away. "You're just jealous!" she scorned. "You're jealous 'cause I experienced something and you—"

"Honey," Mom interrupted. "Just because you've experienced something doesn't make it—"

"I *saw* things! I was there! I was Louis XVI!"

"They were illusions," Scott argued. "They were hallucinations that couldn't possibly be—"

"They were *not* hallucinations! They were real!" Becka's eyes started to fill with tears. Why was he doing this? Why was he taking away the only power she'd ever had? "I saw things! I saw things only a person who had lived back then would know!"

"Only a person living then ...," Scott said quietly, "or a demon."

"What?!" She couldn't believe her ears.

"It's just like the Ouija board, Beck. The board knew stuff, remember? From different places, different times. It knew stuff, not because it had supernatural powers of its own, but because of the demons controlling it. The demons who had actually been at those places, who had actually seen those things."

A sneer curled Becka's lips. "*I* saw those things. Not Maxwell. Not demons. But *me!* I saw them."

"With Maxwell's help."

Becka would not cave in. "What about my dreams? On my own bed? Here, in my own room!"

"Dreams you had after Maxwell hypnotized you."

"What's that got to—"

"Dreams are cool," Scott continued. "They helped me remember all that stuff Dad tried to teach us. But—" He took a deep breath, and Becka knew she was going to hate this next thought even more. "Somehow ... I don't know how, but somehow, you're letting Maxwell influence ... even control you. Maxwell or ... whatever critters he has with him are trying to—"

"You're telling me all this is done by demons?!" Becka shouted.

"Honey." Mom started toward her.

"What about my power?" Becka stepped back. "What about the light?"

Again Mom and Scott looked at each other. This time they had no answer. This time Becka had them, and she knew it. "Ha!" she mocked. "You don't know, do you? You don't know about the power. You don't know about the light. And you know why? Because you're not chosen. Because you haven't lived my past, you're not worthy of the power that's going to be mine. You're not ready for the light!"

"Becka," Mom said, approaching. "What power? What light are you talking about?"

Becka laughed. "I've experienced more power than you will ever know. And it's only the beginning. There's plenty more waiting for me. All I have to do is—"

"Becka." Scott edged closer.

She whirled at him. "You don't believe me?"

"I believe ..." Scott chose his words carefully. "I believe you think you've experienced some sort of—"

"Think?!" she shouted. "You think I've just imagined all this?" Her mind raced. She had to show him, to make him eat his words. Suddenly an image filled her mind. The train. Its glaring headlight. The roaring engine, the thundering power. She didn't know where that image came from, but she knew what it meant. Of course! Let them witness it firsthand! She turned to Mom. "What time do you have?"

Mom glanced at her watch. "It's nearly eight. Why? What does that—"

"You have to take me somewhere."

"Becky, I don't think now's the—"

"If you take me somewhere, I can show you. I promise."

"Beck—"

"I promise. And if I'm wrong … If I'm wrong, then you can talk to me all you want and I'll listen."

Again Mom and Scott exchanged glances.

"But you've gotta let me show you first."

"Where?" Scott slowly asked.

"Not far. But we've got to hurry."

Mom and Scott hesitated, but not Becka. She snatched her hoodie off the bed. "Come on," she ordered. "You want proof; I'll show you proof!"

❧ ❧

The van cut through the fog as it followed the road, dipped under the Death Bridge, and rose back up.

"Right here," Becka ordered.

"Here?" Mom asked doubtfully.

"Stop the car," Becka insisted. "We have to get out here!"

Mom slowed the van. Before it even came to a stop, Becka slid open the side door and jumped out.

"Becka!"

"Hurry," Becka called back. "We don't have much time!" She

turned and started toward the grade leading up to the tracks. She couldn't explain the energy rushing through her body. Or its connection to the train. But she knew they were the same. And then there were Maxwell's words: *"To fully experience the power, you must let go; you must let it have its way."*

Finally, she was doing that. Finally, she had quit questioning. And as she did so, the power grew. The closer she came to the tracks, the more the urgency within her grew. Something was pushing her, driving her forward.

"Becka!" Mom called. "Becka, slow down!"

"We don't have time!" Becka shouted. She arrived at the grade leading up to the tracks. "Hurry!" Her feet slipped on the gravel as she scrambled up the hill, but she dug in and continued climbing.

Scott was climbing right behind. "Beck! Becka, wait up!"

And then another voice, farther away. "Hey ... Becka! Rebecca!" It was Ryan.

"Pretty lady, what are you doing?" And that, of course, was Ryan's little friend, Pepe. She'd almost forgotten. Ryan had said he was going to visit Pepe that evening. The two were probably nearby when they heard the shouting from her mother and brother. And now they were coming to investigate.

Perfect. Ryan can see this too.

She didn't look back, but kept climbing. When she reached the top of the grade, she quickly crossed to the center of the tracks. Already she could feel the faint vibration under her feet. The 8:10 was right on time.

"Becka!" She turned. Ryan and Pepe were closer now. She could almost make out their shapes through the fog as they ran down the road toward her. "Rebecca!"

She stared at them a moment, then redirected her attention back up to the tracks. To the bend. Everything was just as she had dreamed. Plenty of fog. No wind. No stars. Just an eerie stillness ... and the distant vibration of the approaching train.

Now she understood. *The dreams were just a preparation—a way of getting me ready for what was coming. But tonight ... tonight will be the real thing.*

Scott arrived beside her, breathing hard from the climb. "What's going on?"

"Do you hear it?" Becka asked. She was also breathless, but more from excitement than exertion.

"Hear what?"

"Listen!"

There was a faint rumbling. Scott looked puzzled.

"It's the train," she said. "It'll be coming around that bend any second."

"What?" Scott asked in alarm.

"Becka!" Mom called from the bottom of the grade. She had tried to climb it, but it was too steep. "Sweetheart, what do you want? What do you want to show us?"

"Just stay there!" Becka called. "You'll see."

"See what?" Scott demanded. "What are you going to show us?"

Becka never turned to him. She just kept staring down the tracks. Her voice was hollow and empty. "You'd better get down, Scotty."

"What about you?"

Becka did not answer. The rumbling grew louder.

"Becka ... what about you?"

"Rebecca!" Ryan's voice was much closer—practically under the trestle. Perfect, just like the dream.

"Becka?" Scott sounded frightened. "What about you?"

She didn't look at him but continued staring down the tracks. The rumbling had grown into a roar—an ominous roar. "You'd better get down," she repeated.

"Not without you." Scott took her arm.

"Let go."

His grip tightened. "Come on, we're getting outta here."

"I said let go." She tried to twist free.

"Not without—"

And then the train appeared. For a moment both Scott and Becka froze. Her heart pounded so hard she found it difficult to breathe. The headlight swept around the bend until it hit them squarely in their faces.

And with the light came the power. She could already feel its approaching energy.

"Come on!" Scott yelled. He pulled her hard, but she resisted.

"Let go!" she shouted.

"Beck!"

He grabbed her other arm and tried to pull, then push her off the tracks. She fought him. She was still just a little bigger, just a little stronger.

The train thundered toward them.

"Becky!" Mom shouted from below. "Scotty!"

But neither heard as they continued the fight. It was a bizarre sight—the two struggling up on the fog-shrouded tracks, lit only by the glaring light of the approaching train.

"BECKA!" Ryan arrived beneath the trestle. Pepe jumped up to the nearest girder and started climbing toward the tracks. Ryan raced to the hillside and started scampering up the grade.

As she fought her brother, the train's roar filled Becka's head. Everything was exactly like the dream. Exactly. She knew her power and the train's power were the same. They were one. She could not be hurt. She could only absorb the power and be absorbed by it. Everything was perfect ... except for Scott.

She knew he was trying to help—to save her from the fate of the other kids who had played chicken up here and lost. But those were stupid pranks. Childish games. Kids who'd been destroyed because they weren't prepared. Because they weren't chosen.

She had to get rid of her brother. Finally she twisted one arm free.

The train blew its whistle—blasting, shrieking, screaming.

There was no other way. Becka was prepared. She could absorb the power. Scotty could not. With all of her strength, she leaned back and hit her brother in the stomach as hard as she could.

"OOOAFF!" he gasped as the air rushed out of him. He staggered backward until his heel caught the rail. He tripped and tried to regain his balance, but she was immediately there to push him the rest of the way. He fell and tumbled down the grade, rolling over and over, arms flailing.

"BECKY!" her mother screamed, but Becka did not hear. At last she was free.

She turned to face the blinding light. It filled her vision. She could feel the power encompass her. Her power. The power she had sensed so many times before. The power for which Maxwell had prepared her.

Once again the tunnel formed.

The whistle screamed, but she did not hear. Voices shouted, but she paid no attention. This was her moment. It was time to receive the power, to step into the light. She would become the power, and the power would become her.

Then she saw it. Movement out of the corner of her eye. "Rebecca!" It was Ryan. The fool was practically at the top of the grade, scrambling toward her!

She had no choice. She began to run. Straight toward the light.

"Rebecca!"

She arrived on the trestle and continued running. The light grew brighter. The center tunnel grew wider. Once again she saw Maxwell inside, reaching his hand to her.

The trestle jolted as the train reached the other side, pounding the tracks, shaking the steel girders.

Maxwell and the tunnel filled her vision. She could feel the wind, smell the diesel, hear the massive steel wheels on the tracks. She reached her arms toward Maxwell. As she ran, she tilted her head back, waiting for contact, waiting for the tunnel to swallow her and make her one. And at the peak of anticipation, at the moment of total freedom ... she was struck.

But not by the train.

A small form had leapt off the bridge and almost knocked her out of the way. Almost, but not quite. A steel rail from the front of the locomotive caught both of them, flinging them off the bridge and into the gravel grade, sending them bouncing and rolling and tumbling down as the machine thundered past.

Becka remembered nothing after that. Only a blur of spinning sky and ground. And a small, dark-haired boy with blood spewing from his mouth and a look of horror frozen on his face.

Pepe.

And then there was nothing.

10

It was nearly three days before Becka started to remember. Oh sure, there were vague recollections of IV tubes, heart monitors, and concerned faces looking down at her. But nothing really came into focus until three days after the accident.

"Hey, crash, welcome back." It was Scott. He was grinning from the left side of the bed. As always, he was trying to lighten the moment.

Becka started to move, but the sudden throbbing in her head made it impossible. "Oooo …," she groaned.

"Take it easy, sweetheart." It was Mom, leaning above her from the other side.

"Where am I …," Becka mumbled. "What happened?"

"You played tag with a train and lost," Scott answered.

Becka groaned again as the memories rushed in. Memories of the Death Bridge, the train, the little form leaping at her from the side of the bridge. "What about Pepe?" She struggled to sit up. "That was Pepe who saved me. Is he okay?"

"Guess you'll have to ask him." Mom smiled as she glanced over her shoulder.

Pepe hobbled into view. His face was still pretty bruised, and the crutches made his movements a little jerky. But it didn't stop the smile. "Hello, pretty lady."

"Pepe! It's you!"

The boy grinned. "Mostly, it's me." He reached up and tapped his front teeth. "These are brand-new, though. Some sort of plastic. What do you think? Do they make me even more irresistible?"

"Pepe ... I'm so sorry."

"No tenga pena," he said, shrugging. He threw a glance over to Scott and Mom. Realizing they'd want some time alone with Becka, he grinned at her. "Ryan's downstairs grabbing something to eat. He wanted to know as soon as you woke up. I'll get him and be right back." With that he turned and hobbled toward the door.

"Pepe?"

He stopped and turned back to her.

"Thanks," she said.

"For a lady of your beauty," he answered with a mischievous smile, "what else could I do?"

Becka couldn't help smiling back. The boy was a flirt to the end. He turned and headed out the door.

As she watched, more memories returned. It was as if she had awakened from a dream ... a dream that began not long after her first experience in the library. She groaned. "I can't believe I was so stupid."

Mom and Scott exchanged glances.

"I'm just glad he's okay," she continued.

"Which is more than I can say for you," Mom answered. Becka looked up to her. "Concussion, broken collarbone, broken leg."

Becka looked down to her body to confirm the fact. Sure enough, she was wearing a few more casts and wires than the last time she remembered. She leaned back on her pillow and sighed. "What was I trying to prove?"

"I don't think it was just you," Scott said. "I think you had a little help from Maxwell and his buddies."

Becka turned to him.

He continued. "I had a long talk with Z. He said the junk you experienced with the light and power and stuff isn't all that unusual—especially for occultists. A little extreme, maybe, but nothing that unusual."

"By occultist, you're talking about Maxwell?"

Scott nodded. "Oh yeah, big-time. Z says the guy was playing off your desire for power—you know, your wanting to be somebody. He says that's pretty common too."

"So all that King Louis stuff?"

"Counterfeit. The devil using Maxwell to con you."

"But what about—I mean, he said he believed in Jesus. He even prayed with us. How can you pray to God if you don't believe in him?"

Mom shook her head. "I've been thinking about that, honey. It could be Maxwell *was* praying, but to his god, not to the real God. Or it could be he just knew the right things to say and do to make us believe and trust him. Either way, he used just enough of what sounded like the truth to put us off guard."

"That's what makes this occult stuff so dangerous," Scott added. "It's just close enough to the truth to fool people—especially those who want to be a somebody."

A sinking feeling began somewhere in Becka's chest and continued down into her stomach. Scott was right. She *had* wanted to be a somebody. A headline-maker. Unfortunately, the only headlines she would have made were in the obituary column. She took a deep breath. "Why would he choose me?"

"Maxwell?" he asked.

She nodded.

"The same reason he chose me," Mom answered. "Either he thought we were really something special, or ..." Mom hesitated, unsure whether she should continue.

Scott saved her the trouble. "Or the Society was using him to hurt us."

Becka threw her brother a look.

Scott shrugged. "They're still pretty steamed about that little encounter with them and their Ouija board."

Becka took another deep breath and stared at the ceiling. Which was it? Was Maxwell deceived about her, or was he—she gave a little shudder—or was he trying to destroy her?

"Where is he now?" she asked. "Maxwell, I mean."

"San Francisco," Scott answered. "Some international 'cosmic gathering.'"

"I was so stupid," Becka groaned.

"No argument there," Scott agreed.

"Well, at least it's over," she sighed. But then she noticed Mom and Scott exchanging looks again. "What's wrong?" she asked. "It is over, isn't it?"

"Not entirely, dear," Mom answered.

There was a brief pause, which Scott broke. "Z thinks maybe we should, you know, pray. To make sure there isn't any leftover demonic junk." Becka looked at him. "I mean, you were into all that power and light stuff pretty deep," he added.

For a split second, Becka's temper flared, but the sincerity in Scott's and Mom's faces cooled it. Maybe they were right. After all, she had gotten pretty cozy with the whole "power" thing, and she had definitely experienced stuff that didn't come from her own imagination. "What ..." Her voice was a little hoarse. "What am I supposed to do?"

"It's just like in Brazil," Mom offered. "Remember the Bible studies? When someone involved in witchcraft wanted to be a Christian, remember how we had them renounce all the power they had experienced and ask Christ to replace it with his Spirit?"

Have I gone that far? Becka thought. She wasn't sure. And she knew her mother and brother weren't, either. Still, after all she'd been through, it definitely wouldn't hurt to play it safe.

She looked back at Mom, her admiration growing. She'd almost forgotten how much she loved and respected her mother.

She turned to Scott. He was doing his usual Cheshire cat grin. She loved him too. Though she'd never go out of her way to bring the subject to his attention.

"Well," she finally sighed, "I guess there's no time like the present. Shall we do it?"

A look of relief crossed Mom's and Scott's faces as they moved in a little closer. They each took one of Becka's hands, and Mom gave the hand she held a little kiss. Scott gave his a little squeeze. And then, right there in the hospital room, all three bowed their heads and started praying.

👁 👁

Later that night, Scott chomped on a carrot as he entered his room and snapped on the light.

"*SQUAWK!* BEAM ME UP! BEAM ME UP!"

"Hey, Cornelius," he said, unzipping his jacket and tossing it onto the bed. "We haven't talked much."

The bird bobbed his head up and down as if agreeing. "MAKE MY DAY. MAKE MY DAY. MAKE MY DAY."

Scott took another bite of carrot and slid into the chair behind his desk. "We're going to have to teach you some hipper sayings, old buddy."

The parrot leaped from his perch and fluttered down onto the desk. "MAKE MY DAY. MAKE MY DAY. MAKE MY DAY."

Scott held the carrot between his teeth and leaned forward. In a flash Cornelius reached over and snatched it from his mouth. The bird quickly waddled to the far end of the desk with his new prize. And balancing on one foot, he held up the carrot with the other and started nibbling away.

Scott glanced at his phone: 9:04 p.m. He turned on the computer, went to his email and opened a chat window.

Hey, Z.

Good evening.

I just got back from visiting Becka.

Before he could continue, Z answered:

I'm glad she finally regained consciousness.

This guy was unbelievable. Scott quickly typed:

Will you stop that? How do you know that this stuff?!

He waited for a reply, but there was none. Finally words appeared on the screen. Once again Z had changed the subject:

Did you enjoy your meeting with Nagaina?

That was pretty sneaky—making us ride all the way out to those houses, thinking we'd finally meet you.

Almost as sneaky as you trying to find out where I live.

Scott raised an eyebrow. The man had a point. But Z wasn't finished:

I thought Nagaina's experiences would be far more beneficial to you than mine.

She sure made her point about reincarnation.

Funny, isn't it? On the surface it seems innocent enough. But when you follow reincarnation to its logical conclusion, you find bigotry, prejudice, indifference toward human pain, and most important, a direct conflict with Christ's purpose for dying on the cross.

Well, at least it's over.

Not entirely.

Scott felt a chill.

What do you mean?

There was a pause. The words formed ... more slowly than before:

For some reason you have been singled out. I am afraid this was just another battle in what appears to be an ongoing war.

Somehow Scott had already guessed as much. He typed:

What's next?

I am not certain. However, I would look into that strange noise and light in your garage before too many more days pass.

Scott caught his breath. The noise. He'd almost forgotten. But with that thought came another:

Who told you about the noise and light?
Z?
Z? Who told you about the noise?

Good night.

No, hold it a minute. Hold it!

He waited, continuing to stare at the screen. But there was no answer. Z had signed off.

"BEAM ME UP, SCOTTY, BEAM ME UP." Cornelius had trotted over to Scott's keyboard. Once again he was bobbing his head up and down for attention.

Scott reached out and scratched under the bird's neck as he continued staring at the screen, wondering.

Discussion questions for
The Deceived:

1. Maxwell Hunter's use of hypnotism seemed harmless. Do you think all hypnotism is dangerous?

2. Reincarnation teaches that you die again and again and keep coming back until you are finally good enough to enter heaven. How is this idea opposite of what the Bible says? (See Hebrews 9:27.)

3. Why do you think Becka was attracted to the idea of reincarnation?

4. When Maxwell Hunter visited Becka and her mom at their home, he assured them that he was a Christian and even prayed before he began hypnosis. What did you think of his actions? Can you think of other situations where evil masquerades as good?

5. Visiting Pepe's neighborhood, Becka looked at the people's poverty with very little compassion because of her new-found belief in reincarnation. If you were her friend, how would you have reacted to her behavior?

6. Maxwell Hunter told mom about the "Christ within" that is present in every person. How do you think this different from accepting Jesus Christ as Savior and having him come into your life?

7. How did believing she had been a king in another life affect the way Rebecca treated her friends and family?

8. How did the Hindu belief of reincarnation impact Nagaina, the woman from Nepal who Scott and Darryl met at the abandoned house?

9. Becka tried to access the light and power Maxwell had shown her by using deep meditation. Why do you think this kind of meditation is dangerous?

10. After Becka's close call at the Death Bridge, Mom, Scott, and Becka prayed together. What do you think that accomplished?

THE SPELL

… the one who is in you is greater than the one who is in the world.

1 JOHN 4:4

1

The train's light blinded Rebecca as it thundered toward her. She lay on her back and felt the locomotive's power vibrating through the tracks. It was nearly there. She could smell the diesel fuel, see the massive wheels rolling at her. She opened her mouth to scream, but no sound came out. There was only the shriek of the train's whistle.

The wheels were nearly on top of her. She tried to move, but the IV tubes kept her pinned to the hospital bed.

IV tubes? Hospital bed?

With a jolt, Becka woke up. She fought to catch her breath. Her eyes darted around the room. There was no train, no glaring light. Only the muted glow from the lights in the hospital parking lot as they shone through her curtains.

With a groan, she fell back against her pillows. It was another dream. Another one of *those* dreams. The type she'd been having every night for the last week. Ever since her little accident with the train.

She adjusted her hospital gown. It was damp with sweat and stuck to her back.

The shrinks (you don't stand in front of a racing train in the middle of the night, almost getting yourself killed, without a few psychiatrists dropping by) said the dreams weren't unusual. After running about a thousand tests on Becka, they assured her she was going to be all right. "Other than major trauma from the accident, and scoring slightly below average in the area of self-esteem, you seem to be a perfectly normal teenager."

Becka didn't feel "perfectly normal." Last week's run-in with the train—and with Maxwell Hunter, the hotshot New Ager—had left her a little shaky. Actually, a *lot* shaky. Maxwell was an acclaimed speaker on reincarnation. To prove his theories of past lives, he had hypnotized Becka in front of an audience and taken her back to her "past lives."

At first Becka bought it. It all seemed so believable ... right up to the end. Right up until she realized the past lives were nothing but demons playing a game with her mind.

But that was all behind her now. Ancient history. The doctors had assured her she was "all right" and "perfectly normal." And if the doctors said that was so, who was she to disagree?

She turned her head on the pillow and looked through the stainless-steel rails of her hospital bed. The digital clock on the nightstand glowed a crimson 3:01. Four hours and fifty-nine minutes left before she could go home. Four hours and fifty-nine minutes before she was finally out of there.

Her eyes drifted from the clock to the get-well cards on the dresser, then stopped at the giant bouquet of carnations. Even in the dim light, she could make out the flowers' vivid reds and whites. Fear from the dream melted, dissolving into a pool of warmth, a glow of happiness that stirred deep inside her chest. It was too dark to read the card attached to the carnations, but she didn't have to. She knew it by heart:

Hurry and get well. I really miss you.
Your buddy, Ryan

She could have lived without the "your buddy" part. Other

phrases would have been much better. Actually, one specific word — the *L* word — would have done the trick. But the sentence "I really miss you" rang in Becka's heart as resoundingly as when she'd first read it:

"I *REALLY* miss you."

"I really *MISS* you."

"I really miss *YOU*."

The glow in her chest spread through her body. She felt cozy all over as she snuggled deeper under the covers. Ryan said he might be there when Mom and Scotty, her little brother, picked her up in the morning. She hoped so.

She glanced at the clock and closed her eyes, smiling. 3:02. Four hours and fifty-eight minutes ...

👁 👁

The six robed figures stood in a secluded clearing of the park. All around them were dense trees and overgrown bushes, making it impossible to see them from the road. This was good. This was exactly what they wanted.

As usual for this time of year, the fog had rolled in from the beach and blotted out all light from the moon. This was good too. Now there was only the glow of six candles — five black, one white — on the picnic table, their orange light flickering and dancing over the young faces around them.

There were two boys and four girls. Teenagers. Dressed in homemade robes, complete with hoods. All of the group had been drinking, and the boys' red, watery eyes gave clear signs that they'd been smoking weed. Lots of it.

The rat had already been killed, its neck broken. Now the group's leader, Brooke, a chunky girl whose black hair was an obvious dye job, carefully drained the animal's blood, filling the bottom half of a torn diet Coke can with the dark liquid.

The boys snickered. It may have been from the booze or the

weed or just from the chill of what they were doing. Who knew? But it was obvious they weren't taking the ceremony seriously.

Laura Henderson, a brooding blonde with acne, gave them a scowl. This was important business. After all, Brooke had called this meeting and was making this sacrifice for a very serious reason. She had been humiliated — not once, but twice! By a couple of zeros who'd moved into the neighborhood barely a month ago. First there was the younger kid, Scott Williams. He'd actually dared to challenge their leader's powers with the Ouija board. And he'd done it right in front of the entire Society!

Then there was the sister, Rebecca Williams ... as plain as they come. And yet, for some reason, she had been handpicked by the famous guru, Maxwell Hunter, for her supposed gifts. How did such a nobody rate that kind of honor? As if that wasn't bad enough, there was that stunt Williams had pulled with the train — proof to all that Rebecca Williams was trying to compete with Brooke's power and position.

Laura turned and watched with admiration as Brooke finished draining the rat's blood into the can. Brooke meant everything to her. She lived for the girl's praise, wilted at her criticism. She glanced around at the group circling the candles. As her eyes returned to Brooke, her expression hardened.

Okay, Williams, you want power? So be it. We'll show you power.

She closed her eyes and began to recite: "Hate your enemies with your whole heart ..."

The other two girls joined in. The chant grew louder, more concentrated: "... and if a man smite you on the cheek, *smash* him on the other!"

The boys smirked and snickered. Laura opened her eyes and cut them an icy glare. After another snicker and a shrug of indifference they also joined in.

"Hate your enemies with your whole heart, and if a man smite you on the cheek, *smash* him on the other!"

Brooke set the rat carcass on the picnic table and reached into her robe, pulling out a feathered quill and a piece of homemade parchment.

The chant continued.

"Hate your enemies with your whole heart ..."

Brooke dipped the quill into the can of blood.

"... and if a man smite you on the cheek, *smash* him on the other!"

And then she wrote:

Rebecca

"Hate your enemies with your whole heart ..."

"... and if a man smite you on the cheek, *smash* him on the other!"

Their voices grew louder. The booze, the drugs, the force of six people chanting together — it all gave them a kind of energy, a sense of belonging. Laura drew a deep breath and felt a surge of exhilaration. The chant grew stronger, more determined, filling the air, filling her being. This was the unity she needed, the power she craved.

"Hate your enemies with your whole heart ..."

Brooke set the pen down and raised the parchment above the flame of the white candle. The chanting grew more and more feverish. All eyes watched now in eager anticipation.

"... and if a man smite you on the cheek, smash *him on the other!"*

Suddenly the parchment ignited into a bright orange flame. The paper curled and crackled as it was consumed, quickly and efficiently, until everything — including Rebecca's name — was nothing but ash.

❧ ❧

"Why so glum, sweetheart?" Mom asked as she turned their clunker Toyota onto their street and headed toward the house.

Rebecca stared out the window at the passing homes. Theirs wasn't the poorest neighborhood in town, but it wasn't the richest either. Usually she didn't notice the sagging screens, the peeling paint, the semi-kept yards. But today she did. Today they bugged her. Today everything bugged her.

For good reason. What had started out as such a great morning had already turned into a major disaster.

First, Mom was late getting to the hospital. Almost an hour late. Second, nobody came with her. Not Ryan, not even Scotty. Obviously their lives were far too busy to squeeze her into their schedule. But that was no big deal compared to the third reason, the one crammed into the Toyota's trunk.

"You still embarrassed about the wheelchair?" Mom asked.

Becka said nothing.

"The doctors say it'll only be for a few weeks."

More silence.

"If you'd just broken your leg, you could use crutches, but—"

Becka impatiently interrupted, "But since I cracked my collarbone, I can't put the extra weight on my shoulders. I know, Mother. I was there, remember?" Becka bit her lip. She hated being a brat. She knew Mom was only trying to cheer her up. But still ...

And then she saw it: the white vintage Mustang parked in front of their house. "Ryan's here!" she blurted.

"Well, what do you know." Mom threw Becka a knowing smile.

Becka grinned back, realizing her mother was part of a conspiracy. For not only was Ryan's car there, but so was her best friend Julie's Jeep and Philip's blue hybrid. Instinctively, her hand shot up to her thin brown hair, fluffing it out, trying in vain to make it look halfway presentable.

The Toyota turned and rattled up the driveway. Mom turned it off, and after a couple shuddering coughs, the engine finally died.

Little brother Scott was the first to spot them. Not that he was so little anymore. In the last couple of months, he had almost caught up to Becka's height. And by his cracking voice and thickening shoulders, it was clear that manhood was lurking just around the corner.

"She's here," Scott called as he threw open the porch door and clambered down the steps. The others piled out after him. First there was Scott's dorky friend, Darryl. Then Becka's best friend, the athletic and always-too-beautiful-and-perfectly-dressed Julie, followed closely by Ryan, who sported a devilish grin. Finally, there were Philip and his airhead girlfriend, Krissi (better known as Ken and Barbie).

Rebecca could feel her ears start to burn and color run to her cheeks. This was the first time most of them had seen where she lived. Not that she was trying to keep it a secret, but let's face it, this was definitely not one of those fancy country-club homes they were used to.

Still, as they headed toward the car, throwing jibes and barbs, she saw no signs of snobbery.

"Hey there, crash, how you feeling?" Ryan brushed the thick black hair out of his gorgeous blue eyes. And if that wasn't enough, he suddenly flashed her his heartbreaker smile.

"Great," Becka answered with a grin as she pushed open the car door. She wasn't lying, either. Suddenly, she *was* feeling better—a whole lot better.

"I'll get the wheelchair," Mom called.

Suddenly, she was feeling worse—a whole lot worse.

"Wheelchair?" Julie echoed.

"Just for a few weeks," Mom explained as she crossed back to the trunk and opened it.

"Don't tell me we've got to push her around like some old person," Scott groaned.

Good ol' Scotty. *Thanks for the support, little brother.*

"Just a few weeks," Mom repeated as she unfolded the chair.

"Here, I can get that," Ryan said, quickly moving in to take it from her.

"That's cool." Philip grinned at Becka. "That means we can, like, escort you all around, then."

Krissi laughed. "The queen on her portable throne."

Ryan hammed it up as he rolled the chair toward her open car door. "And I, her loyal servant, shall take her wherever she bids." Before Becka could protest, he swooped down and scooped her from the car seat and into his arms. Then, ever so gently, he set her into the chair. "Welcome home." He grinned. Becka felt her heart do a little flip-flop.

When she had first met Ryan, she and Mom agreed that she would just hang out with him as a friend—nothing more. It made no difference how many backflips her heart did when she saw him or that he just happened to be the cutest and nicest guy in school (no prejudice there). The point is she was a Christian and he wasn't. And until that changed, she knew she had to guard her heart and just stay good friends—no matter how difficult it was.

Ryan pulled the chair away from the car and started pushing Becka toward the open garage. Everyone followed, talking and making jokes, while Krissi, once again proving her incredible airheadedness, asked, "Does this mean you won't be running in any more track meets?"

More laughter and wisecracks as they passed through the dozens of stacked boxes in the garage and headed toward the kitchen door.

"So this is the famous haunted garage?" Philip asked as he slowed to a stop and glanced around.

"It doesn't look so scary," Krissi chirped.

"Not in the daylight," Scott said. "But try hanging out here at night."

"All alone," Darryl added, pushing up his glasses and giving a little sniff, "with all those sounds and that light and stuff."

And then, as if on cue, there was a gentle whine. Becka stiffened. Even now, with all these people around, she was still a little skittish. "Did you hear that?" she asked.

"Hear what?" Ryan asked.

The sound repeated itself: a high-pitched whine, accompanied by scratching.

"Don't you hear that?" she asked.

Ryan looked puzzled, then shook his head. "You guys hear anything?"

Everyone quieted down and listened.

"I don't hear a thing," Philip said.

"Me neither," Krissi said.

Becka looked up to their faces and fought off a shiver.

The sound recurred.

"There." Becka pointed toward the closed kitchen door. "It's coming from behind there."

"Here?" Ryan asked as they rolled to a stop in front of the door.

The scratching and whining grew louder.

"Can't you guys hear that?" Rebecca demanded.

There were more baffled looks, this time accompanied by some raised eyebrows of concern. "We, uh, we don't hear anything, Beck," Julie ventured cautiously.

The scratching grew louder. "Guys—" Becka tried to smile, thinking it was some kind of joke—"you mean to tell me none of you hear that?"

But no one smiled back. She shifted uneasily, her fear and self-doubt starting to grow.

Ryan dropped to his knees and put his ear to the door. "You're talking about this door, right here?"

"Yes," Becka said, fighting off her impatience. "There's something behind it. Can't you hear that?"

Cautiously, Ryan reached up to the knob and turned it. It was unlocked. He looked at Becka, then, suddenly, he threw open the door.

Becka gasped as a little ball of black-and-brown fur scampered out and leaped into Ryan's arms. It immediately began covering the boy with slobbery licks and kisses. "Easy, fella," Ryan laughed. "Down boy, easy."

"You guys!" Becka cried as a wave of relief washed over her. She watched as the puppy continued washing Ryan's face. "He's so cute. What kind is he?" she asked.

"Got me," Ryan said, trying in vain to dodge the wayward tongue. "Heinz 57, a mix of everything." He stood up and placed the squirming bundle of fur on Becka's lap. It took the animal half a second to find her face and resume the licking.

The group laughed and Becka giggled, trying to fight off the kissing attack. "Where'd he come from? Whose is he?"

"He's yours," Julie laughed. "Ryan got him from the pound."

The kitchen phone started ringing, but Becka barely heard. She looked up to Ryan. His eyes were sparkling. He said only four words, and they were so soft no one else heard: "I'm glad you're back."

She reached out and took his hand. "Thank you," she whispered. His eyes sparkled even brighter. As far as Rebecca was concerned, the moment could last forever. Unfortunately there was Krissi. "Do you like him?" she blurted. "Hey, Becka, do you like him?"

"Like him?" Rebecca looked back down to the pup and was met with another licking attack. "I *love* him."

Everyone moved in, kneeling and petting the animal who grew even more hyper from all the attention.

"What are you going to call him?" Julie asked. She leaned

in and was met with a wet tongue right across the mouth. "Oh, gross." More laughter.

"What am I going to call him?" Rebecca giggled. She paused a moment to look him over. Ryan was right, the little scamp was a mix of just about every breed of dog imaginable. "What am I going to call him?... How about ... Muttly."

Everyone agreed. It was the perfect name.

Suddenly Scott was shoving the cordless phone through the crowd of faces toward her. He looked a little perplexed. "It's for you," he said.

Still laughing and still fighting off the puppy, Becka took the receiver. "Hello?"

At first there was no response.

"Hello?" she repeated.

Then came the voice. It was low and raspy. "The spell has been cast, Rebecca Williams."

"I'm sorry?" She motioned for the others to quiet down. "What did you say?"

Now she heard the voice distinctly. "The spell has been cast. Your destiny belongs to me."

Rebecca swallowed. It took a moment for her to speak. "Who—who is this? What are you talking about?"

There was no answer, only the click of the receiver followed by the dial tone.

2

It was Thursday morning—Becka's first day back at school. Ryan had kept his word about playing chauffeur. He had shown up bright and early and was helping her into the front seat of his Mustang. She was nervous about returning to school. Real nervous. Call it a wild hunch, but she figured standing on railroad tracks and waiting to get hit by a train had probably started a few people gossiping about her. Then, of course, there was the little welcome-home phone call she had received: *Your destiny belongs to me.*

Ryan sensed her tension and tried to keep things light. "So how's Muttly?" he asked as he slid in behind the wheel.

"Great," Becka said, trying too hard to be cheery. "Well, except for the whining and whimpering and scratching all night long."

"Sorry about that," Ryan chuckled. He started up the car and pulled into the street. "Maybe you should keep him in the garage at night."

"I couldn't do that," Becka protested.

"Why not?"

"He'd get too lonely. Besides ..." She hesitated, unsure how to continue.

"Besides, what?"

"Well, you know."

Ryan threw her a mischievous look. "You mean the haunted garage?"

Becka half shrugged.

"Come on, Beck, you really don't buy into all that ghost stuff."

Rebecca took a deep breath and finally spoke her mind. "It's not just the garage ..."

Ryan glanced back to her. She said nothing, but he knew what she was thinking. "You're still worried about that phone call?"

Becka looked down and nodded.

Ryan answered, "It's just a bad joke someone is playing. Don't let it bug you. Besides, aren't Christians supposed to be protected from curses and all that junk?"

Rebecca turned to him in surprise. "How'd you know I was a Christian?"

He chuckled. "That stuff's kinda hard to hide."

She continued to stare.

"Hey, relax." He smiled. "I think it's cool. I mean, I wish I had something like that to believe in." Becka noticed the slightest trace of sadness in his voice. He shrugged. "Maybe we can check out church together sometime—you know, maybe you can show me the ropes."

You could have knocked Rebecca over with a feather. This guy never ceased to amaze her. He glanced at her and smiled again. It was the killer smile—the one that caused her heart to flutter. He looked down to her hand and reached for it. The flip-flops increased.

Suddenly something caught Becka's attention. A fat tabby cat darted off the curb directly in front of them. "Look out!" she cried.

Ryan looked up, his eyes widening. He swerved hard to the left, barely missing the animal. The car slid, and for a brief second Becka looked out her window to see she was heading directly for a parked car. She started to scream, bracing herself for the crash, but Ryan managed to straighten his car, missing the parked one by only a few inches.

He quickly pulled to a stop. "You all right?" he asked in concern.

Becka took a deep breath to steady herself.

"Beck?"

She took another breath. "Yeah ... I'm fine."

"You sure?"

She nodded.

He looked at her a long moment before putting the car into gear and slowly pulling away.

She was still shaken. The past few days—make that the past few weeks—had definitely taken their toll. Still, she tried to make a joke. "You were saying something about curses?"

Ryan forced a laugh. "Good thing that cat wasn't black."

Becka didn't return the laugh.

Once again Ryan looked at her with concern. "Beck ... not everything that goes bump in the night is the devil. Just because stuff goes wrong doesn't mean something's out to get you." He flashed her a reassuring smile. "That's why they call them accidents."

Becka took another breath and tried to smile back. She wanted to answer, but she didn't trust her voice. *I hope you're right* was all she could think. *I just hope you're right.*

❧ ❧

Scott had barely entered Crescent Bay High when Darryl joined him. As usual, his little dorky friend was sniffing, pushing up his glasses, and rattling on about something ... and, as usual, Scott, the nice guy, was trying his best to be interested. Trying, but not succeeding. Then he heard his name:

"Scott ... Scott, wait up."

He turned to see a gorgeous redhead maneuvering her way through the crowded hallway toward him. They'd met before. At the Ascension Bookshop. Even then he remembered thinking she looked incredible — shoulder-length copper hair, beautiful green eyes, mischievous smile. Of course, at the time, he had been a little preoccupied with fighting Ouija boards and casting out demons to pay too much attention.

"Hi." She smiled as she bounced up next to him and flipped her hair to the side. "I'm Kara. We met at the Society a couple of weeks back." Before Scott could answer she leaned past him and offered a perky "Hi" to Darryl.

"Hi," Darryl's voice squeaked. Darryl's voice always squeaked — especially when he talked to gorgeous girls. At the moment he sounded halfway between a rusty hinge and a cat stuck in the dryer.

She turned her attention back to Scott. "How've you been?" she asked, sounding as if they'd been friends for years.

"Pretty good," he answered.

"Great."

They walked on in silence. Scott wasn't sure what was going on, but he figured if he waited long enough, he'd find out.

"Sorry about your sister," Kara offered. "But I heard she's out of the hospital now."

"Yeah," Scott said, still waiting. Then another thought came to mind. And with the thought, a trace of anger. "Listen, you guys in the Society, you're not the ones who called her when she got home, are you?"

"Called her?" Kara asked.

Scott looked at her carefully. "Yeah, something about casting a spell and taking away her destiny."

Kara shook her head. She was still light and breezy, but there was also a trace of sadness to her voice. "No, that wasn't us ... at least it wasn't me."

"But you know something about it?"

"I know that Brooke is pretty mad about all the attention your sister's been getting."

"Brooke?"

"Yeah, you know, the leader of the Society. And I know that she and a few of the kids are getting real heavy into this satanism."

"Satanism?" Scott asked.

"Yeah."

"But not you, huh?"

Kara laughed, "No way."

Scott glanced at her. She sure seemed to be telling the truth. "Well," he continued, "if you should happen to see Brooke, tell her to lay off, will you? Becka's pretty shook up already, and she doesn't need somebody playing with her mind."

"I will, Scott." Kara held his gaze. "You have my word on it. I'll definitely tell her."

There was something about the sincerity in Kara's voice and the twinkle in her jade green eyes that caught Scott off guard, that made him realize he was definitely mad at the wrong person. It also made him realize it was time to change gears and dig up some of that world-famous Scott Williams charm. "Hey, how 'bout the homework Mr. Patton is laying on us?" he asked.

"Yeah," Kara said, suddenly sounding as chipper as ever. "That's what I want to talk to you about." She nodded to a couple of passing boys and continued, "I was wondering—I mean, you're so good at algebra and everything—could you ... I mean, could we, like, get together sometime, and maybe you could ... tutor me a little?"

For a split second Scott was surprised. Then came the grin. He'd heard rumors about California girls and how forward they could be, but he'd never seen one in action. *Tutor her?*

Who's she kidding? He knew when a girl was flirting. But that's okay; if that's how the game was played, he could play it as well as the next guy.

"Sure," he said slowly, pretending to think over her request. "I'm sure we could, you know, work something out."

"Great!" She beamed and pulled her cell phone out of her bag. "Can I get your number?"

She tapped the numbers into her phone as Scott said them out loud.

"Cool!" She dropped her phone back into her bag, spun on her heels and headed off in the opposite direction. "I'll give you a call."

"Yeah, right —," Scott said, trying to cover his surprise. "You give me a call." He continued to stare after her, marveling, until Darryl brought him back to reality with one of his irritating sniffs.

"You're good," Darryl said, shaking his head in admiration. "Real good."

"Yeah," Scott chuckled, although he still wasn't sure what he had done or how he had done it, "I guess I am pretty smooth."

❧ ❧

Becka's face was on fire as Ryan wheeled her through the doors of Crescent Bay High. She'd known returning to school would be tough. She just hadn't known it would be this tough.

As they started down the hall it reminded her of the old Ten Commandments movie where Moses parts the Red Sea. Ryan pushed her through the crowd and everyone stepped back, giving her space. One or two murmured a greeting, but most just stopped talking and stared. Those in the front looked down at her and gawked, while those in the back shifted for a better view.

Rebecca bit her lip and stared hard at her lap. Maybe getting smashed on the train tracks wouldn't have been such a bad idea after all.

"Look up," Ryan whispered, so softly that she almost didn't hear. She wanted to glance at him, to confirm what he'd said, but she was too embarrassed.

"I said, look up." His voice was firmer now, yet just as gentle. "I'm right here with you, Becka. You have nothing to be ashamed of. Look up."

Rebecca stared even harder at her lap, hoping no one would hear him.

"Becka ..."

His voice was louder now. She wanted him to shut up. Didn't he know he was asking the impossible? Didn't he know that she was incapable of looking up?

"Don't let them do this to you," he said. "You're just as good as they are. Look into their faces."

Why was he pushing? Why didn't he just let her be? Why didn't he let her melt into the wheelchair? Then she heard another voice: Julie's.

"Hey, Rebecca! Welcome back to the living!" Becka stole a glance and saw her best friend making her way through the crowd toward her. Julie was all smiles, just as bright and cheery as if nothing had ever happened. "I love that sweater," she said as if seeing her friend in a wheelchair was an everyday occurrence. Before Becka could respond, Julie had joined her and Ryan, and was walking along with them. Suddenly she spotted a kid from student council—one of the most popular guys in school. She flashed him her cover girl smile. "Hey Brian, have you met my good friend Becka Williams?"

Brian stared.

"Well, have you?" she persisted.

"Uh, no ... not yet."

"Then come over and say hi. She's cool."

He hesitated.

If Becka thought she'd been dying of embarrassment before, she knew it was time to start planning the funeral now. *What are you trying to prove?* she thought. *Aren't we friends? Why are you doing this to me?*

But Julie pressed on. "Don't be shy," she said to Brian, her voice teasing. She motioned to him. "Come on."

Brian threw a look at his buddy, shrugged, then pushed through the crowd to join them, falling in step beside Julie, Ryan, and the wheelchair.

But before introductions were made, Julie was calling out to somebody else. "Karen, I want you to meet Rebecca Williams. She's the one who gave up her position at the track prelims so I could win. Remember?"

"Yeah, I heard."

"Come over here and meet her."

The girl hesitated, but Julie's persistence and cheerfulness were overpowering. "Come on, it'll only take a minute."

If there was one thing Karen could tell, it was when something important was happening. And if there was one thing Karen hated, it was being left out of anything important. So she joined them.

Now there were five.

A lump swelled in the back of Becka's throat. She looked up at Julie, appreciation washing over her. Her friend was cashing in on her popularity to build up Becka's acceptability.

"Hey, Philip, Krissi," Ryan called out. "Look who I've got!"

"I see," Krissi chirped as she pulled Philip through the crowd toward them. "You look awesome, Becka," she said loud enough for everyone to hear. She turned to Philip and continued, "Doesn't she look awesome?"

Philip nodded as they joined the procession. "She's right, Beck, you look great."

Becka's face was still on fire, but there was no missing the moisture of gratitude filling her eyes. Just like the day she'd come home from the hospital, this had been a conspiracy from the beginning. Something they had planned all along. Her friends were standing up for her, making it clear she was not a freak or some nutsoid crazy.

And if they could go out on a limb for her, then the least she could do was hold her head up for them. She raised her eyes. She wouldn't lower her gaze again. Not now. Not after all they were doing for her. Instead, she met the curious gazes around her head-on. She stared back at those who were staring, at those who were murmuring—and she held their gazes until they were the ones who suddenly grew uncomfortable and looked down.

By the time they arrived at her locker, Becka was feeling a thousand percent better.

"I told you there was nothing to be embarrassed about," Ryan said, playfully nudging Becka's head as she dialed her combination.

She laughed, "You guys really pulled out the big guns."

Julie grinned. "For you, girl, anything."

Becka looked at her, then to Ryan, and finally to the others. She tried to hide her emotion with a smile. But when she spoke, her voice was hoarse. "Thanks, guys."

"No sweat." Philip shrugged.

Becka turned back to her locker and opened the door. It was so great to have friends like—

Her smile froze. She wanted to scream, but no sound came. She wanted to gasp, but she could not breathe. Instead, she started to shake. All over.

There, on the center coat hook, hanging from a string by its broken neck, was a dead rat. A note was pinned to the carcass. Scrawled writing, which looked like it was in blood, read:

YOUR DESTINY IS MINE.

3

Cornelius strutted back and forth on his perch in agitation. "MAKE MY DAY, PUNK! *SQUAWK!* MAKE MY DAY, MAKE MY DAY!"

The reason for his anger was simple: Muttly. Obviously the little fur ball hadn't read the handbook on puppyhood. Especially the part that says dogs and parrots are not best friends. It seemed no matter what Cornelius did, Muttly would find him, sneak up on him, and start yapping in delight—which always sent the bird flapping and squawking back to his perch in horror.

It was all fun and games for Muttly, who now sat on his haunches, panting and grinning for joy. But it was sheer terror for Cornelius, who paced back and forth, screeching at the top of his lungs.

"MAKE MY DAY, PUNK! MAKE MY DAY, MAKE MY DAY! *SQUAWK!*"

Rebecca laughed as she patted her lap for the puppy to join her in the wheelchair. "Come here, boy, come on." Muttly scampered up her leg and into her lap. Immediately he set his wet tongue into action. "Okay, fella, settle down," she said, trying to avoid the kisses.

After turning several tight circles and going through plenty more squirmings and lickings, he finally found his place — perched as far up Becka's chest as he could go, snuggling in as far under her chin as he could get. Becka could feel his tiny puffs of warm breath, and when she remained still, she could feel his little heart tripping away.

She treasured this little guy. Not just because he was from Ryan, but because he never seemed to run out of love. No matter what she did, or failed to do, Muttly was always there with his wagging tail and busy tongue.

Right then, she and Muttly were hanging out in Scott's room, while her brother messed with his computer.

"I texted Z earlier today," Scott said. "He said he could chat around nine."

Becka glanced at her cell phone. "It's just about time."

Scott nodded. He was munching on a piece of cold pizza.

"You really think he'll know about the rat and the threats adn stuff?" Becka asked.

"He hasn't let us down yet."

Scott had a point. Whether it was Ouija boards, reincarnation, or just your basic, run-of-the-mill demonic possession — if it was anything dealing with things supernatural — somehow Z knew about it. But he knew more than that. He knew about Becka and Scott. Their personal lives. They'd never met him (not that they hadn't tried), and he would only talk to them through texting and email—and occasionally chat—but somehow, someway, he always knew what they were up to. Sometimes it was comforting.

Other times it was eerie. Real eerie.

"He's online!" Scott opened a chat window in his email.

Hey Z. Are you there?

Scott and Becka waited, staring at the screen. There was no

answer. Muttly gave a little whine and snuggled closer under Becka's chin. She scratched behind his ears.

Z—you there?

More waiting. Finally the words appeared:

How is Rebecca?

Becka swallowed. It was kind of unnerving to see her name typed up on the screen by someone she didn't even know.

Scott typed back:

Today was her first day of school.

I know. I'm glad her friends are helping her get adjusted.

Scott threw a look over to Becka and shook his head in amazement. Was there anything this guy didn't know? Becka took a slow, deep breath, then spoke. "Ask him about the note and stuff. Ask him what your redheaded friend said about them being satanists."

Scott turned back to the keyboard and typed:

Z, what do you know about satanism?

The response formed:

Are you being bothered by the Society again?

Not the whole group. Just some kids who claim to be satanists. What do you know about them?

There was no answer. Scott typed:

Z ... are you there? Z?

Finally, the response came:

I believe satanists are given more credit than they deserve.

How's that?

For the most part, satanists are outcasts who find it difficult to fit in to society. So they indulge in drugs, sex, music, anything leading to self-gratification.

Scott quickly fired back:

What about human sacrifices and curses and spells and that sort of stuff?

Opinion is divided. Many so-called satanists are usually looking for a shortcut to control and power. They feel their ceremonies provide them with those things. Others are just in it for the thrill. But as for actual spiritual authority, I have strong doubts they can do anything supernatural.

"I don't know about that," Becka said. "Tell him I disagree." Scott nodded and typed:

Becka has her doubts.

The words formed:

Hello, Rebecca.

She fought back a wave of uneasiness. This was the first time Z had directly addressed her. The words continued:

After your ordeal I can appreciate your fears. But understand that everything that goes wrong is not necessarily satanic or supernatural. I believe the only power satanists have is the power you give them through your fear.

Before Rebecca could respond Scott typed:

What about the human sacrifices we always hear about?

They are very, very rare.

But possible?

There was a pause, then the words formed:

Why haven't you two started attending church?

Scott threw a look to Becka and typed:

Are you changing the subject?

Yes.

"Well, at least he's honest," Scott sighed. He typed the words:

I guess we haven't had the time with moving in and all that's been happening. Besides, we've got each other and Mom ... and, of course, the great Z, our private answer man.

The response quickly returned:

I am no substitute for surrounding yourself with other believers. You need them for growth. You should also have a place you can invite your friends to visit.

Becka fought off a little shiver. Wasn't it just this morning that Ryan had mentioned going to church with her? "Ask him—" She took a breath. "Ask him how he knew."

Scott turned back to her. "What?"

"Ask him how he knew about Ryan."

"What are you talking—"

She cut him off. "Just ask!"

Scott turned back to the computer and typed:

Becka wants to know how you knew about Ryan.

There was another pause. And finally:

Good night, you two.

Quickly Scott typed:

Z —hold on a minute.

But before Scott could finish typing the sentence, Z had gone offline.

"I hate it when he does that," Scott said.

Becka stared at the screen, feeling colder than ever. "Me too," she muttered, pulling Muttly closer. "Me too."

❧ ❧

It was three o'clock in the morning when his cell phone rang. Scott, who was known for his weird dreams, was in the middle of a doozy: He was giving an oral book report on *A Tale of Two Cities* to a classroom full of all the world leaders. Nothing too unusual there, except that he was dressed only in his boxers.

The phone continued ringing until he awoke. Grateful for the interruption (he hadn't even read the book), he fumbled to pick up the phone from his bedside table.

"Hello?" he mumbled.

"Scott, is that you?"

"I think so. Who's this?"

"Kara."

"Kara?"

"From Algebra." She paused. "I talked to Brooke early this evening.

"Can't this wait till tomorrow?" Scott asked, rubbing his eyes, trying to clear the last of the world leaders out of his mind.

"I asked her if she was the one putting the curse on your sister."

Suddenly Scott was wide awake. "And?"

"And she said no."

"So that's good."

"Not necessarily. It was the way she said it: 'Us not is it.'"

"What?"

"She was speaking backwards. Sometimes they do that. It could mean just the opposite of what she said."

"So ... she was lying?" Scott frowned, trying to bring the pieces together.

"I wasn't sure, so I tried to call her just now and she sent me straight to voicemail."

"What's that got to do with—"

"Usually when they make their sacrifices and cast their spells it's around three in the morning."

"What time is it now?"

"3:15."

Out of the corner of his eye, he saw someone in the doorway. He spun around to see Becka sitting in her wheelchair. Even in the dim light he could see how concerned she was. And how frightened. He covered the mouthpiece and asked, "Hey, Beck, what's up?"

She said only three words. They were exactly the ones he didn't want to hear: "You tell me."

☜ ☞

The cemetery was covered in a thick, cold fog. Tiny droplets of water collected on the kids' clothes and heads, condensing into larger drops that streamed down their coats and faces. There was only one light, a single neon vapor that hung from a pole above the adjacent Community Church parking lot. The fog absorbed most of it before it reached the open grave. Not only did the fog absorb the light, but it muffled the clanks and thuds of the pickax and shovel too.

"How much farther?" Brooke demanded as she shone her flashlight into a hole at the boys.

The two guys leaned against their digging tools, waist deep in the pit, gasping for breath. At first the idea of sneaking into a graveyard and digging up a corpse sounded pretty exciting. But now, between the booze, the freezing fog, and the heavy clay dirt that resisted every hit of the pickax and shovel, both the excitement and the guys' strength were gone.

"Should be any time," the meatier of the two boys growled. The other guy, a kid with a shaved head and more earrings than a jewelry store, looked at him doubtfully. But he didn't say anything. He knew what happened when Meaty Guy drank, and there was no way he was going to become the brunt of all that anger.

He watched as Meaty Guy wiped the cold moisture from his face, raised the pickax over his head, and gave another swing.

Thud.

Without a word, Shaved Head resumed his digging.

Not far away, Laura, the brooding blonde, was knocking over small upright tombstones. Brooke had nodded in grim approval when the first one toppled, so Laura continued. Some of the markers were easy. Others took five, six, even seven kicks before they broke and fell. It was something Laura would never do on her own. But the whiskey and the approval in Brooke's eyes had opened new doors for her. Now, as each tombstone collapsed, she felt a little surge of power.

Two other girls stood across the hole from Brooke. The younger and more frail looking of the two shivered when she spoke. "Brooke?" Her voice was thin and slurred. "Can I wait in the car? I don't feel so good."

Brooke shot her a look that made the girl cringe.

"Here," her friend said, producing a half-empty bottle of Jack Daniel's from her parka. "Have some more. It'll keep you warm."

Frail Girl took the bottle and eyed it warily. She wasn't so much cold as she was sick, and she was pretty sure the whiskey wasn't going to help in that department. But she couldn't refuse. Not with the others, especially Brooke, watching her. She tilted her head back and drank. It was all she could do to keep from gagging.

"Aughh!" Meaty Guy grunted.

"What?" Brooke flashed the light back into the hole but saw nothing except the damp clay and some darker earth.

"It's what's left of a coffin." He raised his pick above his head and slammed it down hard. The dark dirt gave way more easily. Everyone moved in for a closer look. "Give me that shovel," Meaty Guy ordered.

His partner handed him the shovel. Meaty Guy carefully scooped three, four, five shovelfuls out of the way. Suddenly, the flashlight caught a reflection of whiteness.

"Is it—?" Shaved Head asked.

"Yeah," Meaty Guy muttered. "A bone."

"Brooke." It was Frail Girl again. This time her speech was worse. "I don't feel so good ... really ..."

No one paid attention. Meaty Guy continued to dig. By now, Laura had also joined the group as they crowded closer to the hole and peered in.

At last Meaty Guy kneeled down. He carefully brushed aside some clay, then took something into his hand. Everyone stared as he slowly rose to his feet. Much of it was still covered in dirt, but there was no missing the gleaming white bone and the two hollow eye sockets.

"Give it to me," Brooke commanded. Meaty Guy reached up and handed her the skull.

The group looked on, enjoying the thrill, the cold tingling that spread through their bodies. No one spoke. The skull repulsed and attracted, frightened and excited. Everyone stared in cautious awe. Everyone but Frail Girl. She dropped to all fours and began to vomit. Deep, gut-wrenching gags, so loud that they set a neighbor's dog to barking.

Laura looked down at her with disgust. She hated weakness. She knew Brooke did too.

Brooke pulled the skull into her parka and ordered, "Come

on, we've got lots to do." She turned, and everyone but Frail Girl headed toward the beat-up Nissan in the church parking lot.

When Frail Girl finally looked up, she realized in terror that she was being left alone at the open grave. "Wait for me!" she cried. "Wait!" She wiped her mouth, struggled to her feet, and staggered after them.

When they arrived at the Nissan, Laura reached into the backseat and pulled out a paper bag. Brooke was gonna love this.

"What's that?" Meaty Guy asked.

"I'll be right back," Laura said. She produced a couple of cans of black spray paint from the bag. They made clicking sounds as she shook them back and forth and started toward the church. "I just want to pay my respects to somebody." She threw a quick look to Brooke, who broke into a grin. Laura's heart swelled.

"Wait a minute," Brooke commanded. "Let's all go."

4

It was Friday. School had just let out. Ryan pushed Rebecca through the front doors and prepared to ease both her and the wheelchair down the dozen or so steps to the sidewalk. Suddenly she looked up from rummaging in her backpack and groaned, "Oh no."

"What's wrong?"

"I forgot my chemistry book."

"No sweat." Ryan did his best to sound chipper. "I'll go back in and get it."

She looked at him and winced. "You don't mind?"

"No problem. I'll be right back." He turned and fought his way against the crowd and back into the school.

Becka rolled her chair off to the side, out of the flow of people. She didn't need someone bumping into her and accidentally knocking her down the steps. Granted, the odds were slim, but after all that had gone wrong today, she didn't want to take anymore chances.

First there was Scotty's little wake-up call at three this morning. It took some work, but Becka had finally pried the information out of him. According to Kara, the curse was still on ...

which had reduced the chances of Becka getting back to sleep that morning to about zero.

Then there was the giant zit forming on the left side of her nose. But not just any zit. No, this was the queen mother of all zits. Tender and so red that, even under makeup, it was practically glowing.

Great, she'd thought as she stared at her reflection. *I'll be able to replace Rudolph this Christmas.*

"It's from all the stress," Mom had insisted. "I wouldn't worry about it."

Wouldn't worry about it? Obviously it had been a while since Mom had been in high school. But it wasn't the pimple that bothered Becka as much as it was the timing. She nervously reached up and touched it. *Pretty coincidental. They cast a spell on me, and I wind up in the* Guinness Book of World Records *for zits.*

Then there was Muttly. Of course, puppies make messes. But right on the carpet? Right in front of her room? Just before Ryan was supposed to pick her up?

And let's not forget the spilled lunch tray at noon. Definitely one of her smoother moves. Chicken Cacciatore all over her jeans and new T-shirt—the one she'd spent so much on to impress Ryan.

Everyone in the lunchroom had seen. Seen? They'd clapped. And of course, she'd turned your basic I'm-a-world-class-fool red. Ryan was immediately at her side. "You're just jumpy," he had assured her as he handed her some napkins. "Try to relax."

She had nodded, too embarrassed to look up, busying herself with scooping the food from her lap and back into the tray.

Then Ryan had suddenly exclaimed, "Becka, look at your hands. You're trembling. You're shaking like a leaf."

Becka had raised her hands and stared at them. *What's happening to me?* She'd bit her lip, then looked up to Ryan. Somehow she was able to hold back the tears, but inside ... inside she was screaming. *Dear God, please make them stop! Whatever they're doing to me, make them stop!*

Now, outside in the front of the school, Rebecca took a deep breath and watched the kids head down the steps. Of course, Mom, Ryan, Scott, even Z would say she was bringing all this on herself with her own fears, her own nervousness. But she wasn't buying it. Not for a second.

She heard a voice call, "Excuse me? Rebecca?"

She looked over to the front doors. A couple of kids were pushing their way toward her. She guessed they were underclassmen, and they definitely were dressed like MORs.

Everyone at Crescent Bay High had their mode of dress: the surfers had their baggy shorts, the jocks had their T-shirts, the preppies had their plaids, the nerds had their hand-me-downs. Then there were the kids like herself, the MORs—Middle-of-the-Roaders. People who tried to stay in style but never went too far out on a limb, either because they couldn't afford it or because their parents wouldn't let them.

The two girls who now approached were definitely MORs.

"Are you Rebecca Williams?"

Becka nodded, figuring they already knew. After today, who wouldn't?

"I'm Jenny Fields," said the smaller of the two, smiling. She had long chestnut hair and a freshly scrubbed look about her. "And this is Kathy."

Becka tried to smile, but something inside was already telling her to be careful. "What's up?" she asked, clearing her throat.

"It's the weirdest thing," Jenny said as she reached into her jeans pocket, "but my dad, he's, like, a pastor ... anyway, he got an email real late last night. And ... uh ..." She hesitated.

"And what?"

"Well, it was about you."

Becka felt herself stiffen. "Me?"

Jenny nodded. "The fax asked my dad to have me give this to

you." She reached out her hand. In it was a slip of paper. Becka eyed it warily. "It's just the address of our church," Jenny assured her.

Becka took the paper and unfolded it. It read:

Community Christian Church
351 Cedar Road
Sunday Service, 11:00

Becka looked back up to her questioningly.

Jenny shrugged. "He just wanted us to let you know. Oh, and to tell you about our youth group. Tonight's pizza night. We're meeting around six."

Becka remained noncommittal. "Who did you say emailed your dad?"

"The guy, he didn't give his name. Just an initial."

Becka drew in her breath. She knew the answer before Jenny finished.

"He called himself Z."

Becka nodded.

"Do you know him?" Jenny asked.

Rebecca sighed, "We're old friends." A brief pause settled over the conversation as Becka looked back down to the note. She could feel Jenny's eyes searching her. Finally she looked up, managed a tight little smile, and said, "Thanks."

"No problem." Jenny grinned. Another pause. "Well, I, uh, I guess we'll see you around."

Becka nodded. The two girls turned and started down the steps. As they reached the bottom and disappeared into the crowd, Becka looked back to the slip of paper. Her hands were trembling again. As they did, the paper slipped away and fluttered to the concrete.

She moaned in frustration. Was there no end to the day's irritations? She bent down to pick it up just as a gust of wind blew it further away, closer to the edge of the steps.

"Come on," Becka muttered as she grabbed one of her chair's wheels and rolled herself forward. She drew precariously close to the edge, but she would only be there a second. She reached down. The wind scooted the paper another half inch. She strained forward, jerking slightly, barely catching the paper's edge between her fingers.

What happened next Becka could never explain. Either it was her jerking forward, or someone had accidentally bumped into her chair, or ...

Whatever the case, the right wheel slipped over the edge.

Becka immediately threw herself backward, trying to keep upright, but she was too late. Everything turned to slow motion as the wheel dropped, dragging the rest of the chair with it.

Becka knew she could not stop the fall, but she also knew she had to straighten out the chair. If she was going down the steps, she would have to face them head-on, otherwise the chair would twist sideways and she'd be thrown out.

She grabbed the left wheel and straightened it. She didn't scream. She had no time. She hit the first step, and as the chair pitched forward, she leaned back with all her might. Somehow she managed to keep the chair upright while fighting the wheels to keep it straight.

She hit the second step, then the third, the fourth — they were jarring, bone-rattling bounces, but she hung on — the fifth, sixth, seventh. She was going too fast. She had to break her speed. She squeezed the wheel rails with all her might and felt the heat sear into her palms ... eighth, ninth, tenth ... two more to go, two more and she'd make it ... eleventh, twelfth, and finally she hit the sidewalk.

She quickly rolled to a stop. She was bruised, her palms were blistered, but she had made it. Of course, everyone stared. A few jerks thought it would be cute to applaud. But she barely had time to be embarrassed before Ryan burst through the doors and raced down the steps toward her. "Becka! Are you all right?"

She nodded and drew a deep, ragged breath. She looked down at her blistered hands. The shaking was worse now. Impossible to stop. So were the tears.

"What were you doing?" Ryan was shouting. Not in anger, but fear. "What were you trying to prove?"

She opened her mouth but nothing came.

"Becka? Rebecca." He reached out and took her hands, trying to stop the shaking. But he couldn't. It was then that they both noticed the crumpled slip of paper in her fist. She was still holding the address of the church.

~ ~

Several blocks away, Scott was making his own exit. It was less dramatic than his sister's, but he still had plenty on his mind. Ever since Kara's phone call that morning, Becka had been in his thoughts. He'd even prayed for her. Was it just coincidence that all of these things were happening to her? Was it just Beck's nerves?

That hanging rat they'd found in her locker was definitely no coincidence. Rats just didn't crawl into your locker and hang themselves—or leave interesting notes. And what about the threats and those satanic ceremonies that were supposedly taking place? Didn't they count for something?

Earlier, he had tried to track down Brooke, the supposed leader. She was in the same grade as he was. But she wasn't in school. It seems she had been missing a lot of school these days. *Probably the late hours she's been keeping,* Scott scoffed.

"Scott ... Scott, wait up."

He looked up to see Kara running toward him. He definitely appreciated the sight of her trim body, her thick red hair, those jade green eyes ... yep, this girl was a breath stealer. And even though he was concerned about his sister, he wasn't too concerned to be flattered by Kara's interest.

"Hey, guy," she said, bouncing up to him.

"Hey, yourself," he said, trying to sound cool and in control. It would have worked too, if his voice hadn't cracked.

"Is this a beautiful day or what?"

Scott looked around. He hadn't noticed before, but now that she mentioned it, she was right, it was beautiful. A crisp, clear day, with sure signs of spring just around the corner. "Yeah," he answered, grateful that his voice was momentarily in control, "it is pretty cool."

Kara closed her eyes. She tilted her face up to the sun and breathed in slow and deep. It was as if she was smelling the day, almost tasting its beauty. By the ecstasy on her face, maybe she was.

"You really get into it, don't you?" Scott chuckled.

She laughed with him, and the sound was as beautiful and carefree as she was. "I get into *everything*," she said with a mischievous twinkle—and Scott suddenly wondered if she was talking about more than just the weather. He immediately looked away, feeling guilty for thinking such a thing.

Kara didn't seem to notice. "So how's your sister?"

"Not much better," he sighed.

"Yeah, Brooke can really be a jerk sometimes."

Scott stole a look in her direction. The sun reflected off the silver beads that hung on the delicate silver chain around her neck while highlighting her long, graceful neck, her determined chin, that cute little upturned nose. Scott seldom used the word *awesome*—he'd never really seen a reason for it ... until now.

Still, he had to ask the question that had been on his mind ever since their meeting yesterday. He took a breath and began. "That's something I don't get," he said. "I mean, if you and Brooke are members of the Society and everything, why aren't you part of her little coven?"

"Satanists don't have covens. That's only for witches."

"Witches, satanists, whatever. What are you?"

"I'm …" She hesitated a second. "I prefer to call myself a pagan."

"A pagan?"

"Right," she said, tossing her hair aside, allowing the sun to sparkle off it like glittering copper. "Life is too sacred for us to go around sacrificing stuff. Besides, pagans don't believe in demons and Satan and devils and all that."

"What do you believe in?"

"Freedom. Freedom to do whatever I want. And Nature. I'm a big believer in Nature."

"Nature?" Scott looked at her, even more perplexed than before.

She laughed. "I believe everything is one, everything is interconnected. You, me—" she swooped down and picked up a nearby pinecone—"this pinecone … everything is the same. Everything is God."

"Everything is God," Scott repeated slowly to make sure he got it.

"That's right. The trick is to harmonize yourself with the natural forces around you and become part of that oneness."

"Welcome to California," Scott said, shaking his head.

"Don't laugh." She grinned. "It does have its advantages."

"Like what?"

"Well, if something feels good and it's natural … I'll always do it."

There was that look again. That twinkle. Once again Scott glanced away, feeling both a rush of excitement and a stab of guilt. He stuck his hands into his jacket pockets and tried to change the subject. "So, uh, how's your algebra coming?"

"That's what I wanted to talk to you about," she answered, as carefree and innocent as if nothing had passed between them. Maybe it hadn't. Maybe it was just Scott's imagination.

Come on, Williams, he told himself, *get your mind out of the gutter.*

Kara continued, "With midterms coming up next week, I'm going to need all the help I can get."

He nodded. "So, uh, when do you want to meet?"

Suddenly he felt both of her arms wrap around his as she moved in closer. It wasn't anything sexual. It was just Kara being her uninhibited, friendly self.

"How 'bout now?" she asked, looking up at him with that smile and those eyes. "How 'bout at your house?"

It may have been Kara being her uninhibited and friendly self, but she was definitely fogging up Scott's thinking. "Now?" His voice cracked again. "My house?"

"Sure, I mean if you're not doing anything."

"Um ..." He was positive she had just said something ... unfortunately he couldn't remember what it was. "Um ..."

Come on, brain, work!

And then, somewhere in the back of his mind, another voice spoke.

Be careful.

It was barely discernible over all the emotion rushing through him, but it was definitely there. He cleared his throat. "My, uh, Mom won't be home till around six. Why don't you come by after dinner."

"You want me to come when your mom is there?" she asked in surprise. It almost sounded like ridicule. Immediately Scott hated himself for sounding so lame. Still, he remembered the rules he and Beck had agreed to months before: no guest of the opposite sex at the house without an adult. It wasn't that Mom didn't trust them, it was just ... well, they all agreed it was just a good policy. Why put yourself in a risky situation if you didn't have to?

Of course, he still thought it was a good policy, but that didn't stop him from feeling like a fool. He quickly scrambled to come up with a better excuse. "I've got a lot of chores to do. You know, work in the garage and stuff." (He *had* promised to empty some of those stacked boxes.) "So, uh, later tonight—" His voice croaked again and he cleared it—"later would be a lot better."

"Okay," Kara laughed as she unlinked her arms from his, "if you say so." Then, with that mischievous grin, she said, "We'll see you tonight." She turned and dashed across the street while Scott stood there, watching her go, feeling very much like he'd just been hit by a truck.

5

Shortly before six that evening, Rebecca and Ryan stopped in the doorway of the Community Christian Church's youth room. They were shocked at the destruction — ripped sofas, broken chairs, smashed speakers, walls smeared with plenty of mud and who knows what else, and lots of black spray-painted graffiti. A dozen high school kids were picking up the debris and scrubbing down the walls as an older, college-aged couple helped and gave instructions.

"You made it," Jenny, the girl who had invited Becka, called from across the room. She had just brought in some pizza boxes and was setting them on a table. She brushed her hands and headed toward them.

Coming here had been Becka's idea. She was grateful that Ryan was interested in church, but she would have come with or without him. The reason was simple. She was mad. Real mad. After recovering from "shooting the rapids" on the school steps that afternoon, she had finally made up her mind. She had told Scott her decision just a few hours earlier as he worked in the garage.

"I'm not going to be a victim anymore. We've beaten these

guys twice already—you against that Ouija board and both of us against all the reincarnation junk. We can do it again. I know we can."

Scott had agreed as he lifted another box and moved it across the room. "They want a war," he said, "we'll give 'em a war."

Becka shook her head. "Not on our own, little brother. We need recruitments. You heard what Z said. We need to get plugged into a church."

"But where? Which one?"

Becka smiled as she unfolded the piece of paper with the address. "As usual, Z's looking out for us." She handed it to her brother, gave him a moment to look it over, then said, "I'm going to give Ryan a call to see if he wants to go. You want to come with?"

"I, uh, I'd like to ..." Scott hesitated, as though he was mulling something over. "But, Kara ... she's coming over later this evening."

"So bring her along."

"I don't think so." Scott avoided her eyes.

"Why not?"

"I just don't think she'd fit in."

Becka watched him carefully. Something was up. Normally Scott was all overconfidence and wisecracks. Now he seemed nervous and cautious. She wanted to ask what was going on but figured he'd tell her when he was ready. She wheeled her chair out of the garage and into the house, where she called Ryan.

That had been just a few hours ago. And now here they were, in the doorway of a church's youth room that looked like it had been struck by a hurricane.

Jenny came up to them, brushing stray wisps of hair from her face. "Sorry about the mess."

"What happened?" Ryan asked.

"We got hit pretty hard last night."

"Vandals?" Becka asked.

"Yeah," Jenny said, "or worse." She motioned toward the walls. "Take a look at that."

On one wall was spray painted the numerals 666. Another wall sported drawings of lightning bolts. A third had a cross inside the universal no symbol, a circle with a slash through it.

"Not very friendly," Ryan said.

Jenny nodded. "We think they could be like satanists or something. A couple of the kids are pretty freaked out."

"What's that?" Becka asked, pointing to two lines of letters spray painted across the front wall. They read:

NEMANATAS

ACCEBERREDRUM

"We haven't figured it out," Jenny said with a shrug. "Probably some sort of code. The cemetery next door got hit too. They knocked over a bunch of tombstones and dug up somebody's grave."

Ryan grimaced. "That's sick."

"Not only that, but they took the skull and —"

"Hi, guys." They were interrupted by the college-aged woman. She wasn't gorgeous by any stretch of the imagination, but there was something warm and genuine about her. Becka liked her instantly. "Who're your friends, Jenny?"

Jenny stepped back and made the intros. "This is Rebecca Williams and her friend . . ."

Ryan stepped forward and shook her hand. "Ryan. Ryan Riordan."

"I'm Susan Murdock," the woman said. "And that good-looking specimen over there —" she pointed to the man scooping up a pile of papers — "is my incredible husband, Todd."

Jenny laughed. "Newlyweds. They've been married all of six weeks, in case you can't tell." Everyone chuckled.

Jenny turned back to Susan. "Becka just moved up from South America. Her dad was a pilot who flew missionaries into jungle villages and stuff."

Becka stared at Jenny. Apparently the girl had gotten this information from Z. She frowned, wondering what else he had told her. Did he mention that Becka's dad had also died in one of those flights? That they had never found his body?

Before Becka could ask, Susan reached out and tapped the cast on her leg. "What happened here?"

Becka shook her head. "It's a long story."

"Who's your artist?" Ryan asked, motioning to the walls. Becka knew he was changing the subject for her, and as always, she was grateful for his sensitivity.

"Pretty sad, isn't it?" Susan sighed.

"Susan thinks she knows the kids," Jenny offered.

All eyes looked to Susan. She shrugged. "Well, one of them, yeah. Laura Henderson. I've been working with her for months. I guess this is her way of telling me to back off."

"Not very subtle," Ryan said, shaking his head.

Susan continued, "She's basically a good kid. Her home life's a mess, though. She's pretty desperate for some sort of control, something to hang on to."

"Okay, everybody," Todd shouted to the room. "That's enough for now. Those of you who want to stick around and help afterward, great. But let's grab some pizza and get started."

"We'll talk later," Susan said as she started toward the front.

Jenny accompanied Ryan and Becka to the pizza table. Becka took a deep breath. She wasn't crazy about meeting new people. In fact, she hated it. But Z had suggested they do this, and so far Z had never been wrong.

❧ ❧

Scott continued rummaging through the junk stacked in the garage. The previous tenants had left dozens of boxes behind, and it was his job to go through each and every one to see if there was anything worth saving. Some of the stuff was pretty strange—used toothbrushes, plastic milk cartons, the bottom half of tennis shoes. Yep, whoever lived here before was defi-nitely unique, in a *Ripley's Believe It or Not* sort of way.

Then, of course, there were the strange noises they'd heard in the garage, along with the eerie streaks of light that flew across the room. It's not that Mom and Becka were scared or anything—they were sure there was a logical explanation for it all. They just weren't crazy about being in the garage alone. So Scott, being the official man of the house, had been assigned the job of working there. He'd muttered something about sexism, but it did little good. He could mutter all he wanted. He still got the job.

But right now the noises and lights were not on his mind. Instead, he was thinking of red hair sparkling in sunlight, incredible green eyes, and a fun-loving smile.

He glanced at his watch for the hundredth time. He had done the right thing, putting Kara off till Mom got home. But the hours and minutes seemed to drag by. She was practically all he could think about. It's not that he hadn't seen beautiful girls before. Or never been attracted to them. But not like this. This one was special. And to top it off, this one was interested in him. Very interested.

What had she said? *"I'm a pagan ... I believe in freedom ... if it feels good, I do it."* Scott forced the thoughts out of his mind. He took a deep breath and heaved another box onto the others. You didn't have to be a genius to know what she meant. You'd have to be deaf and blind not to know what she meant. Deaf and blind ... and dead!

Scott sighed. For most of the guys at school, this would have been the opportunity of a lifetime. Something they dreamed about. But Scott knew what he should do: Cut her off. Don't get involved. Run from temptation.

But even as he thought that, he heard another voice: *Maybe I can help her. Maybe take her to church. Who knows, she might even—*

"Hey, guy."

He started, and immediately felt his heart begin to pound. "Hey, yourself," he said, turning toward her.

"Sorry I'm early." Her smile said she wasn't sorry in the least.

"No sweat," Scott replied, trying to stay nonchalant.

Suddenly, right on cue, there was a loud *SCREECH!*

Scott's eyes darted to the rafters. Fortunately it was bright enough in the garage that they couldn't see the darting light that always accompanied the sound.

"What is that?" Kara asked, stepping closer.

"Don't worry," Scott said, still staring at the rafters. "Just our pet ghost."

"No, really, what was that?"

"We're not sure."

SCREECH—SCRAPE.

"That's so weird." But instead of backing off, Kara moved in to investigate. "It sounded like it came from up there in the ceiling."

Before Scott could respond, she hopped up on some nearby boxes. Her impulsiveness didn't surprise him. Nothing she did surprised him anymore. She crawled to the next level of boxes, almost even with the bare bulb that hung down. Then she stood up, balancing herself precariously.

Scott didn't mean to stare. But even in the harsh light of the bulb she looked gorgeous. The flowing gauze skirt and tank top didn't help matters. It was a struggle, but at last Scott forced himself to look away.

"Nothing here." Kara sounded disappointed.

"Hmm," Scott said, pretending to examine the contents of his latest box. Not that he knew what he was looking at. If it had been gold coins, he wouldn't have seen them.

"Aren't you going to help me down?"

Scott looked up. Kara stood on the box above him, holding

out her hands. Somewhere in the back of his mind he heard, *Be careful,* but the voice was growing fainter by the second.

"Oh ... uh, yeah. Sure." Scott fumbled to close the box lid and quickly moved to her aid. He reached up; she reached down. It was the first time their hands had touched since that afternoon. Then, before he could react, Kara placed his hands on her waist and gave a little hop. He had to move closer to catch her weight, and suddenly, as he lowered her, they were nice and close. Too close.

"Thanks," she said, shaking her hair back and gazing up at him.

Scott said nothing. He wasn't sure he could speak even if he wanted to.

Holding his gaze, Kara wrapped her arms around his neck, rose up on her toes, and brought her lips toward his. The voice in his head was screaming, but he paid little attention.

Until another voice broke in:

"Hey, Scotty. Who's your friend?"

Scott spun around. Mom was standing in the kitchen doorway. The look on her face showed surprise—and disappointment.

❧ ❧

The youth meeting at the church was good. Becka had forgotten how much she missed being with other believers. Oh sure, some of them were just hangers-on, guys and girls scoping out each other, but there was a handful of kids who were really committed to God. You could tell by the way they got into the singing. The songs weren't just the fun, hand-clapping, I'm-glad-to-be-a-Christian-aren't-you type of stuff. There were also some worship tunes that were really directed to Jesus—songs that told him how much they loved him.

Becka didn't know many of the words (being stuck in remote South American jungles kind of keeps you from learning the latest hits). As the new kid with a non-Christian friend at her elbow, she was definitely on the self-conscious side. But eventually she was able to force that stuff out of her mind long enough to start worshiping a little herself. It felt good. Real good.

The teaching wasn't bad either. "The one who is in you is greater than the one who is in the world." That was the Bible verse Todd kept referring to. He was obviously trying to comfort the kids who were upset and nervous about all the damage. He talked a lot about the authority Christians have over Satan ... the promises Jesus made to Christians that they can stomp on the devil if they believe and use that authority.

But as Becka tried to concentrate on what he was saying, she kept being distracted by the writing scrawled across the wall behind him.

NEMANATAS

ACCEBERREDRUM

Maybe it's a foreign language, she thought. Or initials. But why are the last two words in English? Red rum. Isn't booze usually clear or brown? Why red? Are they talking about blood?

Becka tried to direct her attention back to Todd. Now he was talking about the need to love and forgive our enemies. He was explaining that most people involved in the occult are looking for love, that they're terribly insecure and searching for some sort of control in their life.

Becka really tried to concentrate. But her mind drifted again. *Maybe the words are English, but just mixed up.* She examined the letters of the first word. Nema. *That could be ... name. Or men with an extra* a ... *or flip the* a *around and make* amen. Her eyes widened. That was it! *Nema* was a backwards *amen!* And if you read the second word backward you got—

Suddenly Becka went cold. She felt her body stiffen. Ryan looked at her. A slight frown crossed his face. As though he sensed her tension, he leaned over and whispered, "You all right?"

Becka swallowed hard and tried to remain calm. "Yeah, uh …"

Ryan looked at her carefully. "What's wrong?"

"I, uh …" Even at a whisper her voice was starting to quiver. "I think I know what those letters mean," she said, not taking her eyes from the front wall.

Ryan shot a glance to the wall, then back to Rebecca.

She continued staring straight ahead. "Remember …," she whispered, "remember I told you that Scotty's friend said sometimes satanists speak backwards?"

"Yeah."

She closed her mouth. She wanted to say more, but she didn't trust her voice. She simply nodded toward the wall.

Ryan looked to the first line:

NEMANATAS

ACCEBERREDRUM

"Satan amen," he whispered. "The first line reads Satan, amen."

He looked at her and she managed to nod, but she couldn't take her eyes from the second line. He looked back at the wall and read:

NEMANATAS

ACCEBERREDRUM

"Mur derrebec ca." He scowled. "I don't get it."

Becka managed a hoarse whisper. "Say it faster." Her head was beginning to throb. "Say it faster."

"Mur derrebec ca … Murderrebecca … Murder rebecca." He gasped loudly, "Murder Rebecca?!"

"I'm sorry." Todd stopped his talk. "Did you have a question?"

Everyone turned to look at them. Rebecca stared down at her lap. Then she noticed it.

The shaking had returned. More violent than ever.

6

A ll right," Mom said, shutting the front door and turning to Scott.

Uh-oh, he thought, *here it comes...*

Mom had been pleasant enough to Kara for the few minutes the girl had remained. She'd asked Kara where she lived, what her interests were, would she like to stay for dinner. But Kara suddenly remembered something she had to do at home. She excused herself and was out the door in less than two minutes.

And now that Kara was gone, so was Mom's smile. "What was that all about?"

Scott figured he had two choices: either play the penitent sinner who promised never to break the rules again, or pretend to be outraged that his own mother didn't trust him. Unfortunately, he chose the latter. "Why do you always have to think the worst?" he accused.

"I come home to find you making out with a girl in the garage—what am I supposed to think?"

"We were not making out."

"You sure weren't finding a cure for world hunger!" Mom strode past him and headed into the kitchen. She'd had a long day of looking for work. He could tell she was cranky and hungry. And Muttly didn't help matters — the way he scampered around her feet, causing her to trip every few steps.

Scott followed her into the kitchen. "Kara's a nice girl. She just wanted some help in algebra."

"You know the rules, Scotty." Mom opened the refrigerator, looking for something fast and easy to fix.

"So you don't trust me, is that it?" Scott demanded. Strategically speaking, he thought this was a good move, to keep Mom on the defense. But Mom had some pretty good moves of her own.

"I don't trust the world," she countered. She slammed the refrigerator and crossed the room to let Muttly out the back sliding-glass door.

"Maybe that's our trouble," he shot back. "Maybe the world knows a lot more than we give them credit for."

"And what is that supposed to mean?"

Scott wasn't entirely sure, but he'd already committed himself, so he couldn't back down. "This is the twenty-first century, Mom. California. But it's like we're living in a time warp." It surprised him to hear the anger in his own voice. "You've got me and Beck living in the Dark Ages."

"Right," Mom countered, both angry and hurt. "And this is one medieval mother who still grounds her kids for mouthing off."

"Fine," Scott snapped. He turned and stormed up the stairs toward his room. "Ground me for life! What difference does it make? I'm living in prison anyway!"

Mom followed him to the steps. "And you think hanging out with that girl, doing whatever she wants — you think that's freedom?"

"I think she knows more about freedom than I'll ever know!" He stomped into his room and slammed the door. He stood there, breathing hard. He wasn't sure how the argument had gotten so out of hand. He believed what God said about honoring parents—and he believed what the Bible said about sex and stuff. But still ...

"BEAM ME UP, SCOTTY, BEAM ME UP! *SQUAWK!* BEAM ME UP!"

He looked over at Cornelius, took another deep breath, and slowly let it out. How had everything gotten so crazy?

❦ ❦

It was 8:55 p.m.

"Shine the light over there," Meaty Guy snarled.

His partner, Shaved Head, tried to ignore the sour smell of alcohol that hung on Meaty Guy's breath and snapped on the flashlight. He carefully ran the beam along the sagging back-alley fence. There had to be some sort of gate or opening. "You sure this is the place?" he whispered.

"Uh, 730 North Sycamore," Meaty Guy grumbled. "Two story, white with blue trim. This is it." They moved closer. The gravel of the alley crunched and popped under their feet. When they arrived at the fence Meaty Guy peered over it, searching. "There!" He spotted a rusting latch at the far end.

Shaved Head shined the light in that direction, but Meaty Guy angrily shoved it away. "Don't be stupid. They're home, can't you see?" He motioned toward the sliding-glass door, where Mom was clearing off the table after her dinner.

"Come on," Meaty Guy ordered. He adjusted the large shoe box under his arm and started for the gate.

❦ ❦

"I think maybe Todd and Susan are right," Ryan said as he wheeled Becka from his car toward the open garage door. Since there were no ramps leading up the front porch, they had to enter and exit through the garage. "Maybe we should call the cops."

"And tell them what?" Becka asked. "That somebody's casting

a spell on me?" She tried to sound strong, though she still hadn't been able to stop the trembling in her hands. "They won't believe it's real. Even you don't believe it."

Ryan pushed the hair out of his eyes. "I believe what's happening is real. I just don't think everything has to be supernatural." They entered the garage. Since the kitchen door was only twenty feet away, Ryan didn't bother to snap on the light. "I can't buy that a bunch of losers can get together and suddenly have supernatural powers over you, that's all. Especially with what Todd was saying about God being greater."

"So I'm just being superstitious, is that it?" There was an edge to Becka's voice, which she immediately regretted.

Ryan chose his words carefully. "I just think … you're … giving them more credit than they deserve."

They had nearly reached the door when they were interrupted by a clear sounding *SCREECH—SCRAPE!* followed by a flash of light that darted across the room and disappeared out of sight.

Ryan and Becka froze. Becka glanced up to him and forced a grin. "So everything has to be logical and rational, huh?"

Ryan gave a weak, halfhearted smile and quickly moved them toward the kitchen door.

Muttly sat on the back porch, panting. Ever since Mom had let him outside, he had worn himself to exhaustion chasing leaves. Then his tail. And most recently, jumping into the air trying to snatch the moon out of the sky. (Mongrel puppies have never been known for their outstanding intelligence.)

Suddenly, a hand reached over the fence toward the latch. Muttly cocked his head.

The hand grasped the latch and pulled it up. The gate swung open with a gentle groan. Muttly rose to his feet and gave a shiver of delight as two humans came into the backyard. From the way his tail wagged, it was plain he figured these were two new friends to play with.

The humans spotted him almost as quickly as he had spotted them.

"Perfect," the bigger of the two sneered. "We don't even have to look for him." Then, stooping down, he patted his leg and whispered, "Here, boy ... come on, fella ... come on ..."

Muttly bounded off the porch and raced toward the beckoning human with eager anticipation.

"Come here, fella, come on ..."

The pup was momentarily distracted by a wayward leaf that crossed his path. But soon his attention was back to the human who kept calling and motioning for him to come. The guy had pulled a box out from under his arm. "Come on, fellow ..." Now he was taking off the lid. "Come on ..."

Muttly was practically there. With two final bounds, he reached the human, who suddenly scooped him into his arms. Muttly wriggled ecstatically.

Then the human stuffed him into the box and slammed the cover on top.

"Perfect," the guy sneered. "Just perfect."

👁 👁

Scott had just sat down at his computer. He'd heard Ryan's Mustang pull into the driveway and the slamming of the kitchen door as Ryan and Becka entered through the garage. Mom was taking a bath. He hoped it would be a long, hot one. She needed to relax. In the meantime, since it was nine o'clock, maybe Z would be online. He typed:

Hey, Z, You there?

Good evening. How was church?

I didn't go.

I know.

The answer didn't surprise Scott. The boy hesitated a moment. The two of them had been through a lot together. And through it all, Z had never betrayed his confidence. Maybe he could help here.

Z, you know I believe in the Bible and stuff. But ...

He paused. After a moment Z typed:

But?

Scott took a breath and went for broke:

There's this girl. I mean she's so free and easygoing and ...

Beautiful?

Well, yeah. And, uh ... she's like really coming on strong ...

Z interrupted:

She wants to have sex with you?

Scott raised his eyebrows and typed:

Yes.

What do you want?

That's just it. I mean, I believe the Bible. If it says sex before marriage is wrong, then it's wrong. But ... times change—and, let's face it, the Bible was written a long time ago.

Scott waited. There was no reply.

Z, are you still there?

The Spell

The words formed:

I'm gathering statistical data. Stand by.

Scott snorted and typed:

Z, I'm talking about my heart here, not statistical data.

The information quickly formed on the screen:

According to current reports, 75% of all AIDS transmissions now take place between males and females having sex. The biggest increase of AIDS cases is among teens.

Scott sighed. He already had the answer and typed:

Condoms.

Z's reply was just as fast:

Condoms fail 16% of the time in preventing pregnancy. That's 1 out of 6 times. Sometimes because of breaks or leakage. Sometimes because of manufacturer defects. A woman can only get pregnant a few days a year, but you can be infected with AIDS or other viruses every day of the year.

Scott was surprised, but Z had more:

Besides pregnancy and the danger of diseases, premarital sex creates emotional damage.

Emotional damage?

The following is statistical information—cold, hard, scientific evidence. Those who have sex before marriage:
—have less happy marriages
—are more apt to divorce after marriage
—are more likely to commit adultery after marriage
—enjoy sex less after they are married

You're telling me all this has been proven?

Through research, yes. I need to go.

But Scott had a final question:

Z, this girl, she calls herself a pagan. Do you know what a pagan is?

Yes, but you do not want to know.

Try me.

The letters formed slowly:

A pagan is many things, but in this context she means—

Suddenly the chat window shut down.

"Oh man," Scott groaned. He tried to bring their chat session back up, but nothing happened. And that's too bad. Because if he had, he would have seen the end of Z's sentence.

It consisted of only one word:

witch.

❧ ❧

"Beck," Scott hollered. "You've got a call."

Becka handed her hot chocolate to Ryan and wheeled herself into the kitchen. She took the phone from Scott. He popped the tab of the soda he'd just grabbed from the fridge and headed back toward his room.

"Hello?"

"We have him," the voice said.

Becka recognized it instantly. It was the same voice that had been threatening her. "Who is this? Who do you have?" Her tone immediately brought Ryan to her side.

The voice calmly answered, "Why, your stupid little mutt, of course."

Becka's eyes darted to the floor, searching for some sign of Muttly—any sign. Her voice shook, but she held her ground. "You're not fooling anybody," she bluffed. "My dog's right here."

"Oh, is he?"

Suddenly Becka heard yelping and squealing through the phone. It was Muttly. No doubt about it. And he was in pain.

"Stop it!" Becka shouted. "What are you doing to him? Stop it!"

The voice answered icily, "He's just the warm-up act, Williams. You're the real show. Better get ready 'cause you're on next."

"Who is this? Who are you?" Becka shouted. Muttly continued whining and barking in the background. "Who is this?"

"Red rum," the voice laughed. "Red rum, red rum, red rum."

"Who is this?!"

"Your destiny is mine." There was a click, followed by the dial tone.

7

They called the police. The officers were polite and friendly, but they had no hard evidence to go on—just a couple of prank phone calls and a missing puppy. When Becka hinted about people casting a spell on her, the officers pretended interest, but she could tell they were simply waiting for her to get back to "the facts." So after a half an hour of taking detailed notes and promising to talk to some of the kids in the Society, the police left.

For the next two hours, Scott, Mom, and Ryan did their best to calm Becka's nerves while combing the neighborhood for Muttly. On both accounts they failed. Becka was more jittery than ever, and no one had seen Muttly.

"Maybe we'll have better luck tomorrow," Ryan offered as they rolled into the garage.

"I wouldn't bet on it," Becka murmured.

"You want to come inside for some popcorn or something?" Mom offered.

"No," Ryan said, "I should be taking off."

"You sure?"

"Thanks, though." He glanced down at Becka, who looked

worn and worried. "Listen, why don't I come back tomorrow and we can give it another try?"

Becka shook her head. "It won't do any good. They're too smart. We won't find him."

Ryan nodded. "I know. I was just looking for an excuse to stick close by during all this."

She looked up to him and forced a smile. Ryan Riordan was definitely a one-of-a-kind guy. "Thanks," she said softly.

"If you need a reason to come over, I've got one," Scott said.

"Yeah, what's that?"

With a dramatic flair, Scott spun around to the dozens of unpacked boxes still in the garage. "These." He grinned as he stretched out his arms. "You can help me finish unpacking all of these stupid … no wait … exciting boxes."

Ryan grinned. "Why not? It's as good an excuse as any. Besides, maybe we'll get down to the real cause of those noises and light."

"You don't believe in our little ghost?" Mom teased.

"Ryan doesn't believe in anything supernatural," Becka said. It was part truth, part jab.

"Not exactly," he corrected. "The stuff they said at the meeting tonight, you know, about Jesus and God, that made a lot of sense. I just don't believe that every time something goes wrong it's the work of the devil. I mean, there's plenty of creeps out there without him always having to get involved."

Becka glanced away. Ryan had taken this line from the beginning. Come to think of it, so had Z. What was it Z said? *"The only power they have is the power you give them through your fear"*?

Maybe. But how do you know? How do you know what are mind games and what are legitimate satanic attacks?

❧ ❧

"Maybe it doesn't matter," Mom said, picking up the conversation exactly where they had left it the night before. It was

Saturday afternoon, and all four had returned to the garage to chip away at the stacks of boxes. They weren't entirely sure why they wanted to work except, like Ryan had said, it gave them a chance to stick together. They still hadn't heard anything about Muttly, but Becka kept the cordless telephone nearby. Just in case.

"Maybe what doesn't matter?" Scott asked Mom as he tore open another box.

"Whether we're fighting spiritual wars or wars of the flesh," Mom answered.

"'Wars of the flesh'?" Ryan asked.

Becka explained, "You know, the stuff you want to do but know you shouldn't?"

"Like punching out the latest satanist," Scott quipped.

Becka continued more seriously, "Or lying or drinking or cheating or—"

"Or having sex outside of marriage," Mom said, throwing a too obvious look in Scott's direction. Scott immediately looked down, pretending he hadn't heard.

Mom continued, "The point is, Jesus not only promised to give us victory over evil spirits, but also over our own flesh. All we have to do is pray and believe."

"So you agree with Ryan and Z?" Becka asked. "That these kids have no real power over me? That I'm just being stupid and superstitious?"

Mom hesitated. "I'm not sure, honey."

"I bet Muttly is sure," Becka grumbled. Her tone was sharp and Mom winced. But before Becka could apologize ...

SCRAPE.

Everyone froze. There was no mistaking the sound. As usual it came from overhead. All eyes moved to the rafters, searching. Everyone stood in silence. Everyone but Scott.

"Casper?" he called. "Casper, is that you?"

"Shhh!" Becka motioned for him to be quiet.

If any of them had been alone, they would have moved for

cover. But as a group they seemed to have more courage, so they held their ground. Their heart rates may have picked up, but they held their ground. At least for the moment.

SCRAPE.

Scott fidgeted. "All in favor of getting out of here, say aye!"

There were no answers. Lots of dry mouths and nervous coughs, but no answers.

SCRAPE.

Ryan was the first to spot it. "There!" he shouted and pointed. "Up there."

"I don't see anything," Scott said.

"It was a light. I only caught a glimpse of it, but it was a light. Right there." He started to climb onto one of the boxes. It crushed under his weight. He found another and crawled onto it.

"Ryan," Becka protested. But it did little good. He was already on a second box, then a third.

"I'm sure I saw it ... right there." He grabbed another box and set it on top of his pile to get closer to the ceiling.

"Ryan," Mom said in her I'm-the-adult-here-so-you'd-better-listen-to-me voice, "be careful."

It was the fifth box that did it. Ryan's homemade mountain was not that stable, and suddenly everything began to lean.

"Watch it!" Scott called.

SCRAPE.

Whether it was the noise or Ryan's reaction to the noise, no one knew. But suddenly the entire pile of boxes toppled.

"Ryan!"

He fell hard and was immediately covered by boxes.

"Ryan! Ryan, are you okay?"

Mom and Scott dug through the boxes and finally pulled him out.

"I saw it," he said as they helped him to his feet. "I saw sunlight." Then without hesitation he motioned to the mound of fallen boxes. "Scotty, hand those to me."

"Ryan, don't be stupid," Becka warned.

But he didn't listen.

"Ryan, we don't want you getting hurt," Mom insisted.

"I'll be fine," he said as Scott began handing him the boxes.

Soon they had rebuilt his mountain—more carefully this time. Much more carefully. Everyone watched as Ryan climbed the boxes. At last, Ryan reached the ceiling. He could actually touch the dilapidated plywood and rafters of the roof. He began to poke and feel and explore.

Everyone waited.

And then he chuckled.

SCRAPE.

"Ryan, are you okay?" Mom called.

The sound repeated itself again. *SCRAPE.* And again. *SCRAPE, SCRAPE.*

"What's going on?" Becka shouted.

Scott joined in. "Ryan, are you doing that?"

Ryan laughed again. His right arm was stretched through the rafters in the roof. He seemed to be spinning something.

"It's a ventilator," he shouted.

"A what?"

"One of those vents for the attic. You know, those aluminum balls on the roofs that spin round and around?"

"No way," Scott scoffed.

"Only this one's a little stuck so it takes quite a gust of wind to make it turn." To prove his point, he tugged harder with his arm, forcing the sound to repeat itself faster and faster: *SCRAPE-SCRAPE-SCRAPE-SCRAPE . . .*

The Williams grew silent, feeling a little foolish and a lot relieved.

Becka was the first to speak. "But . . . what about the light?"

"What about it? It's sunlight."

"What about at night, when there is no sun?"

"Got me," came the answer.

"Unless..." Now it was Scott's turn to smile.

Mom and Becka looked at him. "Unless what?" Mom asked.

"There's a streetlight in front of the house, right?"

"Yes..."

Ryan completed the thought. "So on gusty nights, when this thing moves, the light reflects through the hole here and—"

"We have flying lights," Becka finished flatly.

"Bingo!" Ryan grinned.

Mom shook her head. "So much for our garage ghost."

"Well," Scott said with a shrug, "it was fun while it lasted."

Ryan gave the ventilator a few more spins—*SCRAPE-SCRAPE-SCRAPE*—and then started down, just as the phone rang.

Becka froze. Everyone exchanged glances. There was no chance for a second ring before Becka lifted the receiver.

"Hello?" But it was neither the police nor the icy voice. "Hi, this is Kara. Is Scott around?"

"Yeah, hang on." Rebecca held out the phone to her brother. "It's your friend Kara."

"Oh," Scott said, fumbling for the phone. "Uh, hello?"

Mom and Becka exchanged uncertain looks as Scott began to talk. There was something about the way he stammered and fidgeted that made them realize the boy was definitely smitten.

Scott edged out of the garage and into the kitchen, making it clear that he wanted his privacy. "Hey, how did you get this number?" Scott asked quietly. Kara had never called him on the landline before.

"Information," she said lightly. "I thought you might not be by your phone, and I wanted to make sure to reach you."

Mom watched as Scott disappeared from sight. Try as she might, she couldn't shake the uneasiness welling up inside her.

She would have felt even more uneasy if she had known what Kara was asking.

❦ ❦

"I still say we should have brought the van," Laura complained as she tossed the strands of rope into the trunk of her Nissan. "No way can we get her wheelchair in here."

"Don't be stupid," Brooke snapped. "She won't need a wheelchair where we're going."

The others snickered. Brooke saw Laura's face redden. She knew the girl hated being ridiculed, especially by her, especially in front of the group. Good. This would make Laura work all the harder. And that was good.

Brooke looked to the sky. It was almost sunset. Tree branches had started to stir. A mass of heavy black clouds approached. "Looks like a storm," she said with grim satisfaction. "You guys don't mind a little rain, do you?"

The six kids voiced their approval as they gathered around the Nissan and a VW Bug.

"What about the brother?" It was Frail Girl, the one who had vomited at the cemetery.

Brooke gave a sly smile. "I just got off the phone with Kara. Little brother is all taken care of."

"And Williams' boyfriend?" Laura asked.

Meaty Guy tossed a sawed-off baseball bat into the back of the Nissan. "I can handle him."

Brooke eyed Meaty Guy. Like Laura, there was something about his anger and energy she liked. As long as he knew who was in charge, he would prove very useful. She turned to the rest of the group. "We've got the robes?"

"Check," Frail Girl said.

"Candles and incense?"

"Got 'em."

"Athamés?"

"Oh, yeah," Shaved Head chuckled nervously as he produced half a dozen small daggers.

"Nightgown?"

"Right here," Laura called, raising a white nightgown above her head.

"Ropes and gag?"

"We've got everything," Meaty Guy grumbled. "Let's get started."

"Not until sunset," Brooke insisted. "The powers of darkness do their best work in the dark." Then, looking around, she snapped, "The mutt. Who's got the mutt?"

Shaved Head grimaced. "Be right back." He ducked into the nearby trailer home and a moment later reappeared with a squirming pillowcase full of puppy.

"Put him in the VW," Brooke ordered.

Shaved Head nodded, opened the VW's door, and threw the bag in the back. It hit the floorboard with a sickening thud. For the moment, all movement inside the pillowcase ceased.

As Shaved Head slammed the door, Meaty Guy repeated, "Let's go. We can wait outside the house till it gets dark. Come on."

Brooke glanced to the rest of the group. They were primed, ready for action. She could feel their power, their anger waiting to be unleashed. This was good. Very, very good.

"Okay." She nodded. "Let's do it."

They climbed into the cars. "Give me the keys," Meaty Guy said to Laura. "Let me drive."

Laura hesitated. The Nissan was her car.

"Let him have 'em," Brooke ordered as she climbed into the back.

"But—"

"Give him the keys."

Without further argument, Laura handed them over. She had been ridiculed by Brooke once this evening. That was more than enough.

Brooke, Shaved Head, Meaty Guy, and Laura rode in the Nissan. Frail Girl and her partner were in the VW.

Brooke rolled down the window and shouted, "Make sure you've got it all set up by the time we get there!"

The two girls in the VW nodded and took off. Meaty Guy followed.

8

As 7:30 approached, Scott grew more and more anxious. It wasn't because Ryan was staying over for dinner. And it wasn't because the guy kept asking all sorts of cool questions about Jesus.

Scott was nervous because of Kara's phone call earlier that afternoon. She had asked if he'd come over around 7:30 to help her with her algebra. Not a major problem except, for some reason, Scott had not gotten around to telling Mom about it. He wasn't sure why. Maybe it had something to do with the little incident between them in the garage last night. Maybe it was because, in the back of his mind, he suspected Kara really wasn't that interested in mathematics.

Don't be stupid, he argued with himself. *You're letting your imagination run away with you again. She just wants help, that's all.* But if he really believed that, why wouldn't he tell Mom? He wasn't sure. The only thing he was sure about was that, the closer it got to 7:30, the harder it was to concentrate on the dinner conversation. And that was a pity because, as conversations go, it wasn't bad.

"I believe Jesus was a good guy," Ryan was saying, "One of the greatest teachers there ever was."

"Not exactly," Mom answered as she dished out a second helping of corn and passed it on to him.

"What do you mean?"

"Jesus couldn't be a great teacher."

Ryan looked surprised. "Why not?"

"Great teachers don't claim to be God."

"Jesus claimed that?"

"Over and over again. 'I am the way and the truth and the life,' 'I and the Father are one,' 'Anyone who has seen me has seen the Father.' Those are all claims he made about himself in the Bible."

Ryan glanced to Becka, who nodded in confirmation.

Mom continued, "No good teacher would make those claims about himself. A fruitcake, maybe. Or some sort of con artist. But no good teacher would claim to be God."

"Unless—" Becka cleared her throat—"unless he really was God." It had been a while since Rebecca had talked to anyone about her faith, but Ryan was so open and interested that it just came naturally. She continued, "All the other so-called spiritual teachers, all they talk about is how to get rid of our sins through reincarnation or transcendental meditation or whatever. But Jesus, he kept saying, 'I'm going to the cross to pay for those sins. Dump your sins on me; I'm going to die and take the punishment for you.'"

"So you're saying his death was no accident?" Ryan asked.

"That's right. Dying on the cross was his main reason for coming."

Ryan's next question came just a little bit slower. "And what exactly is our end of the deal? What are we supposed to do?"

"Just ask."

"Ask what?"

"Ask Jesus to take your punishment. Believe that he died on the cross for you."

Ryan looked at Becka skeptically. "That's it?"

"That's it." She held his gaze, feeling more confident than she had in days. "That's why he came and died—to take our punishment."

Ryan looked down and shook his head in quiet amazement.

"But there's a price," Mom added.

Ryan looked up.

"You have to let him be your boss ... your Lord."

A brief scowl crossed Ryan's face—but it wasn't from anger, or even from concern—it was from thinking. Deep, earnest thinking.

The conversation continued, but Scott barely heard. He fidgeted nervously and gave another glance at his watch. 7:10. He looked back up just in time to meet his sister's eyes.

"You okay, Scotty?" she asked. She could read him like a book. Sometimes that was good. Sometimes, like tonight, it was lousy.

He did his best to cover with a smile and a shrug. "I promised to meet a friend at 7:30."

"Darryl?" she asked, her eyes still searching. "I haven't seen him around for a while. Not that I'm complaining, you understand ..."

Scott forced a chuckle. "Yeah, well he's been swamped studying for midterms. I thought I'd go over and give him a hand." Scott wasn't sure how the lie slipped in—he hadn't planned on it; it just came. And so did the guilt. He had to get out of there. He had to leave. He pushed himself from the table and stood.

"You're going to do homework on a Saturday night?" Mom asked skeptically.

"Oh, I'm sure we'll squeeze in a couple video games along the way." He forced another smile.

Mom returned it, not entirely convinced. "There's supposed to be a storm tonight," she said, watching him head toward the door. "Take your jacket."

Scott nodded. He could feel their eyes on him as he grabbed his jacket from the coat rack and slipped it on. "See you guys."

"Later man," Ryan said.

Scott opened the kitchen door and headed out. He didn't know why he was in such a hurry. It only took a few minutes to get to Kara's. Maybe it was the guilt he felt closing in around him. Maybe it was Becka's questioning eyes. Or maybe it was because the very stuff they were talking to Ryan about was stuff he believed—but right now it was stuff he was trying to push out of his mind. At least for tonight.

He headed down the driveway and started up the sidewalk. Dark billowing clouds hid the last traces of daylight. The storm would be there soon. He felt no better out here than he had inside at the table. In fact, he felt worse. And by the time he crossed the street at the end of the block, he was so preoccupied that he barely saw the speeding Nissan squeal around the corner and swerve wide to miss him. Of course the car honked and the kids inside swore, but Scott barely noticed.

He had more important things on his mind.

❧ ❧

The Nissan raced past Scotty, then came to a stop ... directly across from the Williams house.

Here they turned off their ignition.

Here they waited for the dark.

❧ ❧

"You've sure given me a lot to think about," Ryan said as he wheeled Becka down the driveway toward his Mustang. They had sat around the table continuing their talk about Jesus—about the life he promised to give, the love he promised to deliver, and the peace he promised to provide. But when Mom and Becka asked if he was interested in that type of life, if he'd like to pray to receive Christ, Ryan had said no.

"It's a big decision," he had explained. "Especially the part about letting him be my boss. If I do it, I don't want to do it halfway. I've seen enough of those type of Christians running around."

The guy had a point. And Mom and Becka agreed that it was better for him to do a little research on his own, to "count the cost," instead of just blindly jumping in. So Mom had dug up a New Testament and suggested he give it a read. He took it and promised he would.

Now Ryan and Becka were calling it a day as they headed down the driveway toward his car. The storm was closing in. Wind was already beginning to blow against their faces and clothes. Although the sun had set, it was still possible to see the clouds churning and roiling above them. Suddenly there was a flash of lightning.

"Looks like it's going to be a big one," Ryan said, staring up at the sky.

The thunder followed, seeming to boom and roll forever. Becka folded her arms against the cold. "You want to stay until it blows over?"

"Nah, if I hurry I'll be able to outrun it." But even as he spoke fat raindrops started to splash on the driveway around them.

There was another flash, followed by an even closer clap of thunder.

They reached the car. Ryan dropped the Bible through the open passenger's window. Then, without a word, he kneeled down and took both of Becka's hands into his. As his deep blue eyes met hers, she instinctively knew what was next. It was something she longed for, something she dreamed about—but she knew the timing wasn't right. Not yet. The rain fell harder. He closed his eyes and leaned toward her. The temptation was overwhelming, but somehow Becka was able to find the strength. She gently put her fingers to his lips.

"No, Ryan …"

He opened his eyes.

She shook her head and said softly, "I'm sorry."

He searched her face, a little surprised, but she saw understanding, not hurt, in those incredible blue eyes.

They continued to hold each other's gaze, the rain splattering on their faces and hair. At last, Becka reached up and brushed one of the rain-soaked curls from Ryan's eyes. "You'd better be going," she whispered.

"Yeah," he whispered back. But neither moved. The rain was pouring now.

Then they heard it. The creak and groan of an old car door. Ryan looked up. Across the street he saw a beat-up Nissan with all four of its doors opening. He thought it weird to see four people stepping out into this deluge. Weirder still that they were all heading toward him.

"Hey, Ryan," the biggest of the group shouted over the rain. "Can we talk to you?"

Ryan peered at them over his car. He could tell they were his age, maybe a little younger. But it was hard to recognize them through the rain. "Do I know you?" he called.

They crossed the street and rounded his car. Two guys and two girls. They stepped up on the curb. The biggest was holding something behind his back and smiling.

Ryan eyed them carefully. "What's going on?" he yelled over the pounding rain. His voice carried an edge—not unfriendly, but definitely demanding.

"It's my car," the big guy shouted. "Battery's dead. Can you give me a jump?"

Ryan didn't believe him for a second. Why would all four kids pile out into this pouring rain to ask for a jump?

"Ryan?" It was Becka. He recognized her tone instantly. It was thin and wavy, like the other times she had been frightened.

He was torn. He did not want to take his eyes off the others, especially the big guy. Yet he knew Becka was scared and needed assurance. It was against his better judgment, but he turned from the group for the slightest second and looked down to her. Before he could say a word, he saw her eyes widen in horror, her mouth opening to scream.

Ryan spun around just as the baseball bat smashed into his chest. For a moment he felt no pain, though the blow was hard enough to send him staggering. Before he could regain his balance, the big guy moved in with another swing. This time Ryan was able to raise his arm, trying to deflect the bat, but it still hit its mark, smashing into his forehead.

The pain arrived. Exploding. Searing.

Ryan heard Becka scream. But it was a distant scream, far away. The lightning flashed as the bat delivered its third and final blow, catching him on his right shoulder. Ryan barely felt this one. It was the second hit that had done the real damage.

He squinted, trying in vain to clear his vision. He felt something warm and wet flowing down his face. He hoped it was rain. He had his doubts. He heard another crash of thunder, directly above them now. At the same time, he felt his legs turning to rubber. Suddenly they gave way as he crumpled onto the wet pavement.

The laughter and screams were from another world now. Barely audible. He could hear some sort of scuffle, but try as he might, he could not make his body move to help. With excruciating effort, he turned his head. The wet concrete felt good against his burning face. As the lightning flashed, Ryan caught sight of Becka in a nightmarish, strobing light as she fought and screamed while they yanked her from her wheelchair.

And then he saw nothing.

❧ ❧

"Hey, guy."

Scott stood in the doorway, dripping wet, looking and feeling very much like a drowned rat. But he no longer cared. For there, inside, stood a smiling Kara. She looked more attractive than ever. Maybe it was the thin silk blouse, or the way the candles from the living room glowed and flickered behind her. Whatever the reason, it was all he could do to croak out the expected "Hey, yourself."

"Looks like you got a little wet." She flashed him her grin and opened the door wider. He sloshed in. As she shut the door, he stood a moment, dripping on the entryway tile, taking it all in. There were no lights. Just the candles. Burning candles on the coffee table, the piano, the bookshelves, the entertainment center. Everywhere.

"I'll grab you some towels," Kara said, turning and heading for a hall closet.

"Guess you're saving on electricity," Scott tried to joke, but his cracking voice betrayed his uneasiness.

Kara disappeared around the corner and down a hall. "I think candles are a lot more romantic than regular light, don't you?"

"As long as your folks don't mind."

"My folks?" She reemerged with an armload of towels. "Didn't I tell you?"

"Tell me what?"

"My folks are out of town for the weekend."

9

"Ryan? Ryan, can you hear me?" The voice was muffled and far away. "Ryan ..." But coming closer and slipping into focus. "Ryan, can you hear me?"

He began to feel the rain — wonderful, soothing rain — washing over his face, cooling the fire on his head. With it came other feelings, less welcome: the throbbing inside his brain, the ache of his shoulder, the stabbing pain in his chest.

"Ryan ..."

The voice was louder now, clearer. He tried to open his eyes, but they were too heavy. They rolled but remained shut. He tried again and kept trying until, at last, they fluttered open.

He blinked rapidly against the splattering rain and saw Becka's mom staring down at him. At least he thought it was Becka's mom — she looked a lot different with her hair wet and plastered against her face. She was kneeling over him, holding his head. "Ryan ..."

Lightning flashed behind her. He tried to move, but the pain in his chest was such a surprise that he gasped.

"Don't move, hon. You're hurt real bad."

But Ryan had to move. He had to see. He braced himself for

the pain and sat up. The pounding in his head was excruciating, but he steeled himself against it. Breathing hard and ignoring the pain as best he could, he looked around. Then he spotted the empty, overturned wheelchair.

"Where is she?" His words came out in ragged gasps.

"I don't know. I heard the screams, but by the time I got outside they were gone."

"We've got—" He broke off, still struggling to breathe. "We've got ... to follow them." He tried to get to his knees, but the pain exploded through his entire body. It was all he could do to hold back a scream.

"Easy now, stay there. Don't—"

"No!" He moved again. The edges of his vision grew white and blurry. He knew he was on the edge of blacking out. He used all of his concentration to hang on. He made it to his knees.

"Ryan ..."

With Mrs. Williams' help he slowly rose to his feet. His legs were unsteady, but with her support he was able to lean against the car. Everything around started to spin, but he drew slow, even breaths until the movement stopped.

"Ryan, we've got to get you to a hospital."

"Call the police," he gasped. "Tell them to look for a brown, four-door Nissan."

"But what about—"

"We can take care of me later."

Mrs. Williams was torn. "But—"

"I'll be okay!" he shouted. The extra energy almost did him in. "Hurry!"

Still torn, Mrs. Williams released Ryan, making sure he was stable against the car.

"*Hurry!*"

His anger overcame the last of her hesitation. She turned and dashed through the rain toward the front door.

Ryan leaned against the car, gasping and wincing, waiting

until she was out of sight. Then, using the car for support, he dragged himself around to the driver's side. By now it was impossible to distinguish between the burning in his chest, the ache in his shoulder, and the pounding in his head. It was all the same. Everything screamed at him.

But Becka had to be found. The Society had to be stopped. And soon. Becka's mom would only slow things down by insisting he go to the hospital. There was no time. He pulled open the door and tumbled into the seat. Pain forced a muffled cry to his throat, but he swallowed it back.

More lightning — a series, one flash after another after another.

He dug out his keys and righted himself behind the wheel.

Now what? Who knew where these kids lived, where they might go? His mind raced. Didn't Scott have a friend from the Society? That Kara girl? She'd know! But where does she live? What was her phone number?

Ask Scott. Yes!

Ryan grabbed his cell phone, found Scott in his contacts and hit send. It went straight to voicemail.

Ryan slammed the wheel in frustration, sending another jolt of pain through his body.

Where was Scott? Where did he say he was going? To help some kid with his homework? Yes! His little dorky friend, Darryl!

Ryan put the key in the ignition and fired up the car. He had taken Darryl home after Becka's welcome-home party from the hospital. He knew exactly where the kid lived. He dropped the Mustang into gear and stomped on the accelerator. The wheels spun against the pavement, caught hold, then thrust the car forward.

He did not hear Mom as she raced out of the house, crying, "Ryan! Ryan, *no!*"

Becka fought and screamed until they shoved the gag into her mouth—so deep she thought she would choke. Then they taped it.

"Now her arms," Brooke ordered.

Laura pushed Becka's face against the back of the seat and cinched her hands. Becka cried out as the girl yanked on the rope, pinching and burning her wrists. But it was a cry no one heard. Besides the gag, there was the noise—the heavy-metal music blaring from the radio, the water splashing under the racing car, the rain pounding on its roof.

There was another burst of lightning. Becka caught only flickering glimpses of rooftops and trees. She had no idea where they were.

The car reeked of alcohol as cans and bottles were passed back and forth.

Suddenly her hair was yanked hard until she was looking, face-to-face, at the chunky, black-haired leader. "So you think you're better than the rest of us?" Brooke demanded. "You think you've got more power than me?"

Rebecca couldn't have answered even if she hadn't been gagged. She was too petrified. All she could do was stare back at Brooke in wide-eyed horror.

Brooke laughed. "A little frightened, are we? Well, just hang on, princess, 'cause you ain't seen nothing yet."

Becka was in a panic. She couldn't think, she couldn't plan. She tried desperately to regain control, but it did no good. What was it Z had said? *"The only power they have is the power you give them through your fear"*? If that was the case, then they had her lock, stock, and barrel. Big time.

And there was nothing she could do about it.

Ryan banged on the screen door a second time. There was still no answer. But someone was home—he could see the lights and hear the TV. He banged a third time, even harder. The pounding sent shock waves through his body.

At last he saw movement behind the curtains. Darryl finally opened the door and peered into the darkness. "Ryan?" his voice squeaked. "You look terrible."

"I've got to talk to Scott."

"Scott Williams?" Darryl gave a loud sniff. "He's not here."

"Where'd he go?"

"How should I know? I haven't seen him all day."

Ryan scowled. "He said he was coming over here—to help you with your homework."

"On a Saturday night? You've got to be kidding."

Ryan wished he was. He closed his eyes and tried to keep his voice calm and even. "So Scott never showed here?"

"No." Darryl was staring at the gash on his forehead. "You want to come in, get that cleaned up?"

Ryan shook his head. "I've got to find Scott." He turned and headed down the porch steps, back out into the rain.

"What's going on?" Darryl called. "If I see him, what should I tell him?"

Ryan reached his car and opened the door. "Just tell him to get home!" he shouted over the storm. "Tell him his sister needs him." Without waiting for an answer, he climbed behind the wheel, started up the Mustang, and took off down the road.

Now what?

He wasn't sure.

Where to?

He had no idea.

If he could just stop the throbbing in his head, maybe he could think. The rain continued to pour, and fog was forming on the inside of his windshield faster than the defroster could clear it.

He glanced to the seat beside him for a rag, anything to clear it off. To his surprise, he saw the New Testament Becka's mom had given him after dinner. An idea came to him. He threw the wheel to the left, and the car went into a skidding U-turn. He straightened it out and headed in the opposite direction—toward the Community Christian Church.

◈ ◈

Laura Henderson's Nissan slid to a stop in the mud beside the VW. They were at the park.

Brooke was the first out of the car. "Strip her," she shouted. "Get her changed and take her to the altar."

Laura pulled Becka out of the car—the booze making her rougher and more eager to please Brooke than ever. Rebecca went completely out of control. Oblivious to any pain, she kicked and thrashed until suddenly she and Laura went down in the mud.

Laura swore as she yanked Becka to her feet and shoved her hard against the car. Frail Girl had seen the struggle and moved to help. Rebecca was whimpering now, sobbing hysterically. Laura grabbed the bottom of Becka's hoodie and started to peel it up over her head. Another wave of panic hit Becka, and she went crazy again, kicking and fighting for all she was worth.

"Stop it!" Frail Girl slurred. "Stop fighting us! You're only making it worse. Stop it! Stop it!"

But Becka didn't hear. She couldn't hear. She was raw terror, squirming and kicking and screaming … until Laura slapped her hard across the face. Becka barely noticed. Laura slapped her again. And again. Until Becka's struggling finally slowed to a stop.

Rebecca stayed hunched over the car, breathing hard. The slaps had done the trick. She was back in control. And with the control came the realization: *I haven't even prayed! How could I be so stupid?* The panic and fear had completely blotted God from her mind. But not now. She took another breath to steady herself, and finally she began to pray. *Jesus, help me, Jesus show me what to do, Jesus . . .*

As Becka prayed, Laura resumed peeling off her sweatshirt. Becka shivered as the rain hit her bare skin.

Jesus, Jesus, help me, help me . . .

Laura got the sweatshirt over Becka's head, then swore again.

"What's the matter?" Frail Girl asked.

"Her hands are tied—we can't get the thing off."

"Should we untie her?"

"Nah, just give me the nightgown. No one will care."

Frail Girl reached into the car and handed Laura the white nightgown. "What about her pants?"

Jesus . . . please, no, Jesus . . . Help me, help me . . .

Laura gave a dubious look at the cast on Becka's leg. "Just throw the nightgown over her. What difference does it make?"

Becka sucked in her breath. It was a small victory, but it was enough. Z had said the only power they had was through her fear—nothing supernatural, just her fear. If that was the case, she had just proven him right. By refusing to give them her fear, she had been able to pray . . . and by praying, she had won a tiny victory.

Thank you, Jesus . . . thank you . . .

They pulled her sweatshirt back down, then forced the nightgown over her head and onto her body. It formed a type of straitjacket, keeping her arms pinned to her sides.

"Come on," Laura ordered.

They half-walked, half-dragged Becka toward the woods.

Jesus, help me, show me what to do . . .

The rain slowed to a stop, but only for a moment.

They rounded the bushes and entered the secluded spot, the one sheltered by a canopy of trees and impossible to see from the road. At its center was a picnic table. Four hooded figures stood around it. They held large flickering candles that were almost blowing out in the wind. On the ground surrounding them was a white circle of rope exactly nine feet across.

Sitting at the center of the table was a stained pillowcase with something moving inside. Scattered around it were more candles, some sticks of burning incense, a wine goblet, and several little daggers. Directly in front of the pillowcase was a large blazing candle stuck on top of a human skull.

Becka felt the fear returning, the loss of control. *NO! Please, Jesus ... help me!*

One of the hooded figures stepped forward. "Welcome, Rebecca Williams." Becka couldn't see her face, but she instantly recognized Brooke's voice. "You have dared to challenge our powers, and it is time you pay the price. Your destiny belongs to me." She turned to another figure beside the picnic table and nodded. The figure reached for a silver dinner bell and rang it.

"Let the mass begin."

One of the figures pulled a card from her robed sleeve and began to read: "Amen. Forever glory the and power the and kingdom the is thine for."

Others from around the table fumbled with their cards and joined her: "Evil from us deliver but, temptation into not us lead."

As they continued, Brooke crossed to the makeshift altar. The rain had started again, but the group paid no attention. The more they read, the louder their chant grew. And the louder the chant grew, the more focused they became on the words—the more detached they became from reality.

"Debtors our forgive we as debts our us forgive and bread daily our day this us give."

Brooke reached for the goblet. Next she reached for one of the daggers on the altar. She pulled up her left sleeve. The blade glimmered in the candlelight. All eyes were riveted on her arm.

She hesitated the slightest moment, then dragged the blade over the back of her arm, slicing it deeply.

Rebecca gasped as the blood oozed. Her panic was nearly overpowering. She could barely hold it back.

Help me, Jesus, help me . . .

"Heaven in is it as earth on done be will thy come kingdom thy."

Brooke reached for the wine goblet.

"Name thy be hallowed, heaven in art who father our."

Making a fist and flexing her arm, Brooke forced the blood to flow faster . . . until two, three, four drops fell into the bottom of the goblet.

Then, with a grin, she passed the goblet to the next figure, who was pulling up his own sleeve, reaching for his own dagger . . . as the group repeated the chant.

"Amen. Forever glory the and power the and kingdom the is thine for . . ."

10

Ryan gunned his car until it skidded into the church parking lot. He pulled himself out of the car, then staggered to the sanctuary, where he threw open the doors and entered.

Susan Murdock, the youth worker he'd met last night, spun around in surprise. She'd been cleaning and preparing the sanctuary for tomorrow's service. Her voice was firm, but there was no missing her alarm as she squinted to the back of the church. "Who is it? What are you doing here? The church is not—" And then she recognized him. "Ryan?"

He stepped to the back pew and leaned against it for support.

Susan started toward him, walking, then running. "Ryan, what happened?"

"They've got Becka."

"What?"

"Becka—the Society—they took her."

Susan reached out and pushed aside his wet, black hair to examine the gash in his forehead. "Ryan, we have to get you to a—"

He shoved her arm away, then forced himself to speak calmly

and evenly. "They've kidnapped Becka. They're going to hurt her. We've got to stop them."

Susan searched his face. He was dead earnest. "Where?" she asked. "How?"

"You said you knew some of the kids."

"One, yes. Laura Henderson. We were getting to be good friends. She even came over for dinner a couple of times. But now ..." Her voice dropped off as she shook her head. "Things have been real tough for her."

"Do you know where they meet? Like, for their ceremonies and stuff?"

Susan frowned. "You think that's where they'd be? On a night like this?" There was a bright flash of lightning outside, followed by ominous thunder. Susan had her answer. Tonight was the perfect night. Without a word, she turned and started for the side office.

"Where are you going?"

"To call the police, to tell them where we'll be."

❧ ❧

The goblet returned to the leader. It had made its rounds and now held the blood of all six satanists. Brooke lifted it high above her head.

"To you, great one, we offer our life's essence in exchange for your life's power."

There was another series of lightning flashes, some illuminating Brooke's face, some throwing her into eerie silhouette. The scene sent chills through Rebecca, yet she managed to hang on, refusing to give in to the fear. Then a Bible verse ran through her mind, and she began to recite it to herself over and over: *The one who is in you is greater than the one who is in the world. The one who is in you is greater than the one who is in the world. The one who ...*

"And now," Brooke said, lowering the cup, "for our final act of sacrifice." She nodded to the two hooded figures beside the table—Meaty Guy and Shaved Head. They reached for the pillowcase in the center. Meaty Guy opened it while Shaved Head pulled out its contents.

Muttly! Becka watched in horror as they tied ropes to each of his four paws. The little fellow whimpered pathetically until he spotted Rebecca. Suddenly his little ears perked up and his tail began to thump.

That was it. Becka could stand no more.

"No!" She screamed through the rag taped in her mouth. *"Noooo!"* She fought and kicked and squirmed for all she was worth. She fell into the mud, dragging down her two captors, Laura and Frail Girl, with her. They did their best to hold her, all the time shouting and swearing, but it did little good. Becka threw them off again and again until Meaty Guy and Shaved Head moved in to help.

In a matter of seconds, they had her in control. All but her mind. "Jesus!" she cried out. "Jesus, please! No! No! *Noooo!*"

Brooke began to laugh as the rain came down harder than ever.

👁 👁

They were in Susan's car. Ryan sat in the passenger seat fighting off the throbbing in his head, trying to take his mind off the pain in his chest. "Why'd you call the police?" he asked.

Susan frowned. "I'm sorry?"

"I thought everything was spiritual with you guys—just say your prayers and call fire down from the sky."

She gave him a look.

"Hey." He tried to smile. "I'm new to this."

Susan smiled back. "God uses the natural as well as the supernatural. Besides, not everything that goes bump in the night is Satan."

"That's exactly what I've been trying to tell Becka."

Susan nodded. "It's tricky to know the difference—I mean, to know what is truly supernatural and what is just man's doing."

"But you can tell?" Ryan asked.

Susan shook her head. "Not usually. But the tools, the weapons of warfare, are pretty much the same. It doesn't matter whether you're fighting against spirits or against flesh and blood."

Ryan looked at her, waiting for more. She continued.

"Our primary weapons are God's Word and our faith and love."

Ryan seemed surprised. "That's it? No supernatural hocus-pocus?"

Susan chuckled. "Once in a while, maybe. But it's not as often as you'd think. Oh, and we have one other weapon. In fact, it's our most powerful."

"What's that?"

"Prayer." She threw him a glance. "Mind if we do a little of that now?"

Ryan nodded. "I wouldn't mind if we did *a lot* of that."

👁 👁

The storm reached the height of its fury. A giant blast of wind suddenly blew out all the candles, even the one stuck onto the skull. The rain came down at a sharp angle. Lightning continued nonstop, illuminating the scene like a thousand flashbulbs.

Becka was held fast by Meaty Guy and Shaved Head. Laura and Frail Girl had moved to the boys' places at opposite ends of the altar. Laura finished tying the last rope to Muttly's paw, then she and Frail Girl pulled the ropes taut, stretching the puppy spread-eagle across the table as he whimpered and whined.

Becka fought and thrashed, but it did little good. Meaty Guy and Shaved Head held her tight. She caught a glimpse of Brooke approaching Muttly, her arms raised high into the air, the wind whipping her sleeves. Lightning flashed, revealing the dagger in her hand.

God! Becka's mind screamed. *Jesus, please!*

And then, just before the knife started its plunge, there was light — bright, moving light, coming through the bushes from the parking lot.

"It's a car!" Shaved Head shouted. "Somebody's here!"

Laura and Frail Girl started, momentarily loosening Muttly's ropes. In a flash, he scampered to his feet.

"No!" Brooke shouted. "We must complete the sacrifice!"

Car doors slammed and faint voices could be heard under the thunder: "Becka! Rebecca, can you hear me?"

"Let's get out of here!" Shaved Head shouted in a panic. The others agreed. All but Brooke.

"Becka! Rebecca, are you in there?"

The group continued to panic. Brooke shouted over them, "Pull those ropes tight! We must complete the sacrifice! We must complete the sacrifice!"

As Rebecca watched their panic grow and spread, the most unusual thing happened: She slowly began to feel a type of peace, a confidence. Granted, the two boys still held her fast, and Brooke was still preparing to kill her dog. But somehow, someway, a gentle peace settled over her ... a calm confidence.

Jesus, show me what to do. Show me ...

As she prayed, the confidence spread through her body, allowing her to relax. The two boys felt her struggling ease and unconsciously loosened their grip. Not much, but enough.

With the fear gone, Rebecca was able to focus her thoughts. They became crystal clear. She knew what to do.

Muttly was starting to get away. Brooke caught one of his ropes with her left hand and jerked the animal toward her. She raised the dagger over him with her other hand. She was about to carry out the sacrifice on her own when Rebecca made her move.

It was instant. Catching the guys off guard, she leaped to her feet and threw herself at Brooke with all her might. She was still encased in the white nightgown and her leg was still in the cast, but she lunged across the circle and hit Brooke like a flying torpedo. The two bounced against the table, and the dagger flew out of Brooke's hands as they fell hard into the mud.

"Get her off!" Brooke cried. "Get her off!"

A flash of lightning illuminated the area, and they both saw the glint of the blade just a yard away. Brooke reached for it, but Rebecca was already spinning her body around. Before Brooke could grab the weapon, Rebecca smashed her cast down with all of her weight, directly onto Brooke's hand.

"*Augh!*" Brooke screamed and grabbed her hand.

Rebecca moved her leg to the dagger and slammed down on it again and again, driving it deep into the mud.

Lightning flashed as Ryan and Susan raced around the bushes and entered the clearing. "Becka! Rebecca!"

Out of breath, Becka started to answer, but suddenly she felt a powerful arm grab her and wrap itself around her neck. It was Laura. Becka felt the sharp, cold steel of a dagger against her throat.

"Go away!" Laura screamed at Ryan and Susan. "Leave us alone!"

Brooke sat in the mud to the right of the altar, holding her crippled hand. Becka and Laura were sprawled in front of the altar, locked in a deadly embrace.

Susan recognized Laura instantly. "Laura ... Laura, is that you?"

"Leave us alone!" she shouted again.

"Laura, what's going on? What are you doing?" Susan took a step toward the girl, and Laura pulled Becka closer, pushing the knife more firmly against her throat.

Susan froze.

"No one asked you to come!" Laura screamed. "Get out of here!"

Lightning lit the clearing.

"Laura ..."

"Kill her!"

All eyes shot to Brooke. She was on her knees, holding her hand, seething in rage. "Kill her! Make the *ultimate* sacrifice."

Laura's eyes locked on Brooke. She seemed unable to look away.

"Kill her! Kill her!"

Susan edged closer. "Laura ... don't listen to her."

"I command you to kill her!" Brooke shouted.

Laura stared at Brooke, mesmerized, held by her rage, her power.

"Laura," Susan continued softly. "Listen to me, Laura. Don't let her tell you what to do."

The words tugged at the girl, nearly drawing her eyes back to Susan, but not quite. She couldn't look away from Brooke.

A police siren began to scream in the distance.

"Laura, I'm on your side."

Laura's eyes faltered, then shifted to Susan.

"Kill her!"

Her eyes darted back to Brooke, whose face was contorted with hatred.

"I command you to make the ultimate sacrifice!"

"Laura, I'm on your side. Laura."

No response. The siren grew louder.

"Laura ... Laura, I love you."

Laura's gaze returned to Susan. The girl was scared, confused — pleading for help.

"I own you! Obey me!" Brooke's voice raised to a screech.

"Laura—" Susan took a step closer—"there's more to life than this."

"Obey me or I'll destroy you!"

Laura's eyes shot back to Brooke. She would not, she could not disappoint the leader.

"Laura, look at me ... look at me. I'm here to help you—I love you." Susan edged closer. "There's no power here. She has no control over you."

"I'll destroy you!"

"I love you." Susan's voice remained calm and in control. "Laura, God loves you."

Laura looked back to Susan. She was trembling, trying to hold back tears.

Susan continued, "I'm your friend, Laura, you know that. I love you."

"*Obey me!*"

"I love you." Susan started to move in again, her voice soothing. "Laura, I love you."

Suddenly Laura pulled Rebecca closer.

Susan slowed but did not stop. "I'll do whatever I can to help you, you know that."

Laura's eyes were blinking rapidly; the tears were coming faster. She turned to Brooke.

"Obey me! I'll destroy you! *I'll destroy you!*"

Then to Susan.

"I love you!"

"*I'll destroy you!*" Brooke's voice rose in fury, but Laura did not look back. Her eyes remained fixed on Susan.

"I love you, Laura. I want to help you." They were less than three feet apart. "Give me the knife, Laura. Give me the knife so I can help."

"I curse you!" Brooke screamed. "I cast your life into everlasting darkness! I curse you!"

Susan reached out her hand. "Just give me the knife so I can help. I love you."

Ever so slowly, Laura reached out her trembling hand.

Panic filled Brooke's eyes. She began to scream, "Hate your

enemies with your whole heart, and if a man smite you on the cheek, smash him on the other!"

Laura hesitated.

Brooke rose to her feet, motioning for her followers to join her. "Hate your enemies with your whole heart ..."

But they would not participate. Meaty Guy, Shaved Head, Frail Girl ... they all looked away.

The siren grew louder. The police were practically there.

"... and if a man smite you on the cheek, *smash* him on the other!"

"Give me the knife, Laura," Susan repeated. "I love you. Jesus loves you."

"Hate your enemies with your whole heart, and if a man smite you on the cheek, smash him on the other!" Brooke stood there, holding her hand, trembling in rage.

Laura was sobbing. Ever so slowly, she released the dagger. It fell into Susan's palm. Instantly, Susan dropped to the mud and threw her arms around Laura.

Rebecca scooted out of the way as the two hugged. Ryan was at her side in a second, his arms around her, holding her so tightly she could scarcely breathe.

Laura leaned into Susan and cried like a lost, frightened child. "It's okay," Susan whispered. "I love you, I love you. Sshh, now." She was crying too.

All watched in silence as Susan and Laura remained on their knees, sobbing and holding one another, their tears mixing with the rain and the mud as the police car pulled into the parking lot, casting blue and red lights on everyone's faces.

11

I should have been there," Scott said, shaking his head. It was almost 4:00 a.m. He sat in the emergency-room lobby with Becka, Susan, and Muttly, whom he'd smuggled into the building inside his zipped-up coat. "If I'd been there, none of this would have happened."

"I wouldn't be so sure of that, little brother," Becka said. She was back in her wheelchair. Her leg and collarbone had already been checked. The wet, soggy cast had been removed, and a new one had been applied. Now they were all waiting for Ryan. Becka continued, "Those guys had been planning it for days. You wouldn't have been able to stop them."

"Still, if I had been over at Darryl's like I said—" Scott looked to the ground, unable to finish the sentence.

Mom had returned from calling Ryan's parents. She reached out and rested her hand on his shoulder. They had already been through his deception, and the punishment had already been given out—something about being grounded until the year 2070. Now it was time to let him know he was still loved. Very much.

"I don't know what came over me." He kept staring at the floor.

"Good old-fashioned lust," Todd volunteered. "It's something even the best of us have to fight." Todd had come to the hospital as soon as he'd received the call from Susan.

Mom nodded. "The important thing is that you won."

"Barely." Scott looked up and sighed.

" 'Barely' counts," Mom said.

"I wanted to stay so bad. But as soon as she told me her folks were gone, something inside clicked. I was out of there in about three point two seconds."

"And that's good, man," Todd encouraged.

"Yeah, till it gets around to everyone. Then I'll be the All-School Joke."

"But not with God," Mom said.

"Or with me, Scotty."

Scott glanced over at Becka. Her smile was full of pride. It helped, but not enough. "Besides," he complained, "I missed seeing you guys pull out the big guns against the Society."

Susan shook her head. "Like I told Ryan, whether we're fighting real spirits or just our own flesh, the weapons God gives us are still pretty much the same: prayer, Scripture, righteousness, faith—"

"And love," Becka concluded.

Susan looked at her and nodded. The group fell silent as all thoughts returned to Susan and Laura hugging each other down in the mud.

Becka looked at Susan and asked what was on everybody's mind: "You think Laura will be all right?"

Susan answered, "I hope so. The police have called her mom. I'm going down there just as soon as we get word on Ryan."

Becka sighed, "It was all just a mind game, wasn't it? Just a way to scare me. They really didn't have any power."

"They thought they did," Mom answered. "But in all truth, probably not."

"Just the power of your fear," Susan added.

"And as soon as I was able to control that, as soon as I put my faith back in God—"

"You won," Scott finished the phrase.

"Seems to me you had a little help from your friends," a voice commented.

All eyes turned to the hall as Ryan appeared around the corner. He sat in a wheelchair with a large bandage over his forehead and his right arm in a cast.

"Ryan!" Becka cried in alarm as she started toward him.

He broke into one of his famous heartbreaker grins.

"Oh, Ryan," she said, blinking away tears. "Are you okay?"

"Yea, just a mild concussion." He smiled.

The nurse who was pushing his chair toward the group continued as if reading a shopping list: "And two cracked ribs, a chipped elbow, a broken arm, a lacerated forehead, and a bruised shoulder."

"Just trying to keep up with the Williams," he laughed as he pulled up beside Becka.

"His and hers wheelchairs," Scott teased. "How cute."

"Now we can do races," Ryan said.

The nurse cleared her throat. "Actually, we'll want to keep him overnight, for observation."

"Oh, Ryan," Becka looked worried.

"It's no big deal."

"But you did all this for me. You're like a hero."

The group oohed and ahhed.

"I think I'm going to get sick," Scott groaned. Suddenly Muttly began squirming and whimpering inside his jacket. The nurse stared at his stomach in shock.

"It's just a little indigestion." Scott smiled sheepishly.

Ryan continued talking to Becka. "I'm sorry you had to go through all that. I wish I could have stopped them at the house."

"You were amazing," Becka said. "When I heard your voice out there in the park, I knew I wasn't alone. Something came over me—like a strength or power or something. Without you it never would have happened."

Ryan shook his head. "It wasn't me."

She looked at him as everyone became silent.

"What I saw there tonight—the faith, the power—" he glanced over to Susan—"and the love ..." He shook his head again. "I've never seen anything like it." Then, reaching beside his leg, he produced the Bible Mom had given him earlier that evening. "I haven't read this yet, but if what I saw tonight is anything like what we talked about over dinner, I think I'm about ready to sign up."

"Ryan." Becka's heart leaped. The news was too good to be true. She wheeled her chair closer. "Are you sure?"

"I've still got some reading to do—and by the looks of things, I'll be having plenty of time for that—but so far, so good."

Muttly could no longer be contained. He squirmed from Scott's coat and leaped to the floor. Scott tried to catch him, but the little guy scampered straight for Becka.

She reached down and scooped him into her lap. He began covering every inch of her face with wet, sloppy kisses. Ryan and the group laughed. Hearing Ryan's voice, Muttly spun around, saw another target, and leaped over the wheelchairs to start a second attack.

More laughter as Ryan coughed and sputtered. Yet he was not too busy to reach out and take Becka's hand. She felt him give her a little squeeze. She returned it, her heart bursting with joy.

☙ ☙

Back at the Williams' house, a message was forming on Scott's computer. A message that came quickly and urgently:

Scott ... Rebecca ... Are you there?

There was a pause as the sender waited for an answer. Finally another message appeared:

The Spell

There is a deserted mansion across town.
Rumor is that it's haunted. My sources say that someone
may challenge you to visit it. Exercise caution. I repeat,
be very, *very* careful. The battle may be over, but the war
rages on.
Z

Discussion questions for
The Spell:

1. Why was Brooke, the leader of "The Society," so angry at Rebecca? Have you ever had someone upset with you because of your beliefs? What could you do?

2. Z challenged Scott and Rebecca to get involved with a church. Why do you think he was so insistent?

3. Kara told Scott that she was a pagan who believed in doing whatever felt good and natural. A lot of people have similar beliefs. How does this belief differ from what the Bible says?

4. What are some reasons people might be drawn to the occult or Satanism?

5. Ryan didn't believe that evil forces were necessarily behind everything that went wrong. What do you think? How much control does Satan have in the lives of Christians? [See 1 Peter 5:8, 1 John 4:4]

6. Scott ended up in a compromising situation with Kara in the garage. How could he have avoided it?

7. Talking about The Society, Z said, "The only power they have is the power you give them through your fear." What did he mean?

8. How did Becka feel after she prayed? Why do you think she felt this way?

9. Why was Laura so desperate for Brooke's approval? Have you ever felt like Laura?

10. Why do you think Laura responded the way she did to Susan's words? When have you seen love make a difference in someone's life?

Author's Note

As I continue writing this series, I have two equal and opposing concerns. First, I don't want the reader to be too frightened of the Devil. Compared to Jesus Christ, Satan is a wimp. The two aren't even in the same league. Although the supernatural evil in these books is based on a certain amount of fact, it's important to understand the awesome protection Jesus Christ offers to all those who have committed their lives to him.

This brings me to my second and somewhat opposing concern: Although the powers of darkness are nothing compared to the power of Jesus Christ and the authority he has given his followers, spiritual warfare is not something we casually stroll into. The situations in these novels are extreme to create suspense and drama. But if you should find yourself involved in something even vaguely similar, don't confront it alone. Find an older, more mature Christian (such as a parent, pastor, or youth leader) to talk to. Let them check the situation out to see what is happening, and ask them to help you deal with it.

Yes, we have the victory through Christ, but we should never send in inexperienced soldiers to fight the battle.

Oh, and one final note. When this series was conceived, there were really no bad guys on the Internet. Unfortunately that has changed. Today there are plenty of people out there trying to draw young folks into dangerous situations through it. Although the characters in this series trust Z, if you should run into a similar situation, be smart. Anyone can *sound* kind and understanding, but their intentions may be entirely different. All that to say, don't take candy from strangers you see ... or trust those you don't.

Bill

Bibliography

Information on the occult for *The Society* came from the following sources:

Pp. 58 – 59 — Bill Myers, *Hot Topics, Tough Questions* (Wheaton, Ill: Victor, 1987) 91 – 93; *Understanding the Occult* (Minneapolis, Augsburg Fortress, 1989) 96.

Pg. 75 — Edmond Gruss, *Cults & Occult in the Age of Aquarius* (Grand Rapids, Mich: Baker, 1974); see also Volney P. Gay, *Understanding the Occult* (Minneapolis, Augsburg Fortress, 1989) 96; Bill Myers, *Hot Topics, Tough Questions* (Wheaton, Ill: Victor, 1987) 91 – 93.

Information on teen sex, AIDS, and condoms for *The Spell* came from the following sources:

Pg. 275: Duane Crumb, "A Guide to Positive HIV/AIDS Education" (American Institute for Teen AIDS Prevention), 36 – 37. See also *Sex, Lies & … the Truth* (Wheaton, Ill: Tyndale House/Focus on the Family, 1994).

Pg. 275: Bill Myers, *Hot Topics, Tough Questions* (Wheaton, Ill.: Victor, 1987) 91 – 93.

POWER TRIP

Everybody has problems.

Problems like finding the perfect boyfriend or girlfriend, fitting in at school, or looking attractive. Then there are the problems, the situations that just seem too big for the average person to handle. Problems like dealing with a bully, overcoming the death of someone you love, or living with a disability or illness.

No wonder people are drawn to the supernatural—a source of power beyond themselves and their ordinary, everyday lives.

One way people seek out this power is through the occult. The word occult comes from the Latin word *occultus*, which means hidden or secret. The occult refers to having knowledge of the hidden, supernatural world.

The Bible tells us that this unseen world does exist. Ephesians 6:12 says: "For our struggle is not against flesh and blood, but against the rulers, against the authorities, against the powers of this dark world and against the spiritual forces of evil in the heavenly realms."

Many of us are aware of the evil forces behind things like animal sacrifices, pentagrams, and reliance on astrology. But sometimes, that unseen world can seem harmless. In *The Society,* for instance, Scott Williams gets an unwanted peek into the spiritual battle around him when he gets involved with some teens from his school who are using a Ouija board to make contact with the spirit world.

The teens in the story are not alone. According to a recent study, three out of ten teenagers have played with a Ouija board. Like Scott, many believe the Ouija board is harmless, but come to find out the "game" is dangerous because of who its power comes from.

Z helps Scott see that there's a reason the Bible forbids divination —the discovery of hidden knowledge through the use of occult powers—as the powers come from Satan. (See Deuteronomy 8:10.) But not everyone has a mysterious friend to help them see the truth. Don't be afraid to read your Bible and share what you learn with others, or warn friends when you think something might be heading in a dark direction. God has given us the Holy Spirit to guide us—when you feel a twinge, trust it.

Scott's sister, Rebecca, learned a difficult lesson about herself and her faith when she opened herself up to dark powers in *The Deceived*, allowing herself to be hypnotized by the smooth-talking Maxwell Hunter. She began to accept the Hindu belief of reincarnation, believing she'd spent a past life as a French king. Even Rebecca's mom was initially fooled by Maxwell's reassuring words and claims to be a believer in Jesus.

Sometimes Satan's tricks aren't obvious at first. They may appear in the form of something or someone really attractive; maybe for you, it's the promise of success, or affection, or having the power to control your life. For Becka, the idea that she might have been someone important in another life was attractive enough to override all her biblical knowledge, because what Maxwell told her—under the guise of truth—made her feel like her current life had more worth.

Maxwell's methods may seem a little transparent from the outside, but in reality his words and promises are ones people under the devil's influence use often, twisting the truth and religion just enough to find a way in. The goal is to make people believe things about themselves and God that aren't true—like the belief that we don't need God and must rely on ourselves. The Bible is clear about Satan's intentions: "The thief comes only to steal and kill and destroy; I have come that they may have life, and have it to the full" (John 10:10).

The truth is, what you think you're getting comes with a dangerous price—and you're often not really getting what you wanted at all. Becka discovered this when her escalating beliefs in hypnotism nearly led to her death. Though Satan's power is nothing compared to God's, the Bible warns Christians not to underestimate God's enemy. Peter compares him to a lion, looking for his next meal. "Be self-controlled and alert. Your enemy the devil prowls around like a roaring lion looking for someone to devour" (1 Peter 5:8).

Throughout the *Dark Powers* volume, as the members of the Society went deeper and deeper into the occult, Satan began to control their actions and lead them to destructive behaviors. Brooke and the other teens believed the power made them special, but it only took them farther away from the One who created them and truly loved them.

Only God can truly give you satisfaction and happiness in your life. And giving your life to Jesus promises a much better future and life than hypnotism, apparent control over darkness, or any lie of Satan's ever can.

Perhaps you are avoiding the occult and are strong in your faith. If so, stay committed ... and be prepared for challenges. In *The Spell*, Becka experiences the fierce side of Satan as a result of what God is doing through her in her community. When the Society—a group of teens influenced by the occult—decides Becka must be punished for opposing them, she becomes the target of a terrifying, deadly plot.

While God is much more powerful than Satan—and has

already defeated the devil—the fact is, Satan will use all the forces he can to oppose those who refuse to follow his temptations and lies, hoping to knock loose our foundations. Becka was shaky after her encounter with hypnoses, and the enemy struck. And Satan is clever enough to use the things that will trip us up the most.

In fact, Scott faced one of the enemy's less obvious ploys— sexual temptation. As long as Scott was distracted by sinful thoughts about Kara, he was unable to see God's direction for his life. For you, it might be busyness, a belief you can be self-sufficient, a new friendship (even if it's a GOOD friendship), or any other thing in your life that can be twisted in order to distract you.

As a result, it is important to find a community that can support you when and if attacks to your faith come. When the Society first began to torment her, Becka was paralyzed by fear, but youth leaders Todd and Susan Murdock reminded her that God has already defeated Satan and offers believers full protection from all of Satan's attacks (Ephesians 6:11–17).

And with Z's help, both Scott and Becka came to realize that God wanted them to experience supernatural power through him alone (Ephesians 1:18–20). Occult stuff, such as Ouija boards, tarot cards, spells, horoscopes, and séances derive their power from Satan. Though the power the occult offers may be appealing, especially during hard times, Satan doesn't solve problems. Only God does.

A community is important for helping others avoid the traps of the occult, but it is also important for helping bring others to the light. When Ryan met Becka, he gained a front-row seat to God's power in action. The more he saw how God protected and helped Becka and her family, the more interested he became in Jesus and the Bible.

Like many people, Ryan believed Jesus was a real person, but didn't have a personal relationship with Christ. Mrs. Williams explained to Ryan that he couldn't simply believe Jesus was a good teacher. Because Jesus claimed to be God, he was either a liar, a crazy person, or who he claimed to be—the only one who could save people from their sins.

The Bible says that every person is born with sin and falls short of God's holiness (Romans 3:23) and is separated from God. Out of his love for us, God sent his Son to earth to live as a sinless human being and pay the penalty for our sin by dying on a cross. Three days after Jesus died, God raised him from the dead.

That is the power that Christians have access to through Jesus Christ! That is the power that Ryan saw in Becka's life— the power that helped him take the first step toward a relationship with Jesus Christ.

Salvation is available to everyone who believes in Jesus and allows him to be Lord. Maybe, like Ryan, you've been checking out Christianity but haven't yet made the decision to follow Jesus and accept his free gift of Salvation. Or perhaps you have a friend who has been wondering about the church and Jesus. The Bible says today—right now—is the day of salvation (2 Corinthians 6:2). All you must do is acknowledge your sin and need of a Savior and believe that only Jesus can save you (Acts 4:12; 16:31). When you've done that, Jesus comes into your life and gives you his Holy Spirit to help and guide you.

Accepting Jesus doesn't mean your problems will be over. After all, there's still sin in the world, and Satan will still try to mess you up. But if you rely on God each day, he will help you stand strong against Satan.

As Scott and Becka discovered, the occult is attractive to those looking for power outside of God. Many people have reported getting involved with occult activity through something small, like playing with a Ouija board at a party or reading horoscopes. But these things give Satan a foothold to take even more control. And his end goal is destruction.

As a Christian, you do not need to be afraid of evil or God's enemy, Satan. God has given believers authority over evil spirits, through the name of Jesus. Like Z told Scott and Becka, "The only power they have is the power you give them through your fear."

God is the one with true power and the solutions to life's problems. He is available and ready to help you today, if you come to him. That's powerful stuff.

Forbidden Doors

A Four-Volume Series from Bestselling Author Bill Myers!

Join teenager Rebecca "Becka" Williams, her brother, Scott, and her friend Ryan Riordan as they head for mind-bending clashes between the forces of darkness and the kingdom of God.

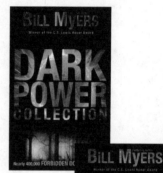

Dark Power Collection

Contains: *The Society,*
The Deceived, and *The Spell*

Invisible Terror Collection

Contains: *The Haunting,*
The Guardian, and *The Encounter*

Deadly Loyalty Collection

Contains: *The Curse,*
The Undead, and *The Scream*

Ancient Forces Collection

Contains: *The Ancients,*
The Wiccan, and *The Cards*

ZONDERVAN®
.com

The Dark Side of the Supernatural, Revised and Expanded Edition

Uncovering God's Truth

You've seen movies and TV shows or read books that have supernatural ideas. A lot of times, it's entertaining. Boys who are warlocks with magical powers, women who see the future, a girl who sees and talks to dead people—as ideas go, these have great potential to tell a good story. But is it real? And if so, what does that mean?

Bill Myers has spent years researching supernatural phenomenon, and has even made movies on the topic. In this book, he'll share his research, along with interviews and true-life experiences of psychics, Satanists, and people who have been possessed, or even abducted by aliens. His encounters with a variety of supernatural topics will open your eyes to what is real and what is fantasy. You'll learn more about:

- Wicca and witches
- Reincarnation
- UFO's
- Ouija boards
- Angels and demons
- Ghosts and near-death experiences
- Satanism
- Vampires, and more

If you're curious about these issues, or have friends who are caught up in them, *The Dark Side of the Supernatural* will uncover the truth and explain how to help.

Available in stores and online August 2012!

Echoes From the Edge

An Exciting Trilogy from Bestselling Author Bryan Davis!

A mysterious mirror with phantom images, a camera that takes pictures of things that are not present, and a violin that unlocks portals ... Each enigma takes teens Nathan and Kelly farther into an alternate universe where nothing is as it seems.

Beyond the Reflection's Edge
Book One

Eternity's Edge
Book Two

Nightmare's Edge
Book Three

ZONDERVAN®
.com